"I should go."

"You don't have to." His pale blue eyes glittered with unmistakable intensity.

"Yes." Her voice was shakier than she'd like to admit, matching her resolve. "I do."

They stared at each other for an instant, the moment awkward, thick with tension. There was a wild and reckless beating in her pulse, one that tempted even as it alarmed. If it had been due solely to animal attraction there would be no choice. She'd be in his bed, wrapped around him, and use him to quench the heat in her blood.

But it wasn't that simple. *He* wasn't that simple.

She took plenty of risks, but only when she could control the situation.

Jake Tarrance didn't appear to be a man easily controlled.

Dear Reader,

Get ready for this month's romantic adrenaline rush from Silhouette Intimate Moments. First up, we have RITA® Award-winning author Kathleen Creighton's next STARRS OF THE WEST book, *Secret Agent Sam* (#1363), a high-speed, action-packed romance with a tough-as-nails heroine you'll never forget. RaeAnne Thayne delivers the next book in her emotional miniseries THE SEARCHERS, *Never Too Late* (#1364), which details a heroine's search for the truth about her mysterious past...and an unexpected detour in love.

As part of Karen Whiddon's intriguing series THE PACK— about humans who shape-shift into wolves—*One Eye Closed* (#1365) tells the story of a wife who is in danger and turns to the only man who can help: her enigmatic husband. Kylie Brant heats up our imagination in *The Business of Strangers* (#1366), where a beautiful amnesiac falls for the last man on earth she should love— a reputed enemy!

Linda Randall Wisdom enthralls us with *After the Midnight Hour* (#1367), a story of a heart-stopping detective's fierce attraction to a tormented woman...who was murdered by her husband a century ago! Can this impossible love overcome the bonds of time? And don't miss Loreth Anne White's *The Sheik Who Loved Me* (#1368), in which a dazzling spy falls for the sexy sheik she's supposed to be investigating. So, what will win out—duty or true love?

Live and love the excitement in Silhouette Intimate Moments, where emotion meets high-stakes romance. And be sure to join us next month for another stellar lineup.

Happy reading!

Patience Smith
Associate Senior Editor

Please address questions and book requests to:
Silhouette Reader Service
U.S.: 3010 Walden Ave., P.O. Box 1325, Buffalo, NY 14269
Canadian: P.O. Box 609, Fort Erie, Ont. L2A 5X3

KYLIE BRANT

THE BUSINESS of STRANGERS

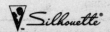

INTIMATE MOMENTS™

Published by Silhouette Books

America's Publisher of Contemporary Romance

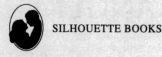 SILHOUETTE BOOKS

ISBN 0-373-27436-X

THE BUSINESS OF STRANGERS

Copyright © 2005 by Kimberly Bahnsen

Visit Silhouette Books at www.eHarlequin.com

Printed in U.S.A.

Books by Kylie Brant

Silhouette Intimate Moments

KYLIE BRANT

lives with her husband and children. Besides being a writer, this mother of five works full-time teaching learning-disabled students. Much of her free time is spent in her role as professional spectator at her kids' sporting events.

An avid reader, Kylie enjoys stories of love, mystery and suspense—and she insists on happy endings. She claims she was inspired to write by all the wonderful authors she's read over the years. Now most weekends and all summer she can be found at the computer, spinning her own tales of romance and happily-ever-afters.

She invites readers to check out her online read in the reading room at eHarlequin.com. Readers can write to Kylie at P.O. Box 231, Charles City, IA 50616, or e-mail her at kyliebrant@hotmail.com. Her Web site address is www.kyliebrant.com.

For Alison, my favorite only daughter. I just knew holding out for a girl would pay off in the end!

Acknowledgments

Special thanks goes to Candace Irvin for all the great military information and for pointing me, not so gently, toward the army! And another huge thank-you to Ben Swank, for your time and patience with my endless questions about the Army Rangers. Your generous assistance is appreciated more than you can know.

Prologue

The tropical blue-green waters of the Atlantic beat in lazy rhythm against the pebbled sand beach of Santa Cristo. The simple lullaby of the flow and ebb of the foamy waves was deceptive, for the constant pattern brought both life and death to the myriad of creatures dependent on it for survival. Each new wash of waves ended existence for some. Each new pull back to the sea gave new life to others.

To the woman in the wet suit, the ocean gave both.

Her unconscious body rode the waves into shore and was deposited on the sand as the water went about its business of tides and lunar cycles. She'd survived, barely, all the dangers the ocean had to offer. The natural buoyancy of her body had helped her elude the churning currents that had tried to pull her under and provide her with a final resting place. The predators of the sea had taken no notice of the black-clad body being tossed from wave to wave, like the rest of the flotsam, after last night's storm.

Perhaps they knew somehow that human predators had already done their worst.

She might have died there, face pressed into the sand, lungs filled with saltwater. Might have slipped from unconsciousness to death in a gradual descent into total darkness that would hold a not unwelcome finality. But dawn had spilled over the nearby mountains and was even now painting the horizon. And on an island gripped by unrest, people rose early, eager to shake off the heavy mantle of darkness that held increasingly ominous threats.

It would be easier to seek oblivion, if it weren't for the never-ending noise above her.

A voice. She identified the sound finally, if not the words. It took awhile longer to recognize the language as Spanish, the voice as belonging to a female. She couldn't explain why both those facts eased a measure of the fear welling up inside her.

"Wake up, Angel. I did not go to all the work of saving you to have you sleep your life away. Wake up now and speak to me."

A soft blanket of darkness summoned, offering to wrap her once again in sweet oblivion. Then she was rolled from her side to her stomach, and white-hot shards of pain stabbed through her, ripping open the cloak of unconsciousness and wrenching a guttural groan from her.

"Estoy apesadumbrado."

The apology didn't register, nor did the deliberate gentling of hands. The pain was gleefully gnawing through muscle, tendon, bone. Unconsciousness shimmered tantalizingly, just out of reach, and she clawed toward it, wanting to dive beneath its cloak again and escape the torment.

"I call you Angel because surely God is smiling on you." A wet cloth, blessedly cool, was laid across her forehead. "How else could you survive two bullets in your back and hours in the ocean during one of the worst storms this year?"

Bullets? Ocean? She waited, but the words summoned no answering memory, and panic began to circle through the pain.

"You must have been on a boat. Were you diving? When my daughter and I found you on the beach, you wore a wet suit. I had to cut it off you to get at your wounds."

Wet suit. Diving. She understood the words. She waited for a mental association to form. None did. The panic surged through the agony.

"I can do little for the pain, I am sorry. When you are well enough I will go for the doctor. He can bring the police."

"No." The woman lunged upward from the bed to grasp her rescuer's hand with surprising strength, given her injuries. All the command, all the urgency she could muster was in her voice. "No doctor. No police."

Luz frowned, her free hand rising to replace the cloth that had been dislodged. "I can do no more than I already have. Luckily for you, I am a nursing assistant. Yours were the first bullets I've ever removed, though, and I have nothing to give you to prevent infection."

"Tell no one." The woman she'd saved clutched at her with burning fingers.

"But this must be reported. I cannot…" Luz began helplessly, then stopped when the woman she called Angel went limp, her eyes sliding closed.

"Is she dead, Mama?" Maria, her eight-year-old daughter, gazed at the stranger with rounded eyes.

"No." *Not yet.* Luz stared down at the unconscious form on the bed, dread rearing. Logic dictated she summon help as soon as she dared leave her patient. Last week the guerillas had overthrown the government in Puerto de Ponce, less than sixty miles away. And with refugees flooding across the porous borders to her country, it seemed almost a given that Angel was one of them.

Except…she was Caucasian, and she hadn't come over the border. How could Luz in good conscience have her shipped back to a country torn apart by fighting, when she'd already come so close to death?

Luz slipped her arm around her daughter's shoulders and hugged her close. She could afford to wait a little longer. Just long enough for Angel to give her some answers.

As the days passed, Angel grew steadily stronger. She insisted on walking on the beach each night, in an effort to regain her stamina. With Luz's help, she cut her hair to the approximate length and style of the other woman's. They were close enough in height and weight for them to pass for each other in the dark, especially with her wearing Luz's clothes. It didn't seem to matter. Angel never saw another person.

She'd begun to think of herself by that name, even as she burrowed deep into her mind for any threads of personal information, without success. She could converse with Luz in Spanish with ease, and the other woman had marveled at her fluency. French, Japanese, Arabic and German came as easily, but her thoughts were in English.

She was almost certain she was an American. She had no accent that she could detect, but education could eradicate that, and so could deliberation. She knew as much about recent events in any number of countries, but her knowledge of American popular culture was by far the greatest.

The mirror told her she must be close to Luz's age, around twenty-four. But the reflection of the woman with tawny hair and wide-set golden eyes sparked no sense of recognition. Her nose was short and straight, her mouth small and full. Other than her injuries, she was in excellent physical shape. She had no identifying marks except for the intricate winged horse she had tattooed on her left ankle. It was small, no more than two inches in diameter, but the detail was remarkable. Had the symbol meant something to her at one time, or had she gotten stupidly drunk one night and awakened with a personal adornment she couldn't recall selecting?

The answer to that question was as elusive as any other she'd asked herself, including her instinctive urge to lie to the woman who'd saved her life. She'd received Luz's promise of secrecy by weaving an elaborate tale of wealth, power and corruption, and an older husband's zeal to guard his political reputation. She didn't question her certainty that going to the authorities would be disastrous—just as she didn't question the knowledge she recalled of this island and both its countries, their cultures, climates and governments. She could recall the name of every high-ranking government official on the island.

What she couldn't do was guess at her own. When it came to personal history, it was as if a sponge had scrubbed her mind clean. She could recall nothing—no name, no country, no family. She had no idea who she was, who had wanted her dead, or why.

All she could be sure of was that they were still out there somewhere. And, if they had even the slimmest suspicion that she was alive, they'd be back to finish the job.

Angel prowled the interior of the small hut, testing her endurance. Luz and the child had been gone for hours. They'd taken to spending their afternoons on the beach. Luz worked at one of the resorts at the nearby town of Cuidad de la Playa, and her two weeks off were nearing an end. She'd go back to work another two months straight, while Maria stayed with her grandparents, who lived a mile away.

Night was falling. To give herself something to do, she lit the candles. The mother and daughter lived simply, without electricity or running water. The roof was thatched, the floor packed dirt, the walls some sort of stucco material. There were rolled up shades above the open windows that were probably only used when it rained. A few miles away, the luxury hotels where Luz worked had every modern amenity, but when she returned home it was to a place bordering on squalor.

Crossing to the door, Angel opened it, stepped outside. The area was secluded, ocean on one side and jungle on the other. A balmy breeze rustled the leaves and she could hear waves lapping against the shore. Despite the simple existence, the place was idyllic.

She stood staring out at the moonlit darkness. Maybe Luz had gone to visit her parents, staying later than expected. At any rate, if Angel went for her evening walk, they'd probably be back by the time she returned.

She headed out at a brisk pace, determined to cover more ground than she had the evening before. But it wasn't long before the same burning question dominated her thoughts.

Who had tried to kill her? A husband, as she'd fabricated for Luz? A lover? Had it been a stranger or someone she'd trusted? She'd seen the wet suit Luz had cut off her. It wouldn't be the type favored by local hotels. The material was insulated, too expensive for the wear and tear it would undergo from a constant stream of tourists. Beneath it she'd worn a simple one-piece bathing suit. Like the outerwear, it was obviously high quality. And like the other article, there was no way to identify it. Neither boasted logos or tags of any kind. An attempt to trace them would likely result in failure. And she couldn't help wondering if that was by design.

Pushing herself, she began to jog. The slugs that Luz had taken from her back had come from a 9 mm cartridge. She found her ability to recognize that fact a bit chilling.

So she knew guns. Her bare feet slapped against the smooth sand as she ran. Trying to retrieve the slightest personal detail resulted in blinding headaches, but facts like that—and her knowledge of languages—were just there, unsummoned.

She needed to get someplace where she could research amnesia, but wouldn't be seeking her answers in a hospital. Her rejection of that idea was as strong as her reluctance to involve local law enforcement. With no memory to work with, she was going to have to trust her intuition. At least for now.

Turning, she started back toward the house. She'd come farther than she'd expected, and slowed to a brisk walk. After an initial wave of exhaustion her body had rebounded with renewed energy. She was well enough to make her way off the island. She just wasn't certain of her destination.

She could make out the hut in the distance, its shape shrouded in shadows. Her scalp prickled. Instinct brought her to a halt, even before comprehension filtered through her.

The house was dark.

The candles she'd lit should have been flickering inside, easily seen through the windows. The light breeze could have extinguished one, perhaps. But not all of them.

She scanned the area, but saw no one. Even so, she made her way to the jungle, took the time to search for something that could be used as a weapon. Her options were limited.

Contenting herself with a stout branch she found on the ground, she quickly stripped it of leaves and twigs. Perhaps she was growing alarmed for nothing. But the absence of Luz and the child began to take on an ominous implication.

She looked down, froze. Two feet away were twin furrows in the sand, leading to the jungle. Adrenaline kicked through her. She raised the stick, prepared to wield it as she followed the marks deeper into the brush. She stopped, barely daring to breathe, and pushed aside a tangle of vines to reveal a body.

Bile pooled in her throat as the smell of fresh death permeated the air. Luz's eyes were open, the gaping wound in her throat resembling a hideous smile.

No! The vehement denial shrieked through Angel, a pitiful shield against reality. It was emotion rather than logic that made her sink to the ground, searching for a pulse that she already knew would be absent. Whoever had slit her throat had done so with minimal fuss. She'd been murdered on the beach and dragged out of sight.

And Luz had died because of her.

Guilt swamped her—if she hadn't washed ashore on this particular stretch of beach, Luz would still be alive. Maria would still have a mother.

The thought had her taking a breath. Where was the child? Had she suffered her mother's fate, or run away to hide deeper in the jungle?

She prayed it was the latter, but there was no time now for a search—she had to concentrate on survival. Whoever was out there wouldn't be claiming another victim tonight.

Angel circled the hut from the cover of the jungle and wondered how long the killer would wait inside. Because he *was* in there. His only hope of taking her by surprise was to ambush her inside.

The thought was so chilling that she didn't consider the

ease with which she'd slipped into the killer's mind-set. She thought only of taking him out before he could strike again.

She'd have to advance on the hut diagonally from one corner, the only blind spot. Still grasping the club, she crept forward an inch at a time, dropping to all fours once leaving the protection of the jungle. She stopped beneath one of the windows, flattening herself against the cool stucco. Should anyone lean out the opening and look down she'd be completely exposed, but she doubted the stranger would be willing to show himself.

Minutes ticked by. There was a slight sound, then a shadow moved across the window. Angel had her answer. He was in there. Now she just needed to draw him out.

If he carried only the knife, she had a chance. A gun would prove more difficult to defend against. Either way, the element of surprise would be her most effective weapon. If she could disarm him, she could neutralize him just as effectively in hand-to-hand combat.

The automatic thought made her pause, a distant part of her now noting the natural way she plotted engaging the man, perhaps killing him. There was a sense of shock at this glimpse into what she was. What she may have been. But the rest of her was grim, focused. And utterly intent on staying alive.

She stood carefully and listened. Hearing nothing, she scooped up some damp sand, squeezed it then threw it up on the roof. She repeated the action a few more times and then rounded the corner, sliding along the wall until she could peer around to the front.

A black clad figure hoisted himself onto the window ledge and straightened. He was about a half foot taller than her, she estimated, around six-three. And the blade of the knife he carried gleamed in the darkness.

He sheathed it at his waist before reaching up to where the wall of the hut met the thatched roof. She figured he'd used the gap there to pull himself up and check out what the person on the roof was planning.

Except no one was there.

She moved swiftly, racing forward with the club raised. Swinging hard, she caught him in the knees just as he turned his head toward her, causing him to fall from the ledge. Her next blow was to his wrist. She wanted to debilitate his grip before he could pull the knife. But while the blow found its target, in the next instant he was rolling away and getting nimbly to his feet. He pulled the weapon with his other hand.

He grinned, a macabre show of teeth against the black cloth of the face mask he wore. "Did you enjoy your swim the other night?" Both of them were crouched, eyeing each other for the best angle of approach. "I was kind of hoping sharks would finish you off, but you always did have the devil's own luck."

He was American, she was almost certain. But she was given little time to reflect on that fact. He feinted toward her with a series of short jabs that she easily deflected with the club. Rather than falling back, she drew nearer to him. By pinning him against the side of the house, she could control his movements to some extent. But he wouldn't be so easily trapped. He lunged toward her, swiping downward with the knife, catching her shoulder.

Red-hot pain sliced through her as she brought the club down on his exposed forearm and heard the sickening crunch of bone breaking. The knife dropped to the ground and she kicked it away. With his injury, the field had leveled somewhat, but she wasn't foolish enough to believe that this was over.

It would be a fight to the death.

As if in recognition of that, he aimed a lethal kick at her femoral nerve. Whirling away, she grabbed the club in both hands and rammed it at his groin. He caught it in one fist and moved sharply backward to pull her off balance. He pounced, spinning her around and pressing the club against her neck in a chokehold. Angel could see gray spots forming before her eyes.

"By the way, Sammy sends his regards." His voice was a poison-laced hiss in her ear. She balled her fist and punched repeatedly at the broken bone in his arm while stomping on his foot. Then she drove her elbow back into his solar plexus and finally felt his grip on the club loosen a little.

He tried a hip shot that threw her to the ground. She rolled with it and lashed out to kick him in the face, scrabbling for the knife while he dived down on top of her.

And as his hands went to her neck, no doubt intent on snapping it and ending the fight, she brought the blade up and rammed it in his heart.

For a moment his hands tightened, his eyes behind the mask going wide. Then his shoulders relaxed, his fingers leaving her to go to the knife hilt. She pushed him off her and, seeing his black and shiny blood in the darkness, kneeled beside him.

"Who are you? Who's Sammy?" she asked urgently.

But he just smiled, a dreadful stretching of the lips that was more of a grimace. "He'll…just send…one of the others. You'll…die…" He released a shuddering breath, the sound rattling out of him. "Traitor…bitch."

"Who *am* I?" Her hands clutched his shoulders and she shook him violently, emotionally. But her efforts were in vain. His body went limp and his eyes stared blankly, mocking her even in death.

She rose, swaying a bit, her breath sawing like razors out

of her lungs. Then she stumbled toward the hut, aware of the pain in her shoulder. Touching it, her fingers came away sticky with blood.

Inside, she wet a towel with a bottle of water and jammed it against the wound. Then she lit a candle. Carrying it back to the body, she dropped to her knees and reached out to remove the man's hood.

Angel waited for a glimmer of recognition, but there was nothing. He was blond, square jawed and his sightless eyes were blue. And he'd known her—his words attested to that. She'd thought that perhaps the sight of something, or someone, familiar would spark her memory, but it remained blank. He might as well have been a stranger.

His clothing had been stripped of tags. A search of his pockets yielded nothing, but the empty knife sheath secured to his belt hung beside a narrow pouch, eight inches long.

She took it off and emptied it. There was a large roll of bills in a sealed clear plastic bag, and a small vial of liquid and a syringe.

With quick movements she undressed him. Holding the candle close, she surveyed his body, looking for any marks that might help identify him later.

She almost missed it. The blood from the knife wound had smeared across his upper chest, leaving only a hint of white showing through the stain. Angel took his shirt and wiped away the blood to discover a small tattoo.

There was a roaring in her ears, and a wave of dizziness hit her. It was a small winged horse, identical to the one on her ankle.

A rumble of thunder reminded her that time was precious. From the little the stranger had said, it was obvious that there were others working with him. There was no way to be sure how long she had before they followed. Grabbing the man's pouch, she rose and made her way back into the jungle, hoping that she'd find Maria.

After several minutes of calling, a bush stirred, and the child crawled out from beneath it. Relief—then grief—swamped Angel. "I'm sorry. I'm so sorry. But it's over now," she said in Spanish as the child approached. "Come. I'll take you to your grandparents' home."

Maria refused to grasp Angel's outstretched hand. "I don't need you to take me. I know the way."

"I'll go with you to make sure you're safe."

Tears poured from the girl's eyes, but the venom in her voice was surprisingly adult. "Like Mama was safe? It's your fault she's dead!" The girl turned and raced out of the jungle toward the beach.

Angel's answer was nearly silent, but it etched a guilt-filled scar through her heart. "I know."

Chapter 1

Six Years Later

Sheriff Kingsley motioned for attention from the deputies and raised a hand to begin the signal. On the count of three, the deputy in front used the entry device to blast the door twice, then stood aside as the sheriff raised a booted foot to send it crashing against the opposite wall. The four people inside were already scrambling.

"Freeze!"

Kingsley went into the farmhouse, followed by Deputies Cook and Ralston. The scene inside was chaotic, the shouted orders mingling with the cries of the suspects. One went for his weapon and the sheriff brought up a rifle, sighted and shot with one fluid movement. The man slumped against the wall, hand clamped to his wounded shoulder. Another was attempting to flee through an open window, and Kingsley let him go. Deputies were stationed all around the house. He wouldn't get far.

"Hands in the air. In the air! Don't make a move toward that weapon!" Three other officers raced by to secure the rest of the house. Kingsley kept the rifle trained on the drug dealers they'd surprised, as Deputies Simpson, Cook and Ralston cuffed them. Only then was the weapon lowered and handed to another deputy.

"Need some help there, Ralston?" Kingsley asked.

The hulking man the deputy was attempting to pat down was huge, over six and a half feet tall, and even in restraints he wasn't proving cooperative. It had taken two officers to put cuffs on him, and he was still actively resisting. Kingsley started forward to assist.

"I got him." Ralston's sullen, barely civil tone was familiar, as it was the one he'd used to address the newly appointed sheriff for the last six weeks.

Because it appeared that the deputy had subdued the man, Kingsley drew on some latex gloves and approached the coffee table. Amid piles of bills was a clear bag containing what looked like shards of glass. Picking it up, the sheriff gave a low whistle. "This just might turn out to be a major bust."

Simpson craned his neck to look. "What is it? Coke?"

"Looks like crystal meth to me." Kingsley dropped it into the evidence bag another deputy produced, while the wounded suspect snarled, "It ain't ours. You planted it. We'll all testify to that." He looked around at his companions, as if for support.

"Better hope none of your prints is on it then, genius." To the deputies, Kingsley said, "Get them in the cars. Simpson, once the medic has your prisoner stabilized, take him to the ER."

One by one the officers led each cuffed man outside. But when Ralston passed by the sheriff with his prisoner, the deputy seemed to stumble a little, loosening his hold. The suspect used the opportunity to pull away, lowering his head and then swinging it hard, connecting with Kingsley's face.

Two deputies leaped to assist, but it wasn't necessary. Kingsley grabbed the man's shirt, using his forward motion to flip him to the floor, and placed a foot on the back of his neck to keep him there. It usually wasn't all that difficult to ignore Ralston's attitude, but the smirk on the deputy's face, coupled with the pain from the blow the suspect had landed, had the sheriff calling, "Meyer. Backstrom. Take over for Ralston here."

The order brought a familiar glower to the deputy's face. "That's not necessary, Sheriff. I've got him under control."

"No, Deputy, *I've* got him under control. Back away." Reluctantly, Ralston stepped aside to allow the other two officers to accompany the suspect to the car. Only after all the cuffed men had been taken outside did Kingsley turn to the deputy.

A hand on his arm stopped Ralston as he started to shove by. "No harm done this time, but making mistakes like that with suspects can get other officers injured or killed. Don't let it happen again."

The deputy wheeled around, his thin face flushed and his eyes narrowed. "Is that what you big city hotshots call a mistake? Reading your press, I figured a cocky dyke like you could take this whole crew single-handedly."

Kingsley nodded. "If I had taken them on, one of the first things I would have done with a large struggling opponent would be to incapacitate him completely. Sort of like this." A stiff-fingered jab to a neural pressure point at the base of Ralston's throat had the man sinking to his knees, both hands clasped to his neck, his breathing strangled.

Sheriff Rianna Kingsley stepped around him. "I wonder which will bother you the most now, Ralston. That you're working for a *dyke* sheriff or that she just kicked your ass?"

It was hours before the arrest and booking procedures were completed. There were reports to be filed, evidence to be labeled and bagged and phone calls to dodge. All of those calls had come from Eldon Croat, local county commissioner and primary reason Ria had been appointed to fill out the prior sheriff's term. She was in no mood to listen to the commissioner's jubilant crowing at this latest bust, or about his own brilliance—even when that "brilliance" had to do with his hiring of her.

Her cheek throbbed where the suspect had nailed her, and the ongoing hostility from Ralston hadn't improved her mood. The man had been a major pain since she'd taken the job six weeks ago, and ignoring him hadn't helped. She doubted she'd improved matters any by embarrassing him in front of some of the others, but it had been completely satisfying for her, so that was something.

She glanced at the clock. It was after six. Saving the report she was typing at the computer, she stood and hung up the navy SHERIFF windbreaker she'd discarded earlier, along with the body armor. Grabbing her purse, she headed out. What she needed right now was a thick steak, two fingers of Scotch and the privacy to enjoy both. That meant traveling beyond the confines of Tripolo, Alabama. And probably even outside Fenton County.

Marlyss, the big blond secretary/dispatcher, looked up from her paperwork as Rianna walked by. "Leaving for the night, Sheriff?"

"Going out for a bite. Where's the best steak to be found

around here?" She'd already learned that Marlyss considered herself a culinary connoisseur. From her talk on Mondays it appeared she and her husband's primary socializing on the weekends centered around discovering new restaurants. Her girth was testament to the success of her search.

"Shakers is about ten minutes from here, and they do a decent fillet. Things can get pretty rowdy there on the weekends, though."

Ria recalled the name. She'd sent a couple deputies on a call there last weekend. "What about outside the county?"

Marlyss reached forward and opened a side drawer on her desk. "If you want to drive on over to Phenix City or even Columbus, Georgia, I've got a few menus from places we've enjoyed. You're welcome to take them with you and decide. Bring them back when you're done though, won't you?"

Recognizing the gesture for what it was, Ria took the menus. She wasn't about to turn aside one of the few offers of genuine friendliness she'd encountered since coming here. "I'll do that, Marlyss. Thanks."

Once she'd showered, changed and got in her car, Ria was in the mood to drive. Glancing through the menus the dispatcher had given her, she decided to bypass Phenix City and cross the Chattahoochee River to Columbus. After six weeks on the job, she knew few people in Fenton County and the vicinity, but many would recognize her, thanks to the local news stories announcing her appointment. Columbus represented relative anonymity, and tonight that was what she craved.

She slowed at the first address Marlyss had suggested, but the place looked too crowded and pretentious for her taste. The second, with the dubious name Hoochees, was more her style, and located on what had to be prime riverfront property.

Once inside, she congratulated herself on her selection. The noise level was muted, the tables were set far enough away from each other to give a semblance of privacy, and the bar looked well stocked.

The service was quick and discreet. Within just a few minutes she'd been seated near a large bank of windows overlooking the river, and had placed her order. Nursing her first Scotch, she let her gaze drift across the room, taking unconscious mental note of its occupants, before she found her attention snared by a man behind the bar speaking to the bartender.

A jolt of pure sexual lust sizzled through her. Surprised, she assessed him more carefully. It had been a long time, perhaps too long, since she'd responded to a man on any level. This one was dressed in black trousers and shirt, the sleeves rolled up to show powerful forearms. He was just a couple of inches taller than her own height of five-nine, with longish, well-cut black hair swept back from a face that was all chiseled hollows and carved angles. It was an interesting face, rather than a handsome one, made more so by the old scar that ran from the corner of one eye halfway across his cheek.

Although it was his bone structure that drew attention, it was his eyes that kept it. A pale ice blue, the look in them was as formidable as his expression.

Some would find it difficult to meet that demanding stare. It turned on her now, just for a moment, and she recognized the male speculation there.

Deliberately, she returned her gaze to her drink. She didn't do long-term relationships, not ever. And when sexual energy demanded that she hook up with a man for a brief explosive sexual encounter, she chose men who were safe and shallow. This one didn't appear to meet either criterion.

Picking up her glass, she swirled the amber liquid pensively. Today could be considered her birthday, in a way. It had been six years since she'd washed up on the shores of Santa Cristo. Six years since her appearance there had signed another woman's death warrant.

Ria drank, the Scotch scorching a path down her throat. If she hadn't already been determined to discover her identity, Luz's death would have convinced her to do so. She may have deserved her fate. It was a hard possibility to contemplate, if a realistic one. But Luz had died because she'd gone out of her way to help a stranger, and the act had robbed her child of a mother, Luz's parents of their child.

And someone was going to pay for that.

After making sure Maria was safe at her grandparents still-empty house, Ria had taken up residence at one of the hotels nearby, casing its clients until she found one who resembled her enough for her to steal the woman's ID and return ticket, and pass them off as her own. The plane had taken her to San Diego, but innate caution had had her purchasing a bus ticket to L.A. There had been every reason to fear she would be followed. She'd made sure the trail wouldn't be an easy one. Once in L.A. she'd found a modest room in a questionable neighborhood and spent her days haunting the computer labs on the UCLA campus.

The waitress delivered some steaming plates of food to the next table, and Ria's stomach responded with a growl of interest. She caught the woman's eye on her way by and raised her empty glass slightly. Smiling, the waitress nodded and continued back to the bar.

The Internet was a well of information for people who knew what they were looking for. Ria never had been able to recall any personal information about herself, but she'd known there were sites on the Net where people could obtain realistic looking documents for making false pieces of identification, and books that detailed how to create a past for herself. She'd had both delivered to a mail drop site she'd opened, and then started the real search.

For who had wanted her dead, and why.

Her nape prickled now and she turned to see the man she'd noticed behind the bar approaching her with a bottle of Chivas Regal. Silently, she watched as he stopped at her table and tipped the bottle to her glass, filling it, his gaze never leaving her.

That skitter was back, an electric current that shimmied down her spine and up again. The man's magnetism was even more apparent up close, those ice-blue eyes even more compelling.

"Was the waitress busy?" she asked blandly, after he'd finished pouring.

His well-formed brows lifted. "No, she would have brought you a refill. I decided to bring you a drink and an invitation to share dinner."

His voice was low, smoky, but she discerned a layer of steel beneath the surface charm. She reached out and raised the glass to her lips, still watching him. When she set it back on the table, she inquired, "And if I just want the drink?"

"Then I'd accept your offer to join you for a Scotch and be grateful for that." Smoothly, he reached over and drew out the chair facing hers, sitting down as he motioned to the waitress to bring another glass.

Ria's lips quirked at the obvious manipulation, but she let it pass. There were worse ways to spend a few minutes than conversing with a fascinating man. And perhaps, upon proximity, she'd discovered he wasn't nearly as intriguing as he appeared.

Even as her mind jeered at the idea, she asked, "Are you the manager here, or something?"

"The owner. Are you a tourist?"

"No, I moved nearby recently." She kept her answer purposefully vague, as much from habit as innate caution. She'd spent the last six years living below the radar. Her current identity had been carefully chosen. It would, and had, withstood law enforcement scrutiny and background checks. But no adopted identity was flawless. She had become adept at giving away as little personal information as possible.

Those pale blue eyes surveyed her as the waitress delivered a glass and poured a serving from the bottle. Their color was made even more startling by the dark lashes surrounding them. His was a rugged face, lined from at least thirty-five years, all of them hard. Most people would believe the scar responsible for the air of danger he carried, but Ria knew better. The danger went deeper. This was a man who had handled trouble and delivered more than his share of it.

"You're not from around here." He swirled the liquor in his glass and aimed a smile at her. His mouth was his best feature, its full, sensuous bottom lip providing an intriguing contrast to the chiseled lines of his face.

Her pulse stuttered, shocking her. It had been a long time since she'd responded to a man this strongly. It had been since…well, never. At least not that she could remember.

"You've got no accent, even though folks 'round here like to claim that it's everyone else who talks differently."

Dodging the question couched in his statement, she brought her glass up, sipped. "*You* don't have an accent."

One side of that well-formed mouth kicked up. "That's because I'm from New York originally. But I've been in Georgia for about eleven years. Another fifty and they might consider me a native Southerner."

Ria smiled. She'd already encountered that distant civility

that clearly stated she was considered an outsider, and probably always would be. That was fine with her. She didn't intend to stay in Alabama forever. Just long enough to finish the quest that had driven her for six long years. "You don't look like a restaurateur."

"No?" He leaned back in his chair, took a drink, pausing as if to enjoy the flavor of the aged Scotch. "Well, maybe that's because I have multiple holdings. This place is just one of my businesses. And as of about ten minutes ago, it's my favorite."

The words might have sounded flirtatious coming from another man. But there was nothing lighthearted about him, or about the heat in his eyes. He was taking no pains to hide the fact that his interest in her was immediate, and frankly sexual. More heady than the Scotch, recognition of that fact fired her blood. One of the things she'd come to know about herself was that she wasn't a woman who appreciated games.

She toyed with the idea of taking him up on the carnal invitation in his gaze. Sexual confidence shimmered off him like heat waves from a scorching tarmac. A quick bout of mind-shattering sex would be far more effective than Scotch and a steak to relieve a little of the stress from the last few days.

But in the next moment she rejected the thought, with no little regret. Although he didn't look like the type to be averse to a no-strings, one-night stand, something about him kept her wary. The man had complication written all over him. And her life was already fraught with far too many complications.

There was a slight sound, and he withdrew a small beeper from his trouser pocket, looked at it and frowned. Glancing at her as he slipped it away again, he said, "I have business to attend to. Are you planning on staying long?"

She was already shaking her head. "Just long enough to devour that steak I ordered."

"Maybe you'll change your mind." He made no attempt to disguise the dual meaning in his words. This wouldn't be a man used to having women turn away from his interest in them. But neither would he be one to brood overmuch when one did. He wouldn't lack female companionship—either from those women too dim to be cautious about the slight menace he emanated, or those, like her, who were attracted despite it.

"I don't think so."

He rose. "Your meal will be on the house tonight."

"That's not necessary."

"No. But maybe it will convince you to come back sometime, give us another try."

"Maybe." The word slipped out before she could prevent it, and a look of satisfaction flickered across his face.

He nodded once more. "Until then."

She didn't turn to watch him leave, although a part of her wanted to. Though she doubted their paths would cross again, fantasizing about a possible next time was harmless enough. There was very little room in her life for foolish wistfulness.

Most of her fantasies involved deadly daydreams of revenge.

Although the owner—they'd never gotten around to exchanging names—had left the bottle on her table, she wouldn't be drinking any more once her glass was empty. She knew her limits, all of them, and stayed scrupulously within them. It had been a reeducation of sorts, every bit of knowledge that she'd learned about herself a prize that could be pieced together with others to get a sense of the whole.

Some had appeared at odd times, disconcerting bits that had formed an undeniably disturbing picture of whom she'd been. She'd had very little trouble devising a plan for getting out of Santa Cristo. She thought it might prove more difficult post 9/11, with all the heightened security. But at the time, she'd never missed a beat, whether it was fighting a masked assailant to the death, breaking into a safe in a resort room or assuming a new identity.

Though her personal recollections had never reappeared, there were plenty of things that she did remember, and those memories were troublesome. How many amnesia victims could claim to recall exactly how to beat a polygraph? She'd been confident in her ability to do so, and had succeeded in the course of her recruitment to the police academy.

It was second nature for her to enter a new place and make immediate note of the exits, while sizing up the occupants with a speed that spoke of training or practice. From just a few glances she knew the bartender here would be as adept with a weapon as he was at mixing drinks; that the couple in the far corner were probably engaged in an extramarital affair; the guy to her right would fold in the face of trouble, but the one sitting at the bar could handle himself in a fight; and that the man on her left was screwing up the courage to approach her.

She no longer questioned where these skills stemmed from. They were merely tools, to be used in her search for answers of a far more serious nature. Although there was very little she could be positive of, she was fairly sure that whatever her identity before that fateful night in Santa Cristo, she'd almost certainly been operating outside the law.

It had been a hard realization to swallow, and she'd done her share of dodging the truth. It would have been easier, far easier, had she been able to manufacture another explanation. There was any number of possible scenarios for her ending up shot and left for dead off the shore of the island. But coupled with her familiarity with weapons, Dim-Mak combat and assassination techniques, there were only a few explanations that made sense.

She'd either been a criminal, a mercenary or some sort of operative, military or government sanctioned. While she'd hoped for the latter, she'd long ago resigned herself to discovering the worst.

Because the pang that accompanied that thought was unwelcome, she pushed it aside. *Happy, happy birthday to her.* Her lips twisted into an expression that should have dissuaded the interest of the man at the next table, before she swallowed some more Scotch, welcoming the fiery path it traced down to her stomach.

Her steak arrived at approximately the same time as the guy beside her, and was much more welcome.

"Looks like you're dining alone." His smile was toothpaste ad bright as he rested his folded arms on top of the chair next to her. "Me, too. Not much fun, is it?"

"Can I get you anything else?" the waitress asked.

Ignoring the stranger for the moment, Ria smiled at the woman, shook her head. "No, thank you. This looks great." The waitress sent a quick glance at the man and moved away.

"It should, for these prices. But they do a decent fillet here. Not as good as Falstead's. Have you been there?"

"No. I'm looking forward to enjoying this one, though." As a dismissal, it was more polite than she was feeling. Spreading the napkin on her lap, she picked up her silverware.

"Be more enjoyable with company, wouldn't it?" The man aimed another smile her way, pulled out the chair next to her. Sinking into it, he continued, "I'm Tyler Stodgill, by the way. I placed my order right after yours. My food should be coming any minute. No reason for us to eat alone."

Looking at him, she said succinctly, "But I want to eat alone."

"Bad for the digestion. Believe me, I know. I'm on the road three or four days a week. I'm a pharmaceutical salesman." He flashed his teeth again. "I hit forty-fifty medical offices a month."

Deliberately, she set her knife and fork down, before she was tempted to use them on him. He wasn't bad looking. He was a little stocky, with short-cropped sandy hair, brown eyes and a rounded jaw. His navy blazer jacket and wheat-colored pants were sharply creased, his white shirt spotless. He could have been a lonely traveling salesperson, looking for a little companionship. She might have believed it if it wasn't for his eyes. This was no dense oaf without the social skills to sense her lack of welcome. This was a man filled with an overinflated sense of self-importance and—a woman's worst nightmare—a gross overestimation of his own appeal.

She sighed and reached for some rapidly dwindling patience. "Look, I've had a hard week. I just want a drink, a steak and silence. I wouldn't be good company."

His expression went ugly. "Looked like your company was fine when Jake was here."

She blinked. "Who?"

"You know. The owner. The guy you were drinking with."

Jake. The name suited the man somehow, tough and nononsense. "I told him basically the same thing I'm telling you." She aimed a pointed look at him. "He took it with more grace."

His face had smoothed. "Whatever it is that's bothering you, I'm just the guy to make you forget about all your troubles." With a sense of disbelief, she felt his hand on her thigh below the table, caressing her leg suggestively through her white slacks. "I'm staying at a hotel not too far from here. After dinner, maybe we could—" Whatever he had been about to say ended in a yelp as she bent his two middle fingers far enough to nearly touch the back of his hand.

She kept her expression pleasant, but her tone was lethal. "You need to learn to pay attention. I'm not interested. Do you understand now?"

With his teeth clenched, he grasped, "You're breaking my damn fingers."

"Not yet. But I could." She exerted just enough pressure on the joints to back up her words, and a whimper escaped him. A man at a table nearby gave them a cursory glance. Ria wasn't concerned. The long table linen would hide her actions.

Stodgill's face was rapidly losing color. She noted the approach of the waitress. "Your food is coming. I want you to take it and ask for a different table. One where I can't see you. If you don't, I am really, really going to hurt you."

"All right! Let go!"

She did, only because the waitress had halted at his table, clearly uncertain about where to set his food. He immediately shoved back his chair, a vicious expression on his face, muttering an obscenity. Ria picked up her silverware again. "I think a table on the other side of the bar might suit your needs best."

He rose, the chair clattering behind him. "I want a different table," he told the server in a loud voice. "I don't like the view from here."

The young woman said, "But you asked for a view of the river, sir. This is the best—"

"Dammit, I said I want a new table! Something over there." He lurched off, leaving the waitress to follow with his tray of food.

While a few diners watched the small scene, Ria reached for her Scotch, drained the glass. The bottle was still there, a silent temptation, one she wouldn't allow herself to succumb to. She couldn't afford weaknesses in her life. Weaknesses led to mistakes. And even one slip could lead yet another assassin to her doorstep, like the one who'd found her in Santa Cristo.

And the second who'd caught up with her in L.A.

She cut another piece of steak and brought it to her mouth, savoring the taste. A woman who had faced death as often as she had had learned to enjoy life's small pleasures. Even now she couldn't pinpoint how the second killer had managed to track her from San Diego to L.A., although she suspected the money she'd taken off the first one had somehow been traced. She hadn't been in Los Angeles two weeks before a man had been waiting for her one night in the room she'd rented.

He'd been as able as the first killer, his intent just as deadly. But instead of a knife, his weapon of choice had been a garrote—a thin wire used for strangling victims quickly and silently. The savage fight had lasted no more than a few minutes, but in the end it had been the stranger who had ended up dead on the floor, without ever having spoken a word.

He'd been dressed exactly as the first would-be killer, down to the pouch at his waist. Again, it had held only a vial, a syringe and a wad of ten one-hundred-dollar bills.

And the tattoo identical to her own, and that of the first killer, had been found on his right shoulder.

This time she'd taken a few precautions before fleeing. She'd gone to a department store and bought a disposable camera, using one of the bills she'd taken off the man. Then, using city transit, she went from one discount store to the next, buying items she'd need, each time carefully exchanging the man's money. When she'd gotten back to her room, she'd taken several pictures of the killer and the tattoo before packing quickly and leaving L.A. behind.

Ria stopped devouring the steak long enough to taste the baked potato, drenched in melted butter. She could practically feel her arteries clogging, but she'd work off the calories the next day at the gym. Tripolo had a new YMCA with a very decent weight room. One of the first things she'd done upon moving there was to join it. Staying in shape was as vital for her new occupation as it had been for whatever her former one had been.

She'd purposefully crisscrossed the western United States in a random manner meant to confuse. When she'd gotten low on money, she'd stolen more, and found herself distastefully adept at it. She'd landed on the campus of the University of Iowa, where it had been surprisingly easy to join a group of prospective new students there for orientation, and obtain a photo ID. And then she'd melted in with the other twenty-nine thousand students and gone back to work. Before she could set about discovering her real identity, she'd first had to manufacture a new one.

"Would you like any dessert this evening?" The waitress was back with a practiced smile.

"No, but I will take some coffee." Ria waited for her to return with it and fill her cup, then had her leave the carafe on the table.

Ria drank pensively, lost in memories that began six years ago. At the U of I she'd haunted the computer labs, careful to use different ones each time, searching for anything that would connect to her.

The discovery of the body she'd left in her L.A. apartment had warranted a three-inch article buried deep in the *L.A. Times*. She'd hoped that a revelation of the assassin's identity would provide clues to her own. She'd even called the news desk at the *Times* on a couple of occasions, talked to the crime reporter who had covered the story. By feeding him some careful details, she was able to whet his interest enough to have him digging further. But the dead man had remained a John Doe, and the case had eventually been shelved as unsolved. The only thing of value she'd learned was that neither of their fingerprints had been on file in the national Automated Fingerprint Identification System. Whoever the would-be killer had been, his death had caused as little stir as had her own disappearance.

Because new identities didn't come cheap, she'd used almost every dime she had left on establishing hers. And she'd been aided, at first unknowingly, by the one person who'd been allowed to get halfway close to her, Benny Zappa.

Something inside her softened at the thought of Benny, with his gangly scarecrow walk and too large Adam's apple. His narrow black-rimmed glasses had been meant to be stylish, but they couldn't disguise what he was—a computer geek through and through, and proud of his abilities, if not of the persona that he could never quite shed. In his awkward, bumbling way he'd offered to help her—in an attempt to hit on her, she'd thought. And at first she'd seen his shy overtures through purely shrewd eyes, as a means to an end. It wasn't until later that she discovered in the process she'd made an invaluable friend.

His genius with computers was coupled with a hacker's love of a challenge. No database—university, state or federal—seemed impenetrable with him at the keyboard. With the information he was able to access for her, she'd chosen a new identity and followed every lead she could think of. And what she appreciated most about him, in all this time, was his willingness to use his skills without asking questions she had no intentions of answering.

Although he must have put some details together about what drove her, he didn't press her about it, and she appreciated his discretion as much as his friendship.

Refilling her cup, she sipped, watching the river churn sluggishly by, as evening turned to dusk. If she headed back now she could get a couple hours of work in. Not at the sheriff's office, but in the office she'd set up in a spare bedroom in the house she'd bought in Tripolo.

Each lead she'd followed about her identity, every fact she'd discovered, was carefully encrypted and kept on her home computer. After six years she had a substantial file with a copy downloaded to CD monthly and sent to a mail drop across the country for safekeeping. So far she had plenty of dead ends, plenty of threads that apparently went nowhere. But she wasn't giving up. She'd never give up.

There were some who would consider her existence lonely. But she thought she must be used to being alone, because it had never bothered her overmuch in the last half-dozen years. What had seemed strange was the openhearted generosity of Luz, the puppy-dog friendliness of Benny. The fact that Ria had first regarded both of them with suspicion was surely an indictment of who, or what, she'd been.

Catching the waitress's attention, she summoned her over, ready to leave. Whatever else she'd learned about herself, she wasn't one to make the same mistake twice. Benny lived halfway across the country and she was excruciatingly careful on the rare occasions she allowed herself to contact him on an untraceable cell phone. She didn't think she'd be able to bear it if another person died because of her.

"Oh, there's no bill, ma'am," the waitress said. "Jake said it's on the house."

Jake. She'd like to pretend she'd already forgotten him, but she wasn't in the habit of lying to herself. He'd hovered in the back of her mind since he'd left, a haunting reminder of a fascinating man she would never see again. Ria opened her purse, took out some bills. "I told him that wasn't necessary. I'd like to pay for my own meal. Could you please tell me how much it was?"

But the woman was backing away, a faintly alarmed expression on her face. "Oh, no, ma'am, I couldn't do that. Jake said specifically, and 'round here, we do what he says."

With a mental shrug, Ria gave up. She folded the bills and handed them to the server. "Then this is for you."

The woman gave her a shocked look, but whisked them into a pocket in her apron quickly enough. "Thank you, ma'am. Hope you come back real soon."

But thoughts of returning were far from Ria's mind as she made her way to the large parking lot outside, keys in her hand. It was full now, much more crowded than it had been when she'd arrived. Walking purposefully toward her car, she heard her cell phone ring and took it from her purse, checking the caller ID. Eldon Croat. With a grimace, she decided against answering it. Tomorrow would be soon enough to meet with the county commissioner and try to talk him out of the press conference he'd want to call about the latest drug busts. Even after all these years, and the attempts she'd taken to change her appearance, she was leery about getting—

He seemed to come out of nowhere, looming from between two cars and taking quick steps toward her. Her hands were full, slowing her response, and before she could react he was behind her, grabbing her nape and smashing her face into the roof of her car.

It was telling in that instant, with stars bursting behind her eyes, that her first thought was of the assassins. And that they'd finally caught up with her.

Chapter 2

Jake Tarrance cruised into the lot and pulled into his private parking spot. Not even to himself was he willing to admit he'd hurried through the problem-solving meeting this evening. It was doubtful the copper-haired woman with the incredible eyes was still at Hoochees, even more doubtful that she'd changed her mind about keeping him company. Still, the memory of taut curves and a tight body had him dispatching his troublesome supplier, Roy Hastings, more quickly than usual. Tonight's solution had been temporary, at best. Hastings was getting to be too much a liability. And Jake had no conscience about dispensing with liabilities.

There were some who would swear he had no conscience at all. More and more frequently these days, he was inclined to agree.

Lights were visible from the security booth installed in the center of the lot, but he didn't see anyone inside. He got out of the car with his hand on the gun nestled at the base of his back. Security might be making rounds, but for a man with a price on his head, caution was a way of life.

After taking a couple of steps, he paused, hearing sounds of a struggle. He withdrew the gun and thumbed off the safety, running in that direction.

He didn't have to go far before he saw the fight going on. He reholstered the gun and reached for his cell phone to alert the still-absent security. But in the next second Jake realized the struggle involved a man and woman, and something inside him went glacial. The phone remained in his pocket. He'd deal with the matter himself.

Racing forward, he became aware of two things simultaneously. One was that the guy was definitely getting the worst end of the battle; the second was that the female beating the hell out of him was none other than the intriguing woman he'd shared a drink with.

The other man rushed at her, his head lowered. She kicked out, catching him in the jaw with enough force to snap his head back. The blow made him stagger, and he stumbled against a nearby car. While he leaned there dazedly, she closed the distance between them, grabbed his shirt to pull him forward and rammed her knee into his groin.

Jake's brows rose in approval. He didn't recall ever seeing a woman less in need of rescuing. Folding his arms across his chest, he watched as the man gave a strangled moan, then in slow motion crumpled to the asphalt.

"That ought to take care of his social life for a few days, anyway."

The woman wheeled around, probably still nerved up with adrenaline. But Jake's amusement fled the moment he caught sight of her face. The blood covering it was still flowing freely, and staining what remained of her yellow blouse. The buttons had been torn off, to leave it hanging loose, revealing the nude, lace-edged bra beneath. The ice abruptly re-formed in his veins.

Jake took a handkerchief from his pocket and held it out to her. When she didn't move to take it, he pressed it into her hands. "Are you hurt as badly as you look?"

She gave him a slight frown, bent to catch a glimpse of herself in a car's side mirror. "Great," she muttered, wadding up his handkerchief and pressing it against her nose. Sending a sidelong glare at the man still clutching himself on the ground, she said, "I ought to hammer him again."

Something inside Jake eased slightly at her tone. It was disgruntled, but she didn't sound as though she was badly injured. "I think at this point that would be redundant, don't you?" He stepped closer, caught her chin in his hand, turned her face one way, then the other, surveying it critically. "Your nose doesn't look broken. How does it feel?"

"Like it got slammed into a car."

When she pulled away from his touch, he let her go. She set down the handkerchief for a moment to tie the front of her shirt together. Taking the cell phone out of his pocket, he pressed a button on his speed dial. Without taking his eyes off her he spoke into it. "Cort, get someone to take over the bar and come out to the parking lot. Bring Finn and Dobbs with you. And find out where the security guard went who was supposed to be on duty out here."

She looked past him to the still empty security booth. "There was no one in it when I left the restaurant. Either this creep has lucky timing or your security isn't all it's cracked up to be."

"Either way, someone has a lot to answer for." Jake looked

at the man on the ground, who was struggling to his feet, then back to the woman. "Feel like telling me what happened out here?"

"It's not what it looked like, I swear."

The man's voice was familiar. Jake peered closer, recognized him as an occasional patron of the restaurant. Taylor something. No, Tyler. That was it. "And what do you think it looks like?"

"She was coming on to me. You know how it is, right?" The man gave him a sickly grin, talking so fast his words practically fell over themselves. "But when I met her out here like she asked, damned if she didn't start talking price. Well, I'm not a guy who pays for it, you know? So things got kind of heated—"

"Stop," Jake advised softly. He knew where the razor-edged fury he felt sprang from. There was a time when it had dictated his every thought, his every action. Surprising that ten years hadn't really dulled it in the least. Surprising, and for this man, unfortunate.

"Uhh…Mr. Tarrance."

Jake looked at the security guard, who had run up, his expression worried.

"Is there a problem?" The man asked. "I just stepped inside for a minute. I was feeling kinda sick. But I wasn't gone longer than that, I swear."

"You're done here. Cort?" He addressed the other man that had appeared silently, already looming over the guard. "Be sure and escort our former employee off the premises."

The guard took a sideways look at the bartender and inched away. "I swear, Mr. Tarrance, I think I got the flu or something. I never woulda left otherwise…"

"Really? Then you won't mind if we go through your pockets."

With a nod from Jake, the bartender quickly searched the man's pants pockets, pulling out a folded fifty that looked a hell of a lot like a bribe.

Jake gave Cort a pointed glance. "I think you ought to drive him home. Have a little talk."

The security guard was still protesting when the bartender took his elbow and led him, almost gently, away.

"Tyler, right?" Jake addressed the man still leaning heavily against a car, dusting off his pants.

His eyes darted nervously as Finn and Dobbs moved silently to flank him. "That's right. Tyler Stodgill. Sorry about all this, but that's the thing about women, huh?" He swallowed hard. "Nothing but trouble."

He seemed to flinch in the face of Jake's answering smile. "You might want to avoid this kind of trouble in the future. It doesn't seem healthy. My men will take you to the hospital, get you checked out. Don't worry. They'll make sure your car gets there, too."

For the first time real fear showed in the man's expression, and he shook his head vigorously. "Hey, that's not necessary. I'm okay. Really."

"I insist. Insurance problems, you know." Jake gave a what-can-you-do shrug. "You could be suffering from internal injuries. Those can be tricky." He made a slight gesture and the two men closed in on Stodgill, his protests trailing behind him as they led him away.

The woman shot him a knowing look. "I have the distinct impression that although he doesn't need a doctor now, he will when he arrives at the hospital."

"Really?" Jake frowned, considering her words. "I could see how a person might think that, if he had a suspicious mind. And if he didn't know what a kind-hearted philanthropist I am."

The handkerchief she was dabbing gingerly at her nose muffled the snort she gave. He reached for her wrist, tugged it away from her face so he could survey the damage. "The bleeding has stopped. C'mon. I'll take you somewhere you can clean up."

"That's not…" He heard a slight sound that might have been her teeth grinding as he cupped her elbow and herded her back toward the restaurant. "You're pushy, you know that?"

"It's been mentioned." Inside the front doors, instead of entering the restaurant he took out his keys and used one to open the discreet private elevator on one wall. "But even given the fate suffered by your last admirer, I'm going risk it. You need some ice for that nose. And if I think it's broken, you're going to see a doctor, too." He ushered her into the elevator and punched in a code. The doors slid closed silently.

"It's not broken."

He had a feeling that her words were laced with more determination than certainty, as if she could will them to be true. The woman had a spine of steel. His mouth quirked. And the self-defense moves of a ninja.

"We never got around to exchanging names." He watched the wariness flicker across her face before she deliberately blanked it. "Mine's Jake Tarrance."

"Ria."

He waited, but it was apparent that was all she was going to offer. With a mental shrug, he waited for the doors to slide open again, then put his hand to the base of her back to nudge her forward.

She went, crossing the large open room to the bank of floor-to-ceiling windows that comprised the west wall. "Nice view." She looked back at him. "Reflective glass?"

He stilled, shot her a look.

"No window treatments." She waved a hand. "Either you're an exhibitionist or the place was designed so you could enjoy the view while maintaining your privacy."

"I do like my privacy." He went to the kitchen and placed some crushed ice in a dish towel, then folded it into a make-shift ice pack. Returning, he passed it to her, taking the handkerchief from her hand. "For the swelling." She pressed it to her face while he studied her. "So he jumped you on your way to your car?"

"I heard him behind me, but he was closer than I thought. Got in one good crack before I turned around." Somehow Jake knew that fact would rankle her for a while. "At dinner he had difficulty understanding I wasn't interested. Must have thought I'd find him more appealing in the dark."

Jake's fist closed, tightened. Ghosts from the past drifted through his memory, carrying with them the sound of distant screams. But Ria wouldn't be the type of woman to cower in a corner while the blows rained down, heavy and punishing. Wouldn't be the kind to make excuses for the man later, smiling through the bruises, with a look in her eyes that was half despair, half hope.

Consciously, he unclenched his fingers. Whatever else this woman was, she was no one's victim. "Guess he found out otherwise."

"You think?" A small satisfied smile settled on her lips, and lust punched through him, just as swift, just as savage as the first time he'd seen her in the restaurant. He knew almost nothing about the woman, but he knew he wanted her, all of her. He wanted to wipe that look of cool competence from her face, to shatter that wariness and have her attention focused only on him as he moved over her, inside her.

The strength of that vicious longing was unexpected

enough to have all his well-constructed defenses slam into place. He wasn't a man driven by impulse. Emotion-laden decisions led to vulnerabilities, and he couldn't afford to be vulnerable. He'd done very well without feeling much of anything at all for the last decade, and hadn't been overly bothered by the void.

It also seemed a shame to develop an attachment for someone who might have to be killed later.

She could have been sent by Alvarez. It wouldn't be the first time an attractive woman had been used to try and set him up. If so, the man had deviated from type this time. Ria was far subtler, both in looks and in manner. She hadn't tried to gain his attention at the restaurant, although the scene outside it could have been a pretense.

Jake considered the thought as she rose and crossed the room to look at a collection of black-and-white photographs on the far wall. Alvarez knew him a bit better than Jake would have liked, and may have staged the scene, guessing how he'd react. But if that was the case, Jake doubted very much that the woman selected would end up beating the hell out of the guy.

The corner of his mouth lifted. No, whoever this woman was, he was willing to bet she hadn't faked anything this evening. Not the spark of awareness that she'd almost successfully hidden. Not the instinctive guardedness that she made no effort to hide.

In any case, this place was swept for bugs daily. The code to the elevator was on a triple circuit pattern that changed upon each use. And Alvarez wouldn't send anyone with lethal intent. He wanted Jake's death to come from his own hand.

Some might consider Jake's swift mental assessment as paranoid. But in his world, paranoia was a necessary tool for survival.

He joined her at the photographs, glancing at her as she stared fixedly at them. Most people found the stark images disturbing. They hadn't been taken to capture beauty, or to celebrate life. But it was impossible to tell her opinion. Her face was expressionless. "You like photography?"

Ria didn't answer at first. She couldn't. They were the sort of photos that made her want to look away, the sort that wouldn't allow her to dismiss them easily. At first glance they would seem disconnected shots. A close-up of a wino shivering in an alley. An old woman leaning out a tenement window. A barely clothed toddler sitting on a ramshackle stoop. A group of teens wearing gang colors and sullen masks.

"I thought at first they were random shots, but I was wrong. The look in the eyes of the subjects is the same. Desolation." She recognized the expression easily enough. She'd faced it in the mirror more times than she wanted to think about. Noting his stillness, she felt comprehension dawn. "You took these yourself, didn't you?"

"What makes you think so?"

After a last glance at the photos, she turned back toward the windows. "Because you have a way of looking through people."

She wouldn't want that cruelly discerning eye turned on her, she thought with vague discomfort. How many times had she felt like little more than a snapshot herself? A carefully presented picture developed to present the image she wished to display to the world. There might be character hinted at in her unsmiling demeanor, but if one were to examine her life, much as they'd hold up a photo to peer at it more closely, they'd find little more than what existed on that flimsy paper. No substance behind the image.

Because in every way that mattered, Ria really didn't exist at all.

Walking to the large, well-equipped kitchen, she placed the ice pack in the sink and then turned to find Jake contemplating her from the arched doorway. "I should go." The thought of her new home lacked appeal, but there was danger here, emotional rather than physical. She recognized the fact even as she wondered where that realization stemmed from.

"You don't have to." His pale blue eyes glittered with unmistakable intensity, but he made no move toward her. Whatever her decision, it would be hers to make. She could respect a man who didn't push, despite the hunger apparent on his face.

"Yes." Her voice was shakier than she'd like, matching her resolve. "I do."

"You can't go home like that. Let me get you a shirt." He turned and walked into another room, while Ria headed toward the chair near the windows where she'd left her purse.

He caught up with her at the door, silently handing her a gray T-shirt with a faded Knicks logo. "Thanks." She took it, appreciating the thought even though she had no intention of changing in front of him. They stared at each other for an instant, the moment awkward, thick with tension. She felt the wild and reckless beating of her pulse, and found it much harder than she'd like to ignore. If it had been due solely to animal attraction there would be no choice; she'd be in his bed, wrapped around him, using him to quench the heat in her blood.

But it wasn't that simple. *He* wasn't that simple. Instinct warned her of that. There was an undeniable connection between them that defied identification, and anything that couldn't be coolly qualified and analyzed was to be avoided. Ria took plenty of risks, but only when she could control the situation. Jake Tarrance didn't appear to be a man easily controlled.

So she tucked away need in the interest of safety. She opened the door, for the first time noticing the tiny cameras in the hallway. Most visitors wouldn't observe them at all, but the miniscule whirls in the oak paneling high on the walls appeared just a little too uniform. He was a careful man. She assumed he had cause to be.

Jake followed her out silently, produced the key that unlocked the elevator. When the door opened, she stepped inside it, turned to face him. He punched in the code that would have carried her away from him. But just as the doors began to slide shut, he stepped forward and slapped his hand over the button that would stop them.

One of his business sidelines—by far the most lucrative one—dealt with rarities of unparalleled value. So he recognized the uniqueness of the woman who was bent on leaving, even if he couldn't have described where the quality came from.

Bracing his hands on either side of the entrance, he leaned in for a taste of her. If this was the last time he'd see her, he'd damn well have this much.

He pressed her lips apart with his, sweeping his tongue into her mouth, and felt the hunger lunge inside him. His fingers clenched on the open elevator doors. It took physical effort to keep from reaching for her. Her flavor was foreign, an intoxicating mixture of desire and caution, but there was a response there to match his own.

Kindred spirits. The phrase drifted across his mind, even awash as it was in a fog of frustrated lust. Something in him recognized a part of her, a part she would have denied existed. Most solitary people were that way by nature, or became so by circumstances.

Then there were people like them, he thought, who allowed circumstance to dictate nature, until the two were so entwined it was impossible to say where one left off and the other began.

Ria gave in to a rare moment of self-indulgence and opened her mouth beneath his. He knew how to kiss a woman, with a single-minded intensity that stripped them both down to their most elemental levels, male and female. He knew how to take while still giving riotous pleasure, sensual hints of the erotic satisfaction to be had if she let passion have its way.

This wouldn't be an easy man to walk away from, although she had every intention of doing just that. But one taste couldn't hurt, could it? Even if it whipped her blood to churning whitecaps and incinerated her control? Every move she made in life was calculated, with the benefits and risks carefully weighed. Stealing a few minutes with an exciting stranger seemed relatively harmless.

But there was nothing harmless about the flames licking through her veins. Absorbing his intoxicating taste was like diving headlong into dark fire.

Without conscious thought she moved closer and caught his full lower lip in her teeth. Scoring it lightly, she felt a measure of restraint slip away. His answering kiss was hard, demanding, but he made no further move toward her. The muscles in the wall of his chest were bunched tightly, his hands still pressed against the open doors.

Emboldened, she leaned against him, took the kiss deeper. How long had it been, she thought fuzzily, since she'd last felt a fever in the blood, temptation stripping layers off her defenses? Had she ever?

This scorching heat was its own kind of seduction for a woman who spent her life—what she could remember of it—in the cold. It was unlikely their paths would cross again. The idea was tantalizing. Despite the shadowy aura of danger that surrounded him, there was something soothing in his very anonymity.

The rationalization shredded caution, struck down logic. He angled his mouth over hers, the pressure almost punishing. The purse and T-shirt dropped from her hands, and she slid her arms around his neck.

The restraint he'd been exerting snapped abruptly. She was pulled against him, the move shattering any sense that she could control this. The kiss turned rawly primitive, even as he walked her backward to press her against the wall of the elevator, sealing their bodies together. Currents of electricity sizzled and crackled between them. One of his hands settled at her nape as his mouth ravished hers, as if to coax her even closer, and he widened his stance so that she was standing between his legs.

He tore his mouth away from hers to bury it at her throat. "I've been wanting to do this since I first saw you." His voice was low, harsh.

"I know." Her answer was nearly a moan, as she arched her neck to allow him better access.

"You, too?"

There was a part of her that wanted to withhold assent, but that would have been pointless. He was a man experienced enough to recognize that the instant attraction that had sparked between them was mutual. And her response to him now was its own answer. "Yes—"

The word stopped on a gasp when he nipped at the sensitive cord of her neck. His tongue soothed the sting in the next instant. "So stay."

It was a demand rather than a plea, and the carnal promise implicit in it made her stomach clutch. He knew exactly how to touch her, his mouth slightly rough, his palm burning the bare skin of her nape, his fingers tangling in her hair. As close as they were, she could feel the unmistakable hard ridge of his erection pressing against the notch between her thighs. She wouldn't have to hold back with him; she could respond with every bit of the explosive arousal churning through her, and he would meet it, match it. But still she was vaguely surprised to hear herself answer, "For a while."

A low sound was torn from him. She felt cool air against her skin and realized dimly that he'd unknotted her ruined shirt. With a quick jerk he had it open, the remaining buttons flying, and his impatience called to a streak of wildness in her, one she was usually careful to keep deeply buried.

There was so little in her life she could claim as her own. Only memories garnered from the last six years. Certainly not her identity, which she'd stolen from another. But this moment was hers. Personal and genuine, it was hers to keep, to remember, to experience to the fullest.

His tongue was tracing the mounds of her breasts where they swelled above the top of her bra as he pushed the blouse from her shoulders, to pool forgotten on the floor of the elevator. Her hands went to his shirt, jerking it impatiently from the waistband of his pants, her fingers flying over the buttons.

When she had them undone, she smiled, satisfied, her breath coming a little faster. The wall of his chest was firm, muscled and bisected by a patch of dark hair. His stomach was hard and ridged. He'd work out, she thought, for the same reason she did—to keep instincts alert and body prepared for whatever dangers awaited. But whatever the reason, the sight of all those well-honed muscles sharpened her desire to a keen edge.

His hands were undoing the clasp of her bra when she leaned forward, tested one hard pec with her teeth. His flesh jumped beneath her lips. Her sudden surge of satisfaction at his involuntary reaction fractured in the next moment when he pulled the straps of her bra down her arms and tossed it aside. Bending his head, he took a nipple in his mouth and sucked strongly.

Colors pinwheeled against her closed eyelids. Her knees went to water. His mouth worked at her ravenously, one hand kneading her other breast, his thumb flicking across her nipple to urge it to a tauter point.

Her muscles took on the consistency of melting wax. To brace herself, she hooked a leg around his hips. With increasing urgency she battled with his shirt, pushing it off his heavy shoulders, over his bulging biceps. Because he wouldn't release her, it remained trapped there, halfway down his arms. Her palms raced over the expanse of flesh she'd bared, exploring the different textures of smooth skin and crisp hair over unforgiving bone and sinew.

There was a primal sort of sensuality to be enjoyed through touch alone. Her hands roamed his torso, discovering every angle and hollow. She traced the shallow indentations between his ribs, scraped a nail over his nipple and was rewarded by his quick shudder.

He raised his head, and when the cool air struck her nipple, still wet from his mouth, she shivered. With quick movements, he struggled out of his shirt, then put both hands under her butt to lift her. Ria clasped her legs around his waist and he carried her that way back into his apartment, swinging the door closed behind them.

Their mouths did battle, tongues darting, teeth clashing as hunger mounted. She slid her hands into his hair to pull him closer, and felt the hot ball of need knot tighter in the pit of her stomach.

When her shoulders were pressed against a cool smooth surface, she arched her back and dazedly opened her eyes.

Rather than his bedroom, they were in the dimly lit living area, her back to a window. Then Jake's gaze caught hers, and her pulse stuttered.

His eyes glittered, intent and predatory. His hair was mussed from her hands, his cheeks flushed with arousal, his expression faintly savage. Her heart pumped, heavy and fast. A normal woman would be having second thoughts, feeling an innately feminine fear in the face of his unvarnished desire.

But Ria reveled in it. It called forth her own unchecked response. There was no holding back; he wouldn't have allowed that even if she'd tried. She could let her own passion rage and know it would be returned in like measure.

Setting her on her feet, Jake stripped her of her slacks and shoes with quick movements, then took a moment to admire the picture she made. She was just a few inches shorter than him, slim, with sleek muscle beneath velvety curves. Her breasts were high and firm, nipples beaded. He fondled them, drawing them into tighter points even as her hands went to his waistband.

He clenched his teeth as she worked the zipper slowly over his hardness, saw the little smile she gave as her hand reached inside the opening to squeeze him lightly. His vision blurred, cleared, and he saw only her.

She wasn't like any other woman he'd had—not shy nor bold, playful or serious. She was, like him, totally focused on the moment, the gut-wrenching pleasure that could be had between two people with no pretenses between them.

And she wasn't, he noticed, as he parted her feminine folds and slipped a finger inside her, a natural redhead.

Her inner moisture eased his way as he probed her gently. He could feel the delicate pulsation as the feminine muscles clenched around his touch, let himself imagine how it would feel when he took her fully.

And then conscious thought shattered as she freed him from his clothes and took him in her hand, clever fingers stroking the length of him in a rhythm guaranteed to send his temperature skyrocketing.

It was a battle to drive each other crazy, and he engaged in it for a few minutes, tasting the pulse at the base of her neck, the crease below her breast. But as the roaring in his blood sounded in his ears, he knew the battle was lost. She'd gotten him hotter, faster, than any woman of his experience, and if he didn't have her soon, he was going to disgrace himself.

Jake broke away long enough to fumble in his pocket for a condom. Ria took it from him and tore it open as he dispensed with his clothes, but the excruciating care she took when she rolled the latex down his length had him gritting his teeth.

His hands less than gentle, he turned her around to face the window, his hormones surging as her sexy form was reflected back for him. Bracing one arm under her against the glass, he pressed her legs apart with one knee and stepped between them. Using his free hand to guide himself, he found the sweet slick opening and entered her.

Their moans mingled. He stopped a moment to haul more oxygen into his lungs, struggling for control. He didn't want this to be over too soon. There was still so much to be savored, rare pleasure to be drawn out as long as possible. But she was just as tight and hot as he'd imagined, and as her hips pressed back against him, forcing him deeper, he abruptly surrendered.

He plunged into her over and over again. He couldn't get close enough, deep enough. Sweat popped out on his forehead. Their position, while erotic, made it difficult to enter her as fully as he wished, and frustration clawed through him. He wanted to be pounding inside her, to feel her struggling to accept every inch of him as they both tried to get even nearer.

He wanted to be buried deep within her when they both came, their climaxes tearing through them.

He withdrew from her, hormones screaming, breath heaving out of his lungs in great ragged gulps. He reached for her hands, bracing them on the glass, elbows bent, her weight forward. Catching her reflection in the glass, he nearly groaned. There was a curve to her lips, a female knowing in her eyes that shredded any thought that he might be in control of this. Whatever he took, she allowed. And he was just desperate enough at that point to be grateful for it.

She moved her legs closer to his, the position bending her a bit at the waist, her hips tilted toward him. And when he surged into her that time, both of them forgot to breathe.

Jake moved, slowly at first, then in hard measured thrusts that drove him deep inside her, almost completely withdrawing before plunging again. He slipped a hand down to stroke her slippery folds, every surge of his hips pressing that taut bundle of nerves against the heel of his palm.

His eyes wanted to close as he lost himself in the motion, but he fought to keep them open, sought to clear his vision. The sight of their reflections moving in the glass was savagely sexy. Her throat was arched, her lips parted, as if a scream might be ripped from her at any moment. The image elicited an unfamiliar primordial possessiveness from somewhere deep inside him. *Mine.* For now at least.

"More." The word was torn from her, sharp with need. "Harder."

Her hips pumped back against him in time with his movements, driving him deeper, faster. His senses were all centered on her. Sight, scent, sound, touch.

When she tensed against him, giving a strangled cry, he could feel her release pulsing around him. Her orgasm unleashed something inside him and he surged against her wildly. There was no thought of finesse as he pounded into her, only an all-consuming passion that wound tighter and tighter until he couldn't tell where he stopped and she began. Ria whimpered, and the small sound had pleasure slamming into him. He gave one last thrust of his hips and joined her, his climax spinning him over the edge in a headlong dive into sensation.

Ria stared at the road, trying to focus on the act of driving. But it was difficult to concentrate when her muscles still quivered with satiated pleasure, and her pulse still kicked at the memory of the last several hours.

She and Jake had made it to the bedroom for the second bout. And the third. And she was ready to admit she'd underestimated his effect on her. Good sex could leave the mind clear and the brain sharp. Great sex, she was discovering, could prove much more distracting.

Leaving him sleeping a couple hours before dawn, she'd silently gathered up her belongings. It had taken her a minute to recall exactly where she'd left her purse and bra, but she found them both, along with her ruined shirt and his T-shirt, in the still-open elevator. Because he'd keyed in the code before stopping it, she was able to press the close button and take the elevator to the ground floor.

She'd spent the better part of the drive home trying to shake thoughts of the evening from her mind. When she pulled into her driveway, she knew there was no use trying to sleep. She was too wired. Instead she took a flashlight from her car and did her customary examination around the perimeter of the house. She had any number of small "tells" that would alert her if someone had sought entry. A hair across the front gate; a paint chip on the doorknobs; trip wires hidden in the yard. But nothing appeared disturbed.

Ria let herself into the house, too used to the need for security to consider the measures she took. Resetting the alarm, she grabbed a quick shower and changed into a fresh uniform before checking the clock. She had a couple of hours before she needed to be at work, so she headed to the office she'd set up in the second bedroom.

Law enforcement wasn't the highest paying profession, but she'd always lived simply. Her furniture was sparse and strictly utilitarian. She bought her vehicles used, with an eye on economy and reliability. This house was the first she'd ever had. Apartments weren't plentiful in the area, and she did like the privacy afforded by its location on the outskirts of town.

She'd been careful with her money, making regular deposits in an offshore account. If she ever had to run again, she wouldn't be doing so without a dime to her name. She had two sets of full ID waiting just in case. But as time went on, she was less and less certain she'd ever use them.

Ria was tired of running. Before someone came for her again, she'd see this thing finished.

Flipping on the light in the office, she sat down in front of the computer. The vast majority of her expenditures were right in this room. A top-of-the-line hard drive, scanner, printer and various other accessories were imperative for a person making her own ID. And the Internet had long been an invaluable tool in her search for answers to her past.

She pulled up her files, smiled at the pop-up header. BENNY'S SECURE-IT ELECTRONIC VAULT: YOU'RE WELCOME! Her friend could make a fortune off his encryption/decryption know-how, but instead preferred to spend most of his time creating increasingly complex video games.

He assured her the market for his products was endless. She'd had to take his word for it. She wouldn't know an Xbox from a Gameboy.

She clicked on the file entitled Tattoo. When she'd first gotten out of the academy, she'd combed the Department of Justice's Missing Person Clearinghouse for pictures and descriptions that matched either her or the man she'd killed in L.A. There were dozens of informal registries available online, as well, but after three years she'd finally admitted the truth: whoever she'd been in her former life hadn't been missed. And apparently neither had the men who'd been sent to kill her. She'd tucked away the desolation that had occurred at the thought and focused on other leads.

Ria had long thought that the identifying mark shared by her and the two assassins was the single best clue to her identity. She'd recognized the intricately detailed image of Pegasus and concentrated a great deal of time on what the tattoo might mean. But chasing that particular lead, too, had proved fruitless.

Aside from the figure in mythology and the constellation by the name, there were Pegasus references to sailboat racing, change systems, software, imaging tools, direct TV, opera and satellite boosters. The companies and products bearing the name were infinite. Trying to find any link at all between her and one of the references had failed.

Nor had she been able to find any artist's rendering that matched the picture on her ankle. When she'd switched her focus to tattoo artists themselves, she'd known it would be a lengthy process. There were an estimated ten thousand in the United States alone. Ria had looked up the licensed designers and sent them copies of the rendering, without finding a match.

Of course, some states didn't require licensing and many

tattooists operated without one. Learning that many left the profession after a few years had underscored the futility of her search. There wasn't even a way to ascertain if she'd gotten the tattoo in the States.

But three months ago she'd found a lead that had sparked a new level of excitement. She'd been working for the DPD when an APB had come across the computers for an escaped convict with family in the Denver area. The name and accompanying photo hadn't rung any bells for Ria, but her attention had been caught by the description and picture of his distinguishing marks. One had been a tattoo of a winged horse. It had been crude, the detail not nearly identical to hers, but close. Far closer than any others she'd seen.

He'd eventually been apprehended in Colorado Springs. She'd contacted the arresting officer, and at her request he'd elicited from the prisoner the origin of the tattoo—a prison artist in the Donaldson Correctional Facility, a maximum-security prison. Tracking down the man had brought her to Alabama, and led to taking this job.

And tomorrow, she'd finally talk to the artist for the first time. He'd proven elusive and decidedly uncooperative to date, but she'd used her position to arrange a private interview with him at the prison. Whatever it took, she was going to get him to tell her what he knew, if anything.

Her heart kicked up at the thought, and she schooled herself to stay calm. She'd been disappointed too many times in the past by promising leads that ended up fizzling. But despite her best attempts, she couldn't downplay the anticipation curling through her. Tomorrow's meeting would probably prove to be yet another dead end. But there was a distant possibility that it might supply her with some of the answers she'd sought for so long.

She scrolled through the information she'd compiled. She might never know which of the numerous references to Pegasus was the connection to the tattoo she bore, but the one she always came back to was the myth. Her favorite variation on the legend identified the famous winged horse, who used to carry lightning and thunder for Zeus, as the son of Poseidon and the Gorgon Medusa.

Staring at the screen, she reread the legend again. She had to keep believing that somewhere the answers to her past existed. And when she discovered the truth, there would be a reckoning.

This time, she'd be the messenger wreaking thunder and lightning on the person responsible for her situation, and for Luz's death.

The thirst for vengeance was a familiar one. But in the next moment a diverting image of Jake Tarrance flashed through her mind, and a sliver of remorse pierced her. There wasn't room in her life for anything, for anyone, but her search. There would be no reason on earth for her to ever see the man again. But try as she might, she couldn't help regretting that.

Chapter 3

"You've been dodging my calls."

Because the truth in the accusation was irrefutable, Ria didn't bother denying it. Instead, she stared calmly at the county commissioner and tried not to focus on his physical similarity to Elmer Fudd. It wouldn't do to antagonize the man, or to underestimate him. She already knew he was a savvy politician, and the driving force behind her predecessor's resignation.

"After the raid yesterday we were pretty busy with booking. It was a fairly large bust. By the time the entire place had been searched we found nearly five and a half pounds of crystal meth." Because his ire still didn't seem dampened, she added for effect, "Street value would be upwards of a million."

The man blinked his slightly protruding brown eyes, and it took him a moment to answer. "Dollars?" His voice squeaked disbelievingly. At her nod, he lunged across her desk, grasped her hand to shake it vigorously. "Good job, Sheriff. Damn good job. You've outdone yourself this time." Face wreathed in smiles, he released her to pump his fist in the air. "Damn, this feels good. If you added up all the busts that no-good Winston made in the fourteen years he held office, you wouldn't come up with half that amount. That man was mightily beliked, but he was all vine, no taters. Wouldn't be a bit surprised if he was getting paid off to look the other way."

Privately, Ria was inclined to agree. From the amount of activity she and her deputies had detected in the last few weeks, she guessed her predecessor had either been deliberately blind or criminally negligent. Of course, the county had gone without a sheriff for two months after Croat had engineered the man's resignation, among very similar accusations, but the drug activity hadn't sprung up over night.

"Once we get this to the DEA, our share should be a hundred grand. The office could sure use a couple of drug dogs." Given the man's jovial mood, she figured timing for the request would never be better. "Once we get them, their handlers will require training, as well. I think it'd be a real benefit to the efforts of our department."

"Drug dogs, huh?" Croat pulled at his bottom lip. She knew he was already thinking of the photo ops the animals would offer. "You might be on to something there, Sheriff. I'll mention it to the other commissioners. I promised to call them as soon as we got the press conference lined up. Might have to expand on that, though. With a haul this big, I'm thinking we could interest the *Birmingham News* in the story. Maybe the TV stations, too."

With effort, Ria kept the dread his words elicited from sounding in her voice. "It's a big bust. I'm sure you'd get a news crew here." She spun her chair to face him as he paced across her small office. "Probably make our job harder, but chances are we've already made the biggest raids we're going to, anyway."

Eldon stopped in midstride and sent a shrewd look her way. "How do you figure that?"

Affecting a shrug, she said, "I'm not going to pretend I wouldn't welcome the attention for the job my deputies and I have been doing. But we've been hitting the manufacturers hard. Media just broadcasts that fact. Probably drive the rest of them further underground, make it more difficult for us to get a handle on them."

The man waved away her argument. "More likely they'll hightail it right out of the county, and that's what we want, isn't it? Make these lowlifes realize we won't stand for that kind of criminal activity in Fenton County."

The man's optimism had Ria smiling. "The only thing that will convince them to move their operation is if the risk of exposure or their expenses grow too great. These guys gravitate to rural counties like this one because they can operate in relative isolation."

She lifted a shoulder again, as if it didn't make any difference to her. "It's your call. Although if you wanted to hold off making a big announcement, say, for six months or so, we'd have more impressive numbers to report, as well as some new equipment to show off. Might make more of a splash. Maybe even warrant national air time."

Clearly torn, Croat said, "National, huh? That'd be something, wouldn't it? Maybe I'll discuss this further with the other commissioners. They're going to be all fired up about this latest news, no doubt about it. A million dollars. Huh."

Wisely, Ria decided against pushing further. She rose. "Just let me know what you decide. I'll have the report done in a couple hours, and have Marlyss send you a copy. I've got business at the Donaldson Correctional Facility this afternoon. Won't be in again until tomorrow."

He nodded absently as he followed her to the door. "Well, that's good then. So how are you finding the help here?"

With little effort, she went along with his change of topic. "I have no complaints." None, at least, that she'd voice aloud. Any problems she had with the deputies, Ralston in particular, she'd handle herself. She'd been in law enforcement long enough to know that department dynamics were best managed without involving outsiders.

"Good, good. We have a saying 'round these parts, that a new broom sweeps clean, but an old one knows where all the dirt is."

Ria had quickly found upon her arrival in town that some of the locals had a saying for just about everything. Nevertheless, she could agree with the sentiment. It was because of her men's prior undercover work that she'd been able to put these busts together so quickly. "I was able to hit the ground running because of the knowledge and training of the deputies. I don't doubt that we'll continue to work well enough together." But if they didn't, she wouldn't be airing their troubles to the county commissioners.

Still the man hesitated, his hand on the doorknob. "Reason I mention it is we had an individual who was vying to be appointed in Winston's place. Won't mention him by name, but I just wanted to be sure he didn't take a distant turn with you."

He had to be talking about Ralston. That scenario would certainly explain his attitude. "I've been pleased with the professionalism of this department," she said evenly. "I expect it to continue."

Croat gave a short nod, plainly relieved. "Good. I'll leave you to your work then."

As he exited she went back to the computer and finished completing the report on the raid, her mind only half on her work. There would be little else she could do to avoid the media spotlight if Croat and the others decided to go ahead with a big announcement.

She calmed the tension in her stomach. It was doubtful she'd be recognized even if anyone was still looking. She'd taken pains to alter her appearance, to match it to the woman whose identity she'd adopted six years ago. She'd dyed her hair and grown it out, donned green contacts and with the artful application of makeup made subtle alterations to the shape of her eyes and face. For all intents and purposes she *was* Rianna Kingsley. At least on the outside.

It hadn't taken her long to figure out that the databases she needed to comb for answers were easily accessible to law enforcement personnel. The killing in Los Angeles had assured her that despite whatever she might be guilty of, her fingerprints weren't on file in the justice system. It was enough to convince her that inserting herself in law enforcement was the most effective way to continue her search.

Her decision had limited her choices for a new identity. Documents could be faked, but background checks couldn't. It wasn't enough for her to present ID supporting her new name. She had to be able to present people who knew her.

Since that hadn't been possible, she'd needed to find someone with an identity she could assume.

Pushing her chair back, she pressed a command on the keyboard and three copies of the report began printing out. Not for the first time, she wondered about the real Rianna Kingsley. Benny had hacked into the University of Iowa student admission files and she had pored over them, until she'd found one that suited. The young woman had been a senior at the college, the product of foster homes in Illinois, with no relatives she had contact with. Their height and age had matched well enough. From there it was a relatively simple matter to befriend her, and learn the pertinent information she'd be expected to know.

She'd gone to Colorado to establish the residency that would be a prerequisite to her admission to the academy there. But she'd kept track of the real Rianna. It wouldn't do to have the woman show up in the same state she was in. But at last check she'd married and was residing in Florida. Perhaps the woman had at last found a family she could call her own.

The new Rianna Kingsley was still, for all intents, an orphan.

Separating the pages as they came out of the printer, she clipped the copies together and slipped one into a file folder. It hadn't seemed as odd as it should have to adopt the identity of a woman who was, for the most part, on her own. There was a solitary core inside Ria that made her think she was used to it.

Hearing a commotion in the hallway, she grabbed the reports and headed to the door. The sheriff's office, rather than being in the century-old courthouse in the town square, was a relatively new, one-level brick building on the northeastern edge of town. The county jail adjoined the offices and boasted top-of-the-line security systems, with a sixty-prisoner capacity, in addition to another half-dozen special management cells. She'd been pleasantly surprised by the first-rate facility and equipment in the department, but as Croat was fond of boasting, no money had been spared to make the county a premiere law enforcement facility.

A couple of years ago Fenton had even joined forces with two neighboring counties and built their own small forensics lab, where less complicated crime scene evidence could be processed far more quickly than at the regional labs in the state. Unfortunately for the previous sheriff, he'd failed to live up to the expectations that had accompanied the expansions.

Rianna handed the reports to Marlyss. "Have this folder sent over to the commissioners. Eldon is expecting it."

The woman beamed a smile at her and took the reports, placing the folder in a manila envelope. "I'll take care of it right away, Sheriff."

Ria detected a degree of warmth in her voice that had been absent up to today. Apparently approving of the restaurant Marlyss had suggested had helped soften the woman toward her.

"What's going on? I heard voices out here."

The secretary jerked her head toward a closed door. "Got some bail bondsmen inside. Simpson took them to the intake desk. Looks like most of that lot ya'll brought in yesterday is 'bout to get sprung."

"Judge Rivers must have come in early this morning." The man wasn't known for keeping the strictest hours, a fact Rianna still wasn't accustomed to.

"More than likely he's got a date this afternoon with his favorite fishing hole and didn't want work to interfere." While she spoke, Marlyss efficiently got up and filed the two extra copies of the report. "He gets flustrated if a day goes by without him catching a mess of catfish to brag on."

"I think I'll check things out," Rianna said, heading toward the door to the intake facility. When she opened it she saw immediately that the waiting area was filled. She recognized a couple of local defense attorneys at the counter. One was arguing with a bored looking jailer, while the other glanced at his watch impatiently. The other occupants of the room must be the bondsmen Marlyss had spoken about. None of them looked familiar.

There was another man standing at the far end of the counter with his back toward her, counting out some bills for the clerk. Ria's brows rose. Even from this distance, she could see that the size of the wad he was holding was impressive. In Denver she'd witnessed people coming into the station to post bail with Baggies stuffed with cash. Cynically, she wondered if the money stemmed from the sale of drugs similar to those confiscated in the raid. Sometimes justice seemed like a vicious circle.

The sight of the prisoner preceding Deputy Simpson down the hallway diverted her attention. It was the large man who had gotten away from Ralston yesterday, the one who had slammed his head against her cheekbone. Boster. His assault had given her a handy explanation for her nose's slight swelling, as well. She'd made a point of adding resisting arrest to the charges against him. With any luck, that had added significantly to his bail.

The man caught sight of her and slowed, sending her an insolent smirk. "Nice bruises, Sheriff. Guess you met up with someone bigger and tougher than you."

"Nope. Just a scumbag drug dealer who's going to be a real popular bunkmate at the state pen."

That wiped the smile from Boster's face. "Well, I ain't there yet, am I? My lawyer will make sure I never do a day of time, so don't…" His words tapered off as his gaze swept the area, and his color abruptly receded. He stopped dead in his tracks, causing Simpson to nudge him forward again.

"Jake?" he croaked disbelievingly. "I mean…Mr. Tarrance. How did you…who called you?"

She went still at the name. Something about the stranger at the counter struck a belated chord of familiarity. With dread circling, she turned in the direction Boster was staring, and found her eyes caught by pale blue ones that sent a shiver of remembered pleasure skittering down her spine.

Jake Tarrance. Their gazes clashed as she struggled to hide the emotion crashing through her. Surely that wasn't a flicker of excitement at the unexpected sight of him? Giving in to her hormones last night had been novel enough for her. Having second thoughts about seeing him again smacked of a dithering indecisiveness that was as foreign as it was unwelcome.

With effort, she schooled her expression to an impassive mask. She wished it were as easy to calm her jittery pulse. What was he doing here? Somehow she doubted those varied business interests he'd hinted at last night included law or bondsman. Remembering the cash with which Jake had paid the bail, she felt a wave of trepidation.

She looked back at Boster. "Good to have friends, isn't it? Just make sure you show up for trial. I'd hate to have to hunt you down again."

The big man flushed, but Jake's presence had apparently defused a great deal of his bluster. Ignoring her, he addressed the emotionless man standing before him. "You didn't have to come here. I can explain everything. It's not what you think."

"We'll discuss what I think in the car."

Jake's tone sent a shiver skating over Ria's skin. It would be impossible to miss the menace in the evenly spoken words, and all appearances aside, Boster wasn't stupid. He swallowed hard and preceded Jake out the door.

Ria stood silently, willing the men to be gone. But on his way past her, Jake's gaze met hers again and she caught her breath at the bitter condemnation she read in his eyes. In the next moment the door closed behind him.

Why in God's name would he be angry with *her?* For leaving in the middle of the night? She doubted it was the first time the man had experienced a one-night stand, so her quiet departure shouldn't have elicited that kind of reaction.

Belatedly, she shook off the thought to focus once again on her surroundings. No one seemed to have noticed the silent exchange between her and Tarrance. Relieved, she caught Ken Simpson's eye and motioned him over just as he was about to go back into holding for another prisoner.

When Ken was beside her, she asked, "Did you know that guy who posted bail for Boster?"

"Not by sight, but I recognize the name. Most law officers 'round these parts would."

The unease in her gut knotted into a greasy tangle. "Why is that?"

The second lawyer had pushed up to the counter now, and was demanding, loudly, for his client's release. Simpson's eyes flickered in that direction as he spoke. "Tarrance runs 'bout the biggest crime organization in these parts. Based out of Columbus, near as I remember. Never known him to do business in Alabama, but wouldn't make book on it."

Ria's throat closed. Images flashed through her mind. Of Jake in back of her, driving into her with savage force. Of her astride him, rocking them both to madness. It took a moment before she trusted herself to speak. "Is he connected?"

Simpson shook his head. "He's not a wiseguy. There's mob activity in Atlanta for sure, but I've never heard that he's got links to them. Columbus PD would know more about him than I do, though." He headed back toward holding for the next release, and Ria left the intake area, her mind in a whirl.

One thought burst through the jumble, however, with blazing clarity. She wasn't in the habit of making errors, but when she did, they were costly. The last time she'd made a mistake of this magnitude, it had led an assassin to her apartment in L.A. Her indiscretion with Jake Tarrance wasn't that serious, she hoped, but it could prove just as damaging.

She didn't even want to consider what would happen to her job here if it were ever discovered she'd been personally involved, however briefly, with one of the most notorious criminals in the area.

Her mood dark, she turned the corner toward her offices and nearly collided with Deputy Ralston. For once the man's face didn't twist into its familiar sneer at the sight of her. His expression and tone were excited. "I thought I just saw Jake Tarrance walking out of here. I didn't read his name on the arrest report this morning."

It seemed everyone knew who the man was. Everyone, that is, with the exception of her. "He wasn't arrested, he was posting bond for Boster, the guy you brought in yesterday."

"So Tarrance is involved in this meth operation, too?" Without waiting for an answer, he turned on his heel and started away.

"Wait a minute." Instinct had her stopping him. "Where are you going?"

"To call the Columbus PD. I'm sure Vice will be very interested in this news."

"We don't have any 'news,' Ralston, and we sure don't have proof that he and Boster were working together." Whatever their connection, it seemed odd that Tarrance would broadcast his association with Boster, rather than just send a lawyer or bondsman to see to his release. "But I'll contact Columbus myself. I'd like a little background on Tarrance." Too little, too late, an inner voice jeered. But before this went any further, she'd apprise herself exactly how serious a mistake she'd made last night.

Ralston's mouth twisted. "Sure, Sheriff. Whatever."

"I'm going to be out of the office this afternoon, so I'd like you to supervise the calls and assignments." She read his surprise in his expression before the more familiar sardonic mask replaced it. "You *are* the senior deputy, aren't you?"

She already knew he was. No doubt that was what had had him certain that her position belonged, by rights, to him. It was clear he didn't know what to make of her offer.

"That's right."

"Good. You can reach me on my cell if there's an emergency. Otherwise, I'll stop in later this evening to catch up on anything requiring my attention." Without giving him a chance to respond, she turned and headed back to her office. Her appointment at the prison this afternoon was less than three hours off. But before making the journey to Bessemer, she was going to learn everything she could about one Jake Tarrance.

Jamie Lee Boster shifted uncomfortably in the leather back seat of the Cadillac Escalade. The luxury of the SUV seemed lost on him. Despite the mild temperature in the vehicle, he was perspiring heavily.

No one spoke. Cort manned the wheel, Finn beside him. Jake sat next to Boster and watched the man sweat bullets, while he tried to contain the fury that churned inside him.

It wasn't all directed at the idiot who used to work for him. No, the worst of it was reserved for himself.

He couldn't remember a time he'd let someone get under his guard as easily as *Ria* had last night. He thought he'd had all the angles covered. The apartment had been swept this morning, just as it was every other day. Whatever else the woman had been after, it hadn't been to plant a listening de-

vice in his home or on his phone. Her intent hadn't been lethal—she'd had ample opportunity to try to slip a blade between his ribs while they lay tangled in bed together. But then,
she hadn't actually had room to hide a weapon, either.

He had a mental flash of her naked, her creamy skin against
his black silk sheets. For a moment his palms tingled, as if he
could still feel the softness of her flesh. Her smell had lingered
in his senses long after he'd awakened, alone in the bed.

And the brief stab of disappointment that had followed that
discovery still haunted him. Taunted him.

He'd been screwed by cops before, but never quite so lit-
erally. The dark humor failed to amuse him. What had she
been after? His alarm system would have alerted him if she'd
tried to search his apartment, and he didn't sleep deeply
enough for any such attempt to be successful, anyway.

"Mr. Tarrance, I know what you're thinking."

Boster's voice interrupted his thoughts. Jake turned to look
at the man. "Somehow I doubt that."

Boster licked his lips. "Okay, I knew you'd be mad, but see,
that's why I went over the state line." He paused, as if waiting for Jake to express his appreciation of that fact. "I figured
as long as I stayed out of your territory, what I did in my free
time was my business, right?"

"Wrong." With the swiftness of a snake striking, he had the
man's shirt in his hand, twisting it tightly so it constricted
around his throat. "You have no free time. *I own you.* Everything you do reflects on me, and I am not happy, Boster." He
twisted the shirt even more, and the man's face grew red as
he struggled to breathe. "What are the two things I told you
wouldn't be tolerated when I hired you?"

Boster moistened his lips and croaked, "Whores and drugs."

"See, you do remember."

He released the man as suddenly as he'd grabbed him, disgusted by his loss of control. "You've got no loyalty, and it looks like you're stupid to boot. A guy like that is a liability in my organization. I'm sure you understand that."

Boster sent a frantic glance toward the silent men in the front seat. "You gotta give me another chance. Maybe I messed up—I see that now. But a good lawyer could make this deal all go away. And then I'd never screw up again, you gotta believe me. I've learned my lesson."

"A bit late, wouldn't you say?" Jake faced forward again, considering his options. When he'd heard of Boster's arrest he'd made damn sure he'd been the first to get to him. There would be no fresh-faced lawyer with ideas of plea bargains in exchange for information, especially when that information might have to do with Jake's own operation. The cleanest way to deal with the man, the best way, would be to make sure he never had an opportunity to talk to anyone. But his disappearance could give rise to difficult questions, especially given their association.

Stress knotted the muscles at the back of Jake's neck. The wisest choice would be to line Boster up with counsel of his own choosing, who could be paid to make sure the man landed in the pen. Jake had contacts everywhere, even in the prison population. The man could still be controlled, even inside.

His decision made, he turned his thoughts once again to Ria—and his punch-in-the-gut reaction when he'd seen her in the sheriff's office after paying the bail. He frowned, remembering something, and turned sharply back to Boster. "What were you saying to that woman, the sheriff, before you saw me?"

Boster lifted a shoulder. "I dunno. Something about that bruise on her face. I managed to land one even though I had

three or four guys on me yesterday." He smirked. "Damn
bitch. No job for a woman, anyhow. I heard one of the cops
say she was butch. Guess them type of women have to have
a gun 'cuz they ain't got a…"

Something in Jake's still expression must have warned
him. The rest of his sentence went unuttered. The mark on
Ria's face had been an angry red welt yesterday, but today it
had bloomed to a sullen shade of blue. And knowing this man
was responsible for putting that mark on her had Jake enter-
taining a brief fantasy of sending his fist crashing into his jaw.

Which meant Jake might be well on his way to crazy. What
did he care if the woman had been knocked around during the
arrest? Given what he'd discovered about her today, his intentions toward her were no less threatening.

What the hell had she wanted from him? He had no business interests in Alabama. They were concentrated in Georgia and stretched east and south to the tip of Florida. Had she
discovered Boster's association with him and been following
up on that? She would have had to work damn fast, since the
arrest had only been yesterday afternoon. Or was she part of
a local task force investigating his holdings? That thought had
merit, and he examined it more closely. He hadn't heard of
any such investigation, and he paid his contacts well to pass
that kind of information on to him.

The surest way to get answers to his questions, he figured,
was to present them to the woman herself.

He smiled humorlessly, even as anticipation tightened in his
gut. Yes, Ria-without-a-last-name had much to answer for. And
he found himself looking forward to their next conversation.

The room Ria was shown to at the Donaldson Correctional
Facility was small and cheerless. The paint on the walls was

of an undetermined age, and its dull beige color wouldn't have brightened the room even when fresh. The floor was institutional tile, the furnishings plain and functional. There was a brown stain in the Sheetrock of the ceiling. She could almost smell the despair.

"Stanton will be brought in shortly. When he is, I'll give you some privacy, but I'll be watching from the other side of the door in case you need me." The blue-clad correctional officer flicked a glance over her, as if doubting her ability to handle herself with a maximum-security prisoner. "Fifteen minutes enough?"

"Should be." She'd need even less than that if Larry Stanton proved no more cooperative in person than he had over the phone. She'd tried more than once to arrange an interview over the telephone from Colorado. But according to the warden, the man had been in the prison medical center for days, and then held in isolation for weeks longer. Even when he'd been capable of taking calls, he'd refused to speak to her.

Nerves knotted in her stomach. She knew better than to count too much on any one lead. She'd chased far too many promising threads that had eventually led nowhere. Stanton was just one in a long line of them. If this interview proved worthless, there'd be another lead. Another clue that would eventually unlock the door to her past.

She told herself that, and tried to believe it.

A small wooden table sat in the center of the room, with a chair on either side. She remained standing until she heard the faint jangle of chains in the hallway. The door opened. A second guard ushered in a man doing the inmate shuffle. Ria's gaze dropped to his feet. He was in leg irons, as well as cuffs, reminding her again that this was a maximum-security prison for Alabama's most violent offenders.

"Sit over there." The guard indicated for the man to take the seat facing the door. Glancing at Ria, he said, "The door will be secured, but the room will be supervised through the window." There was a large double-glass pane with a wire inset in the center of the door. "Just give a knock when you're done. The inmate is to remain seated at all times." His attention shifted to Stanton. "Is that clear?"

"Yes *sir*."

Apparently the guard caught the sardonic inflection in the prisoner's voice, because his expression darkened. "Don't give me any trouble, Stanton. You've already caused enough 'round here."

Ria waited until the guard had exited the room before turning to survey the inmate she'd come to see. Her first thought was that this man didn't look capable of causing much of a stir. Gaunt to the point of emaciation, he was slightly stooped, shaving a couple inches off his above average height. His skin bore a sickly pallor that was only a shade darker than the white prison-issue uniform he wore.

He had full sleeves: tattoos running up and down both arms. Unlike the tat on the convict caught in Colorado, this work had obviously been done on the outside. They were in full color. He even had the back of each knuckle tattooed.

He swiped at a lock of sandy-blond hair clinging limply to his forehead, and pushed it back along his receding hairline. His eyes were a muddy shade of hazel, and right now they were raking her form in a slow insolent way that left no secret about his thoughts.

"Larry Jay Stanton?" Her voice was crisp, commanding, exerting her authority.

"That's right, doll. This must be my lucky day. I was sure due for one."

Ria crossed to the table and braced her hands on it, leaning toward him. "You will address me as Sheriff Kingsley. Is that understood?"

Eyes alight with laughter, he responded, "Sure, I got that, *Sheriff.* I'll call you anything you want."

Pushing away, Ria pulled out the opposite chair and sat. "I represent Fenton County, Alabama. During the course of an investigation, your name came up."

Wariness crept into his expression. "Don't see how. I been in here going on five years now. Even you cops can't pin something on a guy locked up."

"I understand you're a pretty accomplished tattoo artist. Ran across an escaped convict in Colorado a few weeks ago that named you as the designer of the tat he had. Ronny Baker. That name ring a bell?"

Stanton shrugged. "I do plenty of tats. So what?"

"It was a winged horse. A little crude, but I suppose you don't have the tools at your disposal that you had when you worked on the outside." Tattoos in prison were often done with a sewing needle and ballpoint ink. "Where did you used to operate?"

The man sat back in his chair, clearly impatient with the questioning. But a glance toward the door had him straightening again. One of the biggest complaints of inmates, Ria knew, was boredom. Despite his less than enthusiastic responses, her presence represented a reprieve from the unrelenting sameness of his days. She was counting on that to sustain his interest.

"I been all over. East Coast mostly. Florida and Georgia, before Alabama."

"Does this look like some of your work?" She took a couple of photographs from her pocket and placed them on the table, nudging them over to him. They were from the film she'd taken of the second assassin before she'd fled L.A. Stanton picked up one, then the other, examining them closely.

"He dead?"

She nodded. "Unsolved. His identity was never discovered. Why, do you recognize him?"

Ria hadn't been aware she'd been holding her breath, until he shook his head. She expelled it slowly, tamping down the disappointment she'd promised herself she wasn't going to experience.

"Never did pay much attention to the guys. The ladies, though, that was always different." One of his eyelids closed in a lascivious wink. "Them I'd remember."

Distaste rose. "I'll bet." She'd researched Stanton thoroughly. He was serving a fifteen-year sentence for multiple counts of rape. Apparently he'd offer his female clients something for the pain, and assault them while they were under the effects of the strong drug he slipped them. Then he'd finish their tattoo, expecting them to remember nothing when they came to again.

But a couple of clients had remembered. Apparently they hadn't ingested as much of the drug as he'd expected, because once they'd left his place, they'd gone straight to the police. Some studies indicated that over ninety percent of all convicted rapists had committed previous assaults. Ria was willing to bet Stanton had had a long career of attacks before committing the two that had led to his eventual incarceration.

"So, you don't remember the guy. What about the tat? Does it look like one of yours?"

But the prisoner didn't look back at the photo. Instead, he stared steadily at Ria. "You know, Sheriff, we never did talk about what this conversation is worth to you. You wouldn't think a guy like me had expenses, but I do. Got me a girlfriend in Mobile with a kid. Plus I ain't been able to work. They don't pay us hardly nothin' anyway, but it keeps me in cigarettes, you know?"

She gave a telling smile. "You want to know what this is worth to me? How about my goodwill, Larry? From the sounds of your last few weeks, you could use some of that, couldn't you?"

From what Warden Udall had said, Stanton had recently been the victim of a brutal attack. He'd been near dead when a correctional officer had interrupted the assault. Once he'd been released he'd requested, and received, protective isolation. But according to the warden, that treatment was rapidly approaching an end.

His gaze centered somewhere in the vicinity of her chest, he said, "Your goodwill ain't gonna cut it. Like I said, I got expenses."

"You've also got someone wanting you dead." Her knowledge of his situation had his gaze swinging to hers. "At least that's what you keep telling the warden. But he's ready to release you back into the general population, isn't he? No way of knowing how long you'll survive there."

"I got someone working on that," he muttered, but his expression was worried.

"I can help. At the very least, I can buy you some time. If I tell the warden you're helping with an ongoing investigation, your life takes on new value. It'll buy you more time in protective isolation, anyway."

Stanton appeared to be mulling over the offer. "I need a couple more months there, for sure."

"I'll do everything I can to see that you get it," she promised. It was quite possible that she'd want to interview him again— dependent, of course, on what kind of information he divulged.

"Okay." Stanton smiled, revealing a set of stained and crooked teeth. "You got yourself a deal, do— *Sheriff*. Like I said, that work there is mine." He tapped one of the photos with his index finger. "It's a Pegasus. You know, like in them Greek stories? A flying horse. Supposed to do the work of some god or something." His shrug said the history was of little importance to him. "Lots of tattooists do different designs of it, but the detail in mine sets them apart. See, the smaller the image, the harder it is to get the detail included. But me, I'm a genius at that. I once did this real complicated flower on a woman's nipple. Work of art, I'm telling you."

"I'm only interested in the Pegasus design." Ria brought him back on topic impatiently. "How many have you done?"

From his wrinkled brow, it appeared that the memory search was painful. "I dunno. Fifty or sixty maybe, altogether."

The number acted as a cold dash of water on Ria's hopes. Trying to trace that many individuals would add months, possibly years to her search. And tracking them might prove impossible if he hadn't kept records.

His next words had her emotions swinging back again, like a pendulum. "Not all of them were like this one, though. Most folks want something larger, with a big wingspan on the horse. I once did one that covered a guy's entire back. Took me three days. This one here was a special design. And I made an agreement that I'd never use it again. Never did, either," he said, with a quick glance toward her. "An artist is only as good as his rep. And I got paid for making this design special."

Excitement rose, nearly choking her. Struggling to keep it from her voice, Ria asked, "What makes this one special?"

"Well, the guy wanted it small. And I had to add lightning bolts to it. Not easy, see, because if you don't do it right, it would look like they were coming right out of the wings, which would be stupid. It took a lot of time to make it seem like the horse is carrying the bolts—"

"What guy?" she interrupted impatiently. "Do you remember a name? Did you keep records?"

Stanton shook his head. "He paid me not to. Got a nice fee for the design, and for overlooking certain, ah, regulations. Closed my place down for the evening and just did him and his friends."

Everything inside her went abruptly, completely still. For an instant, she imagined she could feel every beat of her pulse. Taste every particle of oxygen stopped up in her lungs. Her nerves quivered at a heightened sense of readiness that felt nearly painful. "His…friends?"

Rubbing his nose, Stanton answered, "Yeah, there were six of them. Or was it seven?" He frowned. "Seems like there were five guys. But there might have been six. Only one woman, though. I am sure about that."

An hour later, Larry Stanton was lying on the lone bunk in his cell, hands behind his head, staring up at the cracked ceiling. Worst thing about isolation was, well, the isolation. No one to talk to but the guards, if one of them was of a mind to be sociable. Nothing to look forward to but the crap served as meals. No exercise privileges. No library visits.

Staying alive didn't come without a price.

But his visitor today had sure been a change from the usual boredom of his days. Yes sirree, the lady sheriff had been the best looking piece he'd laid eyes on in years, even in that butt ugly tan-and-brown uniform she'd been wearing.

He fantasized about what had been under that uniform, and felt himself hardening. He'd never much fancied redheads, but then, he'd never been overly fussy when it came to the female persuasion. He'd been an equal-opportunity kind of guy. If he were to get a few minutes alone with her sometime, he'd pull her hair free from that braid she had it scraped back into, and wrap his hands in it while he pounded himself into her.

Pressing a hand against his crotch, he daydreamed for a few minutes more before a single thought nudged through the porn-rated fantasy.

He hadn't had any luck getting a promise of money from the cop, not that he'd held out much hope of one. But he could think of someone who might want to know about her visit. Some tattoo he'd done eight or nine years ago didn't have a thing to do with Enrico Alvarez, but Jake Tarrance might like to know that he wasn't the only one interested in ol' Larry Stanton. He might even get more money out of him in return for the information, although he'd have to be careful how he played that. Tarrance wasn't the kind of man it was smart to piss off.

Larry knew he wasn't exactly NASA material, but he took his time thinking things through, and being careful usually paid off for him in the end. So he studied the angles in his mind for some time before reaching the conclusion that Tarrance was probably going to learn about this visit himself even if Larry didn't tell him.

Dismay filled him as his hopes for turning the information into cash vanished. The man seemed to have eyes and ears everywhere. Larry was going to have to tell him before someone else did, unless he wanted to take his chances of drying up the cash cow that allowed him some measure of comfort in this hellhole.

He swore silently, cracking his knuckles in frustration. No use putting it off, either, because it just didn't pay to hold back from Jake. Not about anything.

Morosely, he sat up, swung his legs over his bunk. Something about all those questions the sheriff asked had other memories crowding in, and he shook his head impatiently. It wasn't like she had been the first one to be interested in that damn tattoo. There had been another guy a long time ago who had tracked him down about it.

What had it been—five years ago? Six? Since Stanton didn't feel like taxing his brain, he let the question go. Like he'd told the sheriff, he didn't recall guys too well, so he wouldn't recollect a name even if the man had given one. What he *did* remember was that this fella had offered him a whole lotta money to let him know if anyone had come asking 'bout that tattoo.

The thought of money took his mind off the ache in his groin as excitement of another kind grew. Even though it had seemed a long shot, the amount of cash involved had convinced him it would pay to keep the number he'd been given handy.

With a broad grin, he clenched his fists. Although he'd embellished the tattoos on his knuckles over the years, anyone who looked closely at them would see that at the center of each was a single digit. He held his fists in front of him, side by side, and gave a cackle. If'n that number was still in service, Larry Jay Stanton just might be about to become the richest inmate in Alabama.

Chapter 4

Ria went through the motions of catching up on the afternoon's activities once she was back at the office, but her conversation with Stanton was never far from her mind. It was nearly eight before she left for the evening, but she headed home without sparing a thought for the fact that there would be nothing edible in the house. Food wasn't even close to a priority.

She wanted to get to her computer files.

It was useless to issue a cautionary reminder that she could be embarking on yet another wild-goose chase. Numerous times over the last half-dozen years she'd thought she was just this close. Had believed she was on the verge of discovering the information that would divulge her identity, and that of Luz's killer. Each time, she'd had to deal with the crushing disappointment that accompanied a dead end.

But this time might be different.

Because it was useless to try to dampen her excitement, she tried to harness it and think logically. The word of a lowlife like Stanton wasn't much to go on, but he had little reason to lie. And the details he'd given about the tattoo made a chilling kind of sense. He'd said he'd been in Georgia when he'd done the group's designs, and that was the home of thirteen different military bases. Had she and the group been stationed at one of them?

She'd tried to follow that line a couple times over the years, each time losing confidence in it. Despite the changing social climate, the U.S. military was still staunchly paternalistic. A woman might be allowed to gain the kind of training Ria had obviously had, but she never would have been selected for any type of special operation.

At any rate, there had never been a way to narrow down a specific military branch. Without names to go on, all she could do was get lists of individuals on active duty at the time she was shot, or those reported missing in action six years ago. The sheer volume of information had been overwhelming, and without a direction, had yielded very little.

Now, though, she had direction. Ria turned her sheriff's car into the lane that led to her house. They may not have been special ops at all, but miscreant misfits that had been gathered up and given individual training and narrowly defined assignments? And if that were the case, who had been calling the shots?

The question was abruptly dismissed when she saw the car pulled up behind her personal vehicle.

A burst of adrenaline surged through her and she brought her car to a halt. She didn't have visitors. Not ever. And she sure as hell hadn't invited this one.

Reaching for the radio, she called in the Georgia license

plate, but she really didn't need the dispatcher's answer a few minutes later to guess at the owner of the low slung sports car. Mouth flattening, she swung out of her cruiser and slammed the door, heading up to the house with long strides. Her front door was slightly ajar, as if to mock her with the ease with which her security had been circumvented.

Withdrawing her gun, she released the safety and entered the house carefully, in search of her unwelcome visitor.

She found him in the small living room, ensconced in the recliner in front of the TV. Its sound was muted, and he had a newspaper spread out in his lap. "Funny." Her voice said it was anything but. "I've never had trouble with vermin in this house before."

Jake Tarrance raised his brows. "I'm not surprised. Do you realize there's absolutely nothing in your kitchen to eat? Your fridge only has a couple moldy oranges and lettuce well past its prime." Which didn't explain, she silently noted, the imported bottle of beer in his hand. "If you had the fixings, I'd have had dinner waiting for you."

The harmless words were at odds with lethal air of the man uttering them. Today he was dressed in jeans and an open necked dress shirt the same color as his eyes. Neither his attire nor his matter-of-fact speech could distract from the aura of menace that was so much a part of him.

"Just as well." She entered the room, keeping her gun trained on him. "I would have had to check it for traces of arsenic."

He looked amused. The only light in the room came from the small television screen. He appeared at home in the shadows, one of Lucifer's demons come above earth to bargain for souls. But there would be no bartering here. Ria had given him far too much already.

"Point taken. But despite our serious trust issues, maybe you could lower your gun. You and I have some things to discuss."

She moved to a lamp and switched it on, all the while keeping Jake in her sights. "Sure. Just as soon as you shove that newspaper to the floor. Slowly."

A long moment stretched. She cocked her revolver, the small sound splitting the silence. Again, a flash of amusement skated across his expression, but with a tiny motion he had the newspaper falling to the floor, revealing the Glock in his hand.

He shrugged. "I really did come to talk, but thought you might need convincing."

"The only convincing I need is a reason why I shouldn't shoot you right now."

"Well, you'd most likely ruin your chair," he pointed out. It didn't escape her notice that his weapon was still aimed in her direction. "But given your choice in furniture, it wouldn't be much of a loss. There is the problem of Fenton County's new sheriff explaining a corpse in her house, but I'm guessing you could come up with plausible story."

"Like shooting an intruder who had broken into my home?"

He ignored the caustic question. "I guess I'm just going to rely on the fact that you really really want to know what I'm doing here." He paused, then added silkily, "Almost as much as you want to keep our relationship private."

His words fired her temper, even as it sparked flickers of concern. It would be easier to explain his dead body than the night she'd spent with the most notorious crime boss in the area. Her conversation that afternoon with the lead detective in the Columbus Bureau of Investigative Services had been illuminating. Among other things, Jake was suspected of running a highly lucrative multistate smuggling ring dealing with antiquities. But according to the detective, they'd never been able to collect enough evidence to make any charges stick against the man.

"You'd be surprised at my creativity." She circled him, her gun hand steady. "Any explanations I need to make will carry a lot more credibility than the word of a common criminal."

His expression was pained. "Common? You wound me, Ria, really." He used his foot to swivel the chair slightly, to keep her in his sights. "Sit down, for God sakes. We may as well have our civil discussion. I'm not leaving here without answers."

"There's nothing to discuss. I won't drop the charges against Boster, or discuss a plea bargain. He's one of yours, isn't he?" The contempt she felt sounded in her voice. "Drugs are always a filthy business, but meth is lower than most. High addiction rate. Psychosis. Irreparable brain damage. Nice little sideline you've chosen."

The semblance of civility vanished from his face. Those pale blue eyes went icy, and the temperature in the room seemed to drop ten degrees. "Boster is an associate of mine, I won't deny that. But I had no knowledge of his activities here. You won't find me protecting him from the consequences. I assume you called the Columbus PD today after I left." When she didn't answer, he arched a brow. "Who'd you talk to? Edwards? Renard? Either one of them would tell you I've never been suspected of drug involvement."

Actually, what Detective Edwards had said was the only illegal activities Tarrance wasn't suspected of were drugs and prostitution. Ria didn't share the detective's curiosity about that fact. It wasn't really Jake's choice of unlawful sidelines that concerned her. It was the fact they existed at all.

And that she'd made the excruciatingly poor decision of sleeping with the most disreputable man in the region.

"So if you aren't here about Boster, what do you want?" she asked bluntly. She rested her weight against the wall opposite him, without lowering the gun she had aimed his way.

"What do I want?" he repeated slowly. She doubted he meant to imbue the words with an intimate heat that set her nerve endings quivering. Whatever else this man was after, it wouldn't be a repeat of last night. "For starters, I'd like to know what brought you to my restaurant yesterday. Who sent you? And before you think about lying, you might want to consider that with one bullet I could shatter your gun hand and disarm you at the same time."

His threat had little effect on her. "You move toward that trigger and the bullet I fire won't be going to your *hand*." She shifted her arm slightly to aim at a much more sensitive portion of his anatomy.

A second passed. Then two. Twin spikes of adrenaline raced down her spine as her breathing grew shallow. Instincts were roused to almost painful intensity as time crawled to a stop.

And then, amazingly, he began to laugh. Rich with humor, the sound was darkly masculine. It crinkled his eyes, creased his face and made him all too appealing. "Damn, but I like you, Ria Kingsley. Did from the first. Before you'd given me your name. Before I knew you were a cop." He managed to imbue the final word with a faint note of distaste that didn't detract from the compliment. "Are you working with the Columbus PD? Some sort of multiagency task force?"

"If I were, do you really think I'd tell you?"

He seemed to ignore her question. "I haven't heard of anything like that, and my sources are usually pretty good. So maybe you sought me out for your own purposes."

"I didn't seek you out," she felt driven to mention. "Unless you consider turning down your offer of dinner and getting attacked some sort of bizarre seduction device."

Immediately she wished she'd chosen different words. The amusement had vanished from his face, to be replaced with a single-minded intensity that reminded her all too clearly of last night.

There had been something primitively sensual about being the focus of that powerful concentration. The rest of the world had slipped away, and for the first time in her memory, she'd indulged her senses ahead of her well-constructed defenses.

An act that seemed destined to haunt her in ways she wouldn't have dreamed possible.

"It was just incredibly poor luck on my part." She gave him a grim smile. "Fate hasn't always been especially generous with me."

"I might have believed that, if I didn't also know how you spent your afternoon." Jake watched her as her expression showed surprise, then suspicion. Both emotions were replaced in the next moment by a carefully blank mask that she apparently donned at will. More than anything he wanted to smash his way through that shield and discover the answers he needed. "What brought you to Larry Jay Stanton?"

The phone call he'd received from Larry had worsened an already bad day. And Ria Kingsley's interest in the man was too coincidental to be overlooked. Jake didn't believe in coincidences. He couldn't afford to.

Her beautiful green eyes narrowed in annoyance. "You had me followed?"

"Larry let me know about his visitor. He and I have…an arrangement. He provides me with certain types of information, in exchange for regular donations to his favorite charity."

Meaning his personal bank account, of course. But as Enrico Alvarez's former cellmate, Stanton had a high value to Jake. And he'd continue to be important until Jake was certain the man had divulged everything he knew about Alvarez's plans upon his release. "What does a horse tattoo have to do with Enrico Alvarez?"

"I would assume nothing, since I don't know who Alvarez is."

Jake smiled grimly. "Try harder, baby. It's a little pat that you came by my place last night, screwed my brains out, then happened to arrange a meeting with an inmate under my protection."

"Any diminished mental capacity on your part is probably genetic," she answered coolly. "And your 'protection' doesn't seem too dependable. From what Warden Udall said, the only thing that saved Stanton from death was a change in routine on the part of the guard. I think he'll fare better dealing with me. I can convince the warden to continue his time in isolation indefinitely. Can you promise the same?"

"You'd be surprised at what I can arrange." His reach went beyond the prison walls, but even his power hadn't been able to save Stanton from near death once Alvarez had found out the man had betrayed his confidences. The trouble with a place like Donaldson was there was a never-ending supply of offenders with nothing to lose. Guarding against all of them would be impossible, even in isolation.

But her promise to Larry could work in his favor. Jake knew Udall's patience was wearing thin. Ria's influence might have more affect than the bribes he was paying the man. Jake wanted to keep Stanton alive, at least until Alvarez was released. Only when Larry was completely free of the man's threat could Jake be certain he'd given him all the information he had. Convicts weren't the most trustworthy of people.

Neither were cops.

He eyed Ria now, noting the steadiness of her gun hand. She was as cool, as emotionless as a professional hit man. There was nothing in her demeanor now that even hinted at the fire she'd displayed last night. A pool of heat formed in his belly at the memory. She'd been wary but not coy. Uninhibited but not unguarded. And she'd twisted him up in knots in a way no woman had ever been allowed to before.

She would be dangerous for that reason alone.

"Who's Enrico Alvarez?" she asked.

"A man who wants me dead."

"Given what I've learned of your activities, he can't be the only one. What's your interest in him?"

For someone so guarded about giving out any information herself, she sure seemed to have a lot of questions, Jake noted. Because she could learn the answers to these easily enough, he saw no harm in responding. "Alvarez blames me for his current residence. He'll be released soon and Stanton agreed to share what he knew of his plans for that time."

She regarded him steadily. "He must be the one Edwards was talking about. It was his operation you took over after his arrest?"

Even after nearly ten years Jake still felt a fierce stab of satisfaction at the thought of the man in prison having lost everything he held dear. What money he hadn't hidden was gone. His operation had been reorganized, parts of it dismantled. The control he'd once wielded in Columbus was largely forgotten. But given what he'd cost Jake, it hardly seemed punishment enough.

No, he wasn't nearly done with Enrico Alvarez. And from what he'd learned from Stanton, the man wasn't done with him, either.

"So you're claiming this tattoo you asked Larry about has

nothing to do with Alvarez?" He'd be a fool to trust her, regardless of her answer. But he found himself waiting for her response, nonetheless.

"My investigation is a completely separate matter. Looks like Stanton is just a guy who gets around."

"He is that. I wouldn't put too much stock in anything he tells you. The guy would sell his grandmother for enough cash."

"Since you're the one paying him, I'd think you'd be wise to take your own advice," she countered. "How do you know you can trust him to tell you the truth about this Alvarez?"

"I don't." The admission didn't bother him. He was too used to living this way to consider it. "But that doesn't matter. I don't trust anyone. Not even you." He raked her form with his gaze, flickers of hunger igniting under his skin. He was determined to ignore them. "*Especially* you. If I find out you've been lying to me, I'll be back."

She didn't seem impressed with the threat-laced words. "I wouldn't advise it. I'm not much for guests, especially uninvited ones. Next time I'll be harder to convince not to shoot you."

He'd surely lived too much of his life in the shadows if he found her statement intriguing. Arousing. Jake had an acquired taste for females who could take care of themselves. That didn't include women who could take on most of the men of his acquaintance and likely come out ahead. At least it never had before.

He rose, noting her sudden readiness at his movement. And he wanted, more than was comfortable, to discover where those well-honed instincts of hers had come from. Before they met again, he was determined to find out.

"Your hospitality leaves a lot to be desired." Because there was nothing wrong with *his* instincts, he remained facing her as he backed out of the room. "At least when you were at my place I offered you ice. A warm bed."

"And I'm not about to reciprocate." She kept her gun trained on him as she followed him out of the room and down the hall, so he didn't lower his own. "Last night..." Was that a hesitation he heard in her voice? "...was a mistake. It won't be repeated."

At the door, Jake felt behind him for the knob, pulled it open. "I've got to say, as mistakes go, it was about my favorite one yet. We're not done with each other, Ria." He watched her eyes widen slightly at the certainty in his words, before going guarded. Good. She'd be wise to be cautious. And so would he. He had every reason in the world to distrust her.

So it was just his own incredibly poor taste that had him wanting her, with an unrelenting fire he'd never felt for another woman.

"By the way, I wouldn't worry about your alarm system being especially vulnerable. It was harder than most to jumper, and I'm not without a certain amount of skill in that area." He paused for a moment to appreciate the storm gathering in her eyes, before slipping silently out the door and into the shadows.

"This is bull." Ria looked up from the sheaf of papers in her hand to glare at the Fenton County District Attorney. "Any of my men coming through that door with me last week will testify that no excessive force was used. That idiot pointed a gun at me."

Richmond Davis raised his hands, placating. "I'm sure they will, miss, er, Sheriff. Trouble is, his lawyer is threatening to take this public, and I don't think the commissioners will take kindly to that kind of negative publicity. You did shoot the man."

He took the papers from her, flipped through them until he found the proper page, then cleared his throat to read aloud, "…did willingly and with malice fire a bullet into Mr. Coomb's left shoulder, specifically the anterior deltoid, causing a life-threatening loss of blood and debilitating muscle damage." He stopped, looked up at her with a worried look on his too handsome face. "Debilitating. That means real serious, miss…I mean Sheriff."

Ria clenched her jaw and mentally counted to ten. The act didn't appreciably affect her rising temper. "Where did you get your law degree, out of a cereal box? The man was shot in the shoulder, for God sakes. A bullet is going to mess up the muscle there, but he got immediate medical attention. The hospital didn't even keep him overnight."

"They're listed on here, too." Davis began shuffling through the pages again. "Where's the name of that doctor…."

A tension headache was rapping at the base of her skull. Rubbing the spot gingerly, Ria strove for patience. "It's a nuisance suit, that's all. We got them all the time when I was on the Denver Police Force. He and his lawyer are blowing smoke. Even if it makes it to court, you have nothing to worry about. That arrest was solid."

But the man's face had gone white. "Go to court? Oh, no, mi—er, ma'am. I can't take this to court. We'll have to plead it out."

She came out of her chair with a speed that had the man shrinking back in his chair. "Under no circumstances will you offer a plea bargain."

Davis's face took on a stubborn look. He straightened and brushed at invisible lint on his suit sleeve. "I'm the district attorney. I decide what cases to—"

"You're a young and untried attorney still building a rep."

It was a shot in the dark, but from the youth of the man's features, she was guessing he hadn't been practicing more than a year or two. "You don't want to give the impression that you're soft on crime." She paused long enough to let the import of her words sink in. "Yours is an elected position, and from what Eldon Croat tells me, this county puts a lot of stock in strict law enforcement. A mistake like this so early in your career can come back to haunt you at election time."

Davis swallowed hard, obviously picturing the scenario she'd just drawn for him. "If I lose this in court that wouldn't do my reputation any good, either."

She was starting to feel like the younger man's cheerleader. "I don't think it will come to that. But if that's the worst that happens, wouldn't you rather be able to run on the fact that you held firm against the threats of a known drug dealer, instead of caving in to them?"

He frowned, and she got the feeling that he wasn't totally convinced. "I guess."

"Let his attorney know that you're calling his bluff. Lots of times they'll let these cases progress right up to the time they're about to choose a jury, and then drop them. In that case, you come out looking like a hero and you barely have to step foot in the courtroom."

Face brightening, he said, "You think?"

"I'm sure of it."

He rose, clutching the copy of the complaint. "Maybe you're right. I'll have to mull this over a bit more before I make any decisions."

"You do that." Ria showed him to the door, then closed it after him, heaving a sigh. Great. All she needed to make this day complete was a nuisance suit and a still-wet-behind-the-ears lawyer with qualms about courtroom work. She shook her head, winced when the action made it pound harder. If Davis needed further convincing, she could always set Eldon Croat on the man. Something told her the commissioner would be outraged at the thought of dismissing what was a clear-cut case against one of the drug dealers.

She went to the filing cabinet and pulled open the top drawer. Withdrawing an oversize bottle of pain relievers, she removed the top and shook a couple out. Swallowing them dry, she replaced the bottle and shut the drawer. Stress-filled days followed by late nights were the likely cause of her tension headaches, and there didn't seem to be an end in sight.

A full moon always seemed to bring out the crazies, and from the looks of the cell occupants, Fenton County had more than its share of them. She and her deputies had had their hands full for the last several nights responding to calls ranging from domestic disturbances to armed robbery. Thinking of the brainiac who had tried to rob the Git N' Go outside of town was a perfect example. After grabbing all the cash, he'd run outside to discover he'd locked his keys in the car.

She smiled at the memory. Simpson had caught that call, and still swore up and down that it was the easiest arrest he'd ever made. He'd picked the man up on the highway, hitching a ride.

Her evenings had been spent doing some surveillance work on yet another suspected meth manufacturer. This one was operating out of her trailer house, which also housed her three children. Ria wasn't going to waste any time gathering the evidence they needed to move in on her, and getting the kids out of that situation.

And what time she wasn't working on official duties, she was reorganizing information from her file cabinets at home. She'd focused on the military as a possibility before, and

Benny had long hacked into the National Personnel Records Center for serving in the various branches at the time she was shot. But the sheer volume of material had made the task impossible, without an individual's name, base, or even a branch to concentrate on.

Now she had a lead. Stanton thought he'd been operating in Columbus, Georgia at the time he'd done these tattoos, so she was concentrating on Army personnel. Fort Benning, home of a U.S. Army Ranger school, was less than ten miles from Columbus.

Larry Stanton's memory of the exact date he'd done the tattoos hadn't been too certain. She hoped the rest of the details he'd given her proved to be more definite. She'd had to do a lot of talking to convince Warden Udall that the man's continued protection was imperative to a case she was working.

Online sites gave basic information on current and ex-military personnel. She'd decided to focus her attention on those reported dead around the time the two assassins had tracked her down, then cross-reference the names to the lists of Army personnel. It was painstaking work, but her excitement hadn't dulled.

Finally, she felt as if she was on the right track. And nothing—not time-wasting lawsuits, not dumber-than-life criminals—was going to distract her.

A mental picture of Jake Tarrance formed in her mind, and she squeezed her eyes shut for a moment, willed it away. She hadn't seen him since he'd left her house several nights ago, through the same door where he'd bypassed the alarm.

The memory still rankled. Locks, alarms—even the "tells" she arranged around the perimeter—all just gave the illusion of security. There was no fail-proof way to ensure safety. She'd always known that, and guarded against becoming complacent. But finding Jake Tarrance ensconced in her easy chair, watching her TV, had made a mockery of her measures. She was prepared for the assassin who would lie in wait, prepared to kill her with minimal fuss. She hadn't expected anyone to waltz in, with no attempt to hide his presence while he made himself at home.

She hadn't expected Jake.

He crowded into her thoughts at odd times, when she least expected it. Could least afford it. He'd caught her off guard by showing up at her house, and she suspected that had been his intention.

Because now she couldn't prevent herself from checking her lane for a strange car. Couldn't help but see him in her chair, an imported beer in his hand from a six-pack he'd left in her refrigerator. The house had been stamped with his presence, and try as she might, no amount of effort could erase that. A part of her was wondering when he'd show up again, and she was certain he'd be very pleased to know that. Perhaps that had even been his intention.

With an air of determination, she forced him out of her mind and concentrated on using the next few hours for paperwork. Checking the clock, she made a mental promise to herself that she'd leave here by seven, at the latest. She got so engrossed in the work she had waiting at home that she rarely ate supper, not wanting to spend the time going to a store for groceries, or to a restaurant. Tonight, she promised herself, as she sat down and pulled out the duty roster, she'd swing by the local StopChop and pick up takeout. Her pants were getting loose, and she could ill-afford to lose any more weight.

With Jake Tarrance firmly off her mind, or at least not at the forefront, she settled into the paperwork.

* * *

But despite her best intentions, it would be closer to nine before she pulled into her lane. Eldon Croat had been in the StopChop when she got there, dining with Max Ewald, another commissioner. They'd waved her over and she'd had little choice but to sit down with them as they hashed over the reason for D.A. Richmond Davis's visit to her office that day. She didn't bother asking how they'd learned of it. The town seemed to have a very reliable grapevine, and it appeared in good working condition. She'd focused on her meal, saying as little as possible as the two men skewered Davis's character, and that of at least three generations of his ancestors.

"Richie Davis always was sissified," Ewald had noted wisely, as he downed a helping of chicken fried steak and mashed potatoes swimming in glutinous looking gravy. It was impossible to tell where the food would be stored on his tall spare frame. "He was the worst quarterback Tripolo High ever had. Every time a tackle came at him, he'd get called for intentional grounding, rather than take the hit. Remember that, Eldon?"

Eldon had. "Comes from havin' a mama with too strong a tongue and a daddy with biggety notions of his own. Never did think Richie was the man for the job, but no one else ran against him. Tomorrow we'll go downtown and talk sense into him."

"Why don't you let me speak to him again?" Ria had suggested. "He's thinking things over tonight. I'll check back with him first thing tomorrow morning. If he needs further convincing, I'll let you know."

It had taken most of another hour, but finally the two men had agreed to try it her way. She'd left the diner later than she'd wanted, but certain that, one way or another, Richmond

Davis wouldn't be offering a plea bargain to the drug dealer who'd filed suit.

Darkness had long since fallen. Ria parked the cruiser next to the house. The full moon would make the flashlight almost unnecessary for her perimeter check. She swung the door open and got out. At the last minute, she ducked back inside for the flashlight. It didn't pay to lower defenses, no matter what....

There was a loud popping sound next to her ear, and in the next moment the driver-side window shattered into a spider-web of tiny cracks. Instinct had her diving into the car before comprehension even registered. Another noise swiftly followed, and a hole appeared in the windshield.

Someone was shooting at her.

She rolled to the floor and angled her way back toward the steering column. If she could manage to turn the car on and put it in gear, she might have a chance at getting the vehicle around the house and out of the line of fire. From the direction of the shots, the gunman had to be behind her, probably across the road. There was no cover on her property. She'd had all the bushes and underbrush cleared away when she'd bought the place.

Awkwardly, she reached up and turned on the ignition, pressing the heel of her hand against the accelerator. The engine roared to life. Shifting it into gear, she attempted to keep the wheel straight as she gave it gas. It lunged forward.

The shots were coming more rapidly. She could hear the metallic ping as they hit the back of the car. Alarm sliced through her. The shooter was attempting to hit the gas tank. If he succeeded, she might be trapped inside an inferno.

Pressing more firmly on the gas pedal, she did a mental count to five, then yanked hard on the wheel, hoping she'd clear the house. Twisting her head to the side, she was relieved to see the back of the structure.

Grabbing the radio transmitter, she spoke urgently into it. "This is Sheriff Kingsley calling base. Send all free units to my place on Old Highway Road. There's a shooter in the area. Use caution in approaching. Repeat, use caution in your approach."

The radio came to life with the responses of deputies and the dispatcher. Ria dropped the transmitter and crawled to the passenger door, eased it open.

It was the eerie silence she noticed first. No more shots sounded, and there were none of the night noises she'd come to expect in the area. Ears straining, she listened, but heard nothing.

In a crouch she ran to the house, unsnapping her holster and withdrawing her gun. Thumbing off the safety, she peered carefully around the side of the building, searching the darkness in vain for any sign of the shooter.

She was at a disadvantage. The sniper likely was equipped with night vision goggles. Scanning the sparse line of box elders across the road, she saw no sign of motion. Would he have had time to cross the street to her property while she was still in the car? She tried to remember how long it had been since she'd heard the sound of bullets hitting the vehicle, but the minutes blurred together.

Staying close to the house, she crawled along its side until she was at the front corner. Ria had a clear view of the other side of the road now, but still saw nothing. Sirens sounded in the distance. She glanced behind her, almost looked away again until she caught the sight of motion from the corner of her eye. Staring hard, she saw it again. A shadow at the back corner of the house. Inching slowly forward.

She scrambled to her feet and dodged around the house, flattening herself against the siding. Carefully, she angled herself so that she had a clear look at the still-moving shadow. A second ticked by. Two. The shadow loomed larger.

Then she wheeled around the house and squeezed off three shots in rapid succession. Something stung her cheek, and she dived back around the corner for cover. The wailing of the sirens grew closer. She peered around the house again, and saw nothing. No shadow. No movement.

The first deputy's car wheeled into her lane, quickly followed by a second. Ria stood and waved an arm at the men, knowing they'd be able to identify her in the spear of their headlights.

"Vinton, you and Simpson drive your car across the lawn on the opposite side of the house. We'll take this side. Be careful. He was around back a few seconds ago." Without a word, both men climbed back into their vehicle. Ria got in with Cook. He pulled the car into the backyard as she scanned the area.

The yard was empty. Her cruiser sat motionless, looking as if it'd been through a war, but there was no sign of the shooter. Frustration gnawed at her. He could have disappeared in any of three directions, and with every passing second, he was farther away.

"Want us to do a foot search?"

Resignedly, she nodded. "Get your flashlights and rifles, and take the right of the property. I'll organize the rest of the men as they arrive. We'll surround the area and maybe we can trap him that way."

But as she headed back to the front to greet the approaching department cars, she already had a sense of foreboding that their search would be in vain.

* * *

Three hours later, Ria's suspicion had proved true. Despite the efforts of a dozen deputies and another ten reserves, the shooter hadn't been apprehended. A couple of investigators took her car back to town to the department garage to examine it. Any evidence would then be turned over to the lab. She didn't hold out much hope that it would yield anything valuable, unless a bullet happened to have gotten lodged in a seat.

Spotlights had been brought in so the scene in her yard could be worked. More had been set up across the road, where she'd assumed the shooter had been hiding behind the stand of trees. No casings had been found there, although indentations in the grass indicated it probably was the spot the shots had originated from.

One of the deputies did suffer a sprained ankle when he tripped over the wire she had stretched around the perimeter of her home. She could only hope that the shooter had suffered the same fate.

Finally, she called the men together and halted the search until daylight. "We'll continue canvassing the neighbors and alert Crime Stoppers that we're looking for anyone with information." She scanned the weary faces of the men surrounding her. "Thank you for your help. We'll start up again tomorrow."

"Might want to take a look at your face, Sheriff," Cook suggested. "Blood looks dry now. You didn't get hit, did you?"

She shook her head, even as her hand went to her cheek. Remembering how it had stung earlier, she said, "Probably nicked by a piece of siding. Worley dug a bullet out of the house there."

He nodded and headed toward his car. Some men were already driving away, others had collected in small groups to talk.

"Sheriff? Sheriff?"

With a sinking heart, Ria looked up to see Vera Wainwright bearing down on her. As the *Tripolo Tribune*'s owner, primary reporter, editorialist and photographer, she had her eyes and ears everywhere. Ria fervently wished they were somewhere else right now.

"I've been very patient, Sheriff, but you haven't answered all of my questions."

The woman's brassy blond curls gleamed like molten gold in the moonlight, painting her with a surreal halo. Ria had dealt with her enough to know that the affect was undeserved. The woman was tenacious about a story, and not always overly concerned with the facts. Ria had learned to be careful about what she disclosed to her.

"Sorry, Vera, but we won't know more until forensics has a chance to analyze the evidence."

The reporter looked unconvinced. "Do you have any idea who was shooting at you or why?"

"We don't know that anyone was. It could have been a poacher who got disoriented in the dark." Even to her own ears the suggestion sounded weak. From the look on Vera's face, she thought so, too.

"Don't know why a hunter would be 'round these parts." Duane Ralston's voice sounded behind her, and Ria ground her teeth. The man had been off duty this evening, so he hadn't been in one of the cars responding to the call. She sure hadn't missed him.

"Most hunters stick to the woods on the southeastern side of the county," he continued.

"Unless they were tracking deer or rabbit in that field across the road," Ria countered firmly. To Vera she said, "Stop by my office in the morning for an update. I'll give you all the details I can then."

She and Ralston watched the woman move away. His voice, when he spoke again, was insincere. "I hope you didn't bring trouble to this county by moving here, Sheriff."

There were only a couple of cars left in the yard. Adrenaline had long since faded, leaving Ria exhausted. She strove to keep her weariness from her voice. It wouldn't do to show weakness before this man. "Why don't you say what you mean, Ralston?"

He scratched at his thinning brown hair. "I read your press. Big city cop like you, all those cases of yours, seems like you might have made some enemies along the way. Just hope none of them saw fit to follow you here to settle up some old scores."

Old scores. The phrase had her flesh prickling. Ralston had effortlessly plucked out her greatest fear and voiced it. It wasn't a Denver gangbanger looking to get even that had her instincts on alert, however. It was someone much more deadly.

Had her identity been discovered somehow? Had yet another assassin found her, meaning to silence her forever?

Ignoring the very real possibility for the moment, she said, "We haven't been making friends in certain circles with the drug busts. If I was the target, we should look closely at some of our recent arrests. Any one of them has reason to want to get even."

"Or maybe we should look at someone we didn't arrest. Someone like Jake Tarrance."

Ice abruptly formed in her veins. It took every ounce of effort she could summon to meet Ralston's gaze squarely. "Why would Jake Tarrance be shooting at me?"

"You tell me, Sheriff." The deputy folded his arms across his chest and rocked back on his heels. "You're the one that called in his plates the other night. What do you think he was doing in the county?"

Sensing a trap, Ria opted for the truth. "He was waiting for me." From the look on the man's face, she knew that she'd guessed correctly. Ralston already knew Tarrance had been here, or he'd guessed as much. Without a qualm, she lied, "He was looking to strike a deal for Boster. I told him it wasn't going to happen. He left unhappy, but hardly homicidal."

The story was plausible and there was no reason for Ralston to doubt it. But her mind kept flipping back to Jake's words before he'd left.

If I find out you're lying to me, I'll be back.

We're not finished with each other, Ria.

Unease snaked down her spine. The shooting couldn't be Jake's doing. What would be his motive? She had nothing to do with Alvarez, and the man seemed to consume Jake's attention.

"I say we take a look at him." Ralston's voice seemed to come from a distance. "He's got a better reason than most to want you out of the way."

"You've got a reason to want me gone, too. I took the position you think should have been yours. Should we take a look at your whereabouts tonight?" At the expression of shock on his face, Ria mentally cursed her lack of diplomacy. It was late. She was tired. And she really didn't want to be having this conversation.

"This isn't doing either of us any good. I'm going to get some rest." She strode away, heading toward the front door, stopping to deactivate the alarm.

Deputy Duane Ralston watched her go, fists clenched at his sides. Uppity bitch. She had the brass to taunt *him* about not making sheriff? That job *should* have been his, damn her. He'd put in the time on the force. He had the seniority and experience to be named as Winston's replacement. Give him a couple years to show the people of Fenton County what he could do, and come election time, he'd have been a shoo-in.

But, no. He spat on the ground, to rid his mouth of the vile taste filling it. Croat had convinced the other commissioners to bring in someone from the outside. And if that hadn't been slap enough, they'd had to hire a *woman*. It was too damn bad that one of those bullets hadn't taken care of her tonight, for good.

But just because she was still here didn't mean she had to stay.

The sly thought crept across his mind, lingered. No matter what she said about Tarrance's reason for coming here, she had knowingly dealt with the biggest crime boss in these parts. Who knew what the two had really been discussing? Could be something illegal. Ralston didn't have to prove that, of course. 'Round these parts, it only took the appearance of impropriety to get folks' tongues wagging. One way or another, the bitch would be *gone*.

The more he thought about it, the more he figured that Sheriff Ria Kingsley would bear some watching. If there were some deal in the making between her and Tarrance, he'd get to the bottom of it. Once he did, she'd be out of this county quicker than she'd come. And this time Croat and the others would see who the best candidate for the job was.

An uncustomary smile creased his face at the thought. Sheriff Duane P. Ralston. Yep. He sure did like the sound of that.

Chapter 5

Alabama State Senator Jerry Grimm accepted a refill of Kentucky bourbon and sat back in his chair, swirling the amber liquor in his glass appreciatively. "You always have the best booze, Tarrance, I'll give you that."

"Nothing but the best for my friends, Jerry." Jake lifted his own glass, tipped it toward the other man in a mock toast. "I hope I can continue to count on your friendship, anyway."

Grimm sipped from the glass. "What you're asking this time goes way beyond our past business. If anyone gets wind of our association, you can count this bill dead in the water. And my political career with it."

"I trust your discretion," he said cynically. What he trusted was the man's single-minded sense of self-preservation. Since his greed was equally great, Jake was certain Grimm would find some way to earn the substantial bribe he was offering, while keeping their connection under wraps.

"I still don't see how this is going to help you. Just because I propose the bill legalizing privately owned casinos doesn't mean it's going to get passed. The last time we started a real gambling discussion in this state, we had all sorts of conservatives coming out of the woodwork."

"Let me worry about getting it passed." Jake already had a rough idea just how many in the state legislature could be counted to vote for such a bill. And there were plenty of others who could be approached for support. Human nature never changed. Everyone had a price. And he was quite good at figuring out what that was for each individual.

"I must be crazy to even consider this." Grimm took another swallow of the bourbon. "Political suicide is what it is."

"Not if you follow my instructions. Remember what happened to our former governor when he refused to support a lottery that would have proceeds going to education?"

The other man nodded. "He was defeated in his reelection bid. But still…"

"These are tough economic times." Jake repeated the lines he needed the man to memorize. "Every state has to do what it can for our children's future. Under your proposal, ten percent of all casino profits will go directly to public education. That's a hell of a lot of money, Jerry. You'll be considered a damn saint."

And Jake Tarrance would be first in line with a casino license. He'd spent years grooming contacts in the governor's office and in the gaming commission. As soon as this bill passed—and he'd see that it did—he was positioned to take immediate advantage. Even after the ten percent and taxes, he still stood to make more profit off one month's take at a legally operated casino than he did in six months on his illegal gaming ventures.

"If word ever got out about our association, we'll be in cells side by side."

"I don't think prison would suit me," Jake drawled. "That's why I've always made a point to avoid it." He'd come as close as he ever wanted to when he was fifteen and spent three years in a juvenile detention center. What he'd learned from that experience was that patience paid off. With foresight and planning, prison could be avoided. He'd never forgotten that particular lesson.

"A little fear is good. It'll make you careful." Because Jake sensed the senator was wavering, he added, "Should I wire the money to the same account as usual?"

The mention of the money wiped the concern from the man's face. Senator Jerry Grimm had expenses. A new young trophy wife, a second family and heavy-duty alimony for his ex. There was never a doubt in Jake's mind what the man's ultimate answer would be.

"That's right. The same account."

A broad smile on his face, Jake rose, stuck out his hand. "A pleasure doing business with you, Senator."

Their handshake was brief. Now that he was committed, Grimm seemed in a hurry to leave. "I'll let you know when the bill is ready to be presented."

"I'll want a look at the first draft so I can give you feedback." Jake wasn't about to leave the wording in Grimm's hands. He had two of the finest lawyers in the state on retainer. With their help, the proposal would sound like a suggestion from Mother Teresa.

"I'll fax it to you."

Nodding, Jake stabbed a finger at the intercom button on his desk. "Cort, show our guest out the private entrance." To the senator he said, "My driver is waiting. He'll take you wherever you need to go." A moment later his employee came in and escorted the senator through a door in the paneling that would eventually lead to the alley.

Hands clasped behind his back, Jake stood in front of the priceless artwork adorning his walls, a sense of satisfaction filling him. He'd set the wheels in motion. There was little doubt that the outcome would be exactly as he desired.

Most men would be thrilled by the imminent promise of success. But Jake wasn't given to wild swings of emotion. He was, he supposed, jaded. Spoiled by years of having his every plan come to fruition. The most feeling he'd experienced in years was at the thought of the upcoming showdown with Alvarez. The man wanted him dead. Jake didn't doubt that before they were through, one of them would be.

But upon the heels of that thought came another. He'd been sucker punched with emotion recently, far more than he would have thought he was capable of. Every time he got near Ria Kingsley his hormones ran riot.

Sexual attraction he could handle, but it was more than that. The enigmatic woman with the unforgettable eyes fascinated him. There was more, far more to her than what her surface would suggest. If he hadn't already suspected that, the recent digging he'd done into her background would have proved it.

He turned from the paintings as Cort reentered the room.

"Did you get the senator sent on his way?"

"I figured you'd want him out of here before showing in your next visitor."

Jake arched a brow. "I didn't know I was expecting a visitor."

The other man went to the wall before Jake and slid aside what would appear to guests as a mural. Behind it was a panel of closed-circuit television monitors. He punched some buttons as Jake came to stand beside him.

"Ever seen him before?"

Peering closely at the image of the man even now pacing his outer offices, Jake slowly shook his head. His guest wore a two thousand dollar suit and an aura of power with equal ease. "Did he give a name?"

"Colton. That's all. No ID on him. We patted him down. He's clean."

"Make doubly sure before you show him in."

They exchanged a long look. "Yes sir." He let himself out.

Using the monitor, Jake watched as his employee walked through a small buffer office that was deliberately kept empty, into the outer area where the stranger waited. Cort performed another physical search, then for good measure ran the compact oscilloscope over the man. The stranger argued for a few seconds as he was ordered to empty his pockets, but all he seemed to carry was a gold pen and a small calculator. Cort dropped the two items into a desk drawer, then pressed the intercom.

"Shall I show him in, sir?"

With a quick movement, Jake had the mural back in place, and strode toward the door, pulled it open. "Thank you, Cort. I'll take it from here."

He motioned the man in and closed the door behind him. Indicating a leather chair next to his desk, he said, "Have a seat. What can I do for you, Mr....Colton?"

"That's right." The man sat, appearing at ease. He was about Jake's height, with a slighter build. His hair had never decided on a color. Some would describe it as blond, others as light brown. His eyes were equally nondescript.

His very ordinariness had Jake wary. It wasn't men who stood out from the crowd who were most dangerous, but those who could blend into the background without notice.

"I've done a little research and discovered you have a certain reputation in these parts."

Adrenaline humming, he leaned back in his chair and hooked one ankle over his knee. "As a rule, I don't pay much attention to my reputation. I've always thought it was a mistake to believe your own press."

A ghost of a smile flitted across the man's face, before it was gone. "I'm satisfied that you're the right man for the job I have in mind."

"And what might that be?"

"I have a problem I'd like you to eliminate for me."

Jake spread his hands, watched the man steadily. "So why don't you tell me about it?"

"Not it, her." Colton straightened his cuffs meticulously. "Rianna Kingsley. I want you to kill her."

There was more, but Jake didn't hear it. There was a deafening roar in his ears. He could see the man's lips move, but the sound didn't register. It took long moments to recover, while he strove to keep his reaction from his face.

Blood glacial, he inquired, "Any special reason why?"

"I don't think that's relevant, is it? You'll earn yourself a substantial fee by completing the job by the end of next week."

"A week." Jake's mind was racing. "That's not a lot of time."

"You don't need much time. I understand you already know of her." Colton's smile held a hint of derision. "You and I have a mutual acquaintance. Larry Stanton. He's told me quite a bit about his association with you."

Fury began to bubble, edging out the earlier shock. The last time Jake had talked to Larry, the man had called him to report on Ria's visit. He'd mentioned he had someone else interested in the information, but Jake had ordered him to keep his mouth shut. As usual, Larry's greed had gotten ahead of his brain.

"Really?" Jake's voice was cool. "Hard to imagine how Larry would interest you."

"You'd be surprised what interests me, Mr. Tarrance. Can I call you Jake? I have a proposition for you that will be advantageous for both of us."

"Let me save you some time. I don't think I'm in the kind of business you're looking for. You'd do better with a professional, one who deals exclusively in these matters."

The other man's stare was unwavering. "You may not take care of these matters personally, but from what I've heard, you certainly have contacts within your organization to carry out such a task. And if you hear me out, I think you'll be interested in what I can offer in return. "

Jake rose. "You're wasting both our time. I can't help you. I'll have my employee see you out."

"Enrico Alvarez." Jake stilled. "I believe there's bad blood between the two of you?" Colton gave a shrug, as if the details didn't matter to him. "He's due for parole in a few weeks, and when he gets out, I understand he's coming for you."

"Old history. What does Alvarez have to do with this?"

"Nothing. And everything. In addition to the money I'm willing to pay for the job, I could also arrange to have his parole delayed by a number of weeks." He raised his brows. "I assume that would be beneficial for whatever it is you're planning."

"What I'm planning, Colton, is to stay alive, and out of prison. That's a little hobby of mine. And taking you up on your offer doesn't seem like a real good move toward either end."

It didn't seem to bother the other man that Jake was still standing. Fussing with the crease in his trousers, he inquired, "No? Not even when I tell you what happens if you don't agree?"

The threat in his voice was impossible to miss, even uttered as it was in that mild, almost pleasant tone. "I'm going to assume that you are unprepared at this point for Alvarez's release." He lifted his shoulders. "Guess that's understandable. You had no way of knowing he'd be among those considered for the nonviolent offender early parole program. Prison overcrowding is a real problem in this state, isn't it?"

Stonily, Jake remained silent. Stanton, the lowlife, had obviously not only told Colton about Ria, he'd spilled his guts about Jake, too. It would have taken very little digging on Colton's part to fill in any missing details from Larry's account.

"I can only expect that it would present a real problem to you if Alvarez was ordered released, oh, say…tomorrow, instead of in a few weeks."

All his plans, years in the making, flashed through Jake's mind, seeming to disintegrate like jet vapor. Alvarez still had much to pay for. Prison hadn't even begun to retire the debt owed. It was merely a time for him to reflect on all he had lost and why. And to consider what awaited him when he got out.

For what he'd cost Jake, he'd pay with his life.

But that kind of preparation took time, care and the utmost caution. Emotion would never again be allowed to catch him in its trap. When people responded emotionally, they paid, along with the guilty party. Jake was done paying.

"How do I know you have that kind of power?"

There was a brief look of satisfaction on Colton's face, as if pleased at the word applied to him. "I think your next conversation with Warden Udall would clear up any qualms about my…power." The man gestured toward the phone. "Go ahead and call him right now. I'll wait. Ask him about our friend Larry."

Crossing the front of his desk, Jake did just that. It took several minutes before the warden came on the line, and their conversation was brief. When it was over, Jake leaned over to replace the receiver, surreptitiously pressing a button under his desk with his free hand.

Straightening, he returned to where Colton was still sitting, and sank into a chair next to him. "Let's talk business."

Ria faced the team of four scene investigators assembled in her office. It was a tight fit. Cook and Simpson sat nearest her. Ronny Decker—six foot four and weighing three hundred pounds—was already fidgeting in his seat by the far wall. Ria doubted there was a chair in the department, other than the custom-ordered one at his desk, that would hold his girth comfortably. Patricia Clark, the only other female officer on the force, sat alongside him, her slender figure nearly obscured by his bulk.

"What's the preliminary report?"

It was Simpson who answered. "We didn't find much trace evidence. We've got the bullet we dug out of the siding of your house. That was fired from a lot closer than across the road."

Although it wasn't phrased as a question, she nodded. "He was in back of me, around the corner of the house when he shot that time." The splinters that had struck her as the bullet lodged had come from the siding. It had taken her the better part of two hours, and a couple swigs of Scotch, to dig them out with tweezers and a needle. Her cheek still bore the ravages of her ministrations.

"It was a .30 caliber bullet. No brass was recovered, either at the original shooting site or on your property."

Ria nodded, grimly. The shooter had been cautious. As she'd suspected, he must have worn night vision equipment, which would allow him to see his target and to search the ground in the dark for the spent casings. That kind of caution spoke of careful planning.

Or the ingrained training of a professional.

She shook off the thought and looked at Simpson. "Anything else?"

"We'd have to send it to the Birmingham lab to be sure, but Weston's something of a gun expert, and he thought the rate of twist was 1:11. Not sure what that would tell us, although most high powered rifles are 1:10 or 1:12."

"Might have been custom made." Some rifles geared for sniper/tactical use had that unusual twist. Ria no longer questioned where those odd snippets of knowledge came from. She'd never had difficulty summoning seemingly random facts about weapons and hand-to-hand combat techniques.

She'd just never been able to associate them to any personal history about herself.

"We shouldn't have any trouble matching the bullet to the gun that fired it if we can find it."

Everyone in the room knew that at this point, that was a big if.

"What'd you turn up on the neighborhood canvass?"

It was Clark who spoke this time. "Several neighbors reported hearing what they assumed were fireworks or something. None of them thought of gunfire until they heard the sirens."

The nearest home to Ria's was probably a quarter of a mile away. Isolation was one of the reasons she'd bought the place, but that same fact had allowed the shooter to set up and operate without fear of being detected until his quarry had shown.

"LaDonna Wilcox did say her son thought he saw a yeti running by his window at bedtime." The men in the room chuckled. "LaDonna put it down to an overabundance of cherry Kool-Aid and too much sci-fi channel. Timeline matches up, though, to shortly after your last visual contact of the shooter, so…" Patricia raised her shoulders in a shrug. "Maybe what he actually saw was the shadow of a man running, and his imagination supplied the rest."

"What direction are the Wilcoxes from my property?"

The woman stopped to think. "Southeast."

It made sense. Ria thought she'd dispatched the deputies first on the scene quickly enough to have apprehended the shooter if he'd gone straight east or west. She figured he'd likely used her car for cover and made his way to the back of her land, south, and then disappeared by crossing a neighboring property.

"Found some fibers along the southern boundary line that matched one we discovered at the shooting site. Lab results indicate they're some sort of burlap, with synthetic dyes applied."

"Might have been from a bag he carried the gun in," surmised Decker.

"Or a mat he used while he waited." This was from Cook.

"More than likely came from something he wore."

Ria's gaze met Simpson's and she knew that they'd reached a similar conclusion. "A Ghillie suit."

"One of those camouflage suits made of layered strips of jute burlap," Cook explained for the benefit of Patricia. "You can get them to match shades of terrain and seasonal conditions."

"I know what Ghillie suits are," she snapped.

Ria barely heard them. The suits were made to blend in with the surroundings. To a little boy's eye, a man wearing one might well look like a hulking, shapeless yeti. "Let's take a look at the Wilcoxes' yard today. See if we can find any more traces of burlap. He had to have had a vehicle somewhere in the vicinity. He wouldn't have run far wearing a Ghillie suit and carrying his gun and equipment. Talk to the neighbors again. Describe the suit and see if anyone else admits to seeing something like that."

"I vote Patty gets to interview the Wilcox kid," Cook said.

"And I'll take you along to keep LaDonna busy," Clark returned. "I hear she's always been sweet on you."

"LaDonna Wilcox is sweet on just about anything male and breathing."

There was a round of laughter, which trailed off as Ria sent a gaze around the room. "It wouldn't hurt to take a look at our most recent arrests. Do some checking to see if any are avid hunters, ex-military, or affiliated with a survivalist group of some type. Check and see if anyplace around here carries the suits and if they keep records."

The four nodded and, seeming to recognize the meeting was over, got to their feet. Ria stopped them before they went out the door. "I'm going to be saying this to everyone, but I'll tell you four right now. If this is a retaliation for our recent activities, I might not be the only target." She paused, saw comprehension settle on each of their faces. "We'll all need to take extra care out there."

She swiveled her chair, watched them file out, pulling the door closed behind them. Staring blankly at the varnished panel, she heard her parting words echo and reecho in her head. They could be true. Any one of their recent arrests had reason to want to even the score with someone in her department.

A chill crept over her skin. But when it came to settling old scores, it wasn't only scumbag drug dealers who might want *her* dead. It was hard to imagine one of their recent arrests having such specialized equipment and garb. Which left only one possibility.

There was an odd sense of déjà vu hovering in her mind, one she hadn't been able to shake since the night of the shooting. Two assassins had been sent for her six years ago, but she had dived so far undercover, she'd thought—she'd hoped—she'd never be found again. After all these years she'd assumed she'd succeeded. But it was possible she'd been found yet again.

The last two assassins had been waiting inside the places she'd been staying. Unconsciously, Ria shoved herself out of the chair, paced the room. Their method of kill had been far more personal. A knife the first time. A garrote the next. Each had required skill, and more importantly, hand-to-hand, face-to-face combat.

In contrast, a sniper's bullet was far more removed, less personal, than the previous attempts. It also attracted far more attention. If the sniper *was* someone from her past, what would have warranted such a departure from the other tries? Were the shots really fired by a disgruntled drug dealer out on bail? Or had that method been selected to make it seem that way?

The answers wouldn't be found within these four walls. But Ria had a knot of foreboding in her gut that warned her time for finding answers of any kind might well be running out.

The intercom on her desk buzzed, and Marlyss's voice sounded. "Someone on line two for you, Ria. Wouldn't give his name, and caller ID just shows unidentified."

"I'll take it." Maybe she was jittery, but if the call was by some chance an anonymous tip on the shooter, she didn't want to discourage whoever was offering the information.

She picked up the receiver, punched the button for the appropriate line. "Sheriff Kingsley."

"Sheriff. We have some unfinished business."

He didn't identify himself. He didn't have to. Her system responded to the low, smoky drawl immediately. Nerve endings quivered. Instincts hummed.

Resolve hardened.

"We have nothing more to discuss, Jake." With Ralston baiting her about Tarrance, the last thing she needed was any further contact with the man. She rested a hip against a corner of her desk.

"I disagree. Meet me at the restaurant in two hours. I'll make sure we have some privacy."

"No." The word was easy enough to say. She just wished she'd said it sooner. If she could time travel back to before she'd ever met him she'd have done things much differently. She'd have selected a different restaurant to eat in that night. Or once meeting him, she'd have tucked away sensitized hormones and gotten in her car, to drive home alone.

She wouldn't have had mind-shattering sex with a relative stranger. Wouldn't have assumed that life would conveniently keep their paths from ever crossing again.

She should have remembered that her life had rarely been convenient.

"Two hours, Ria." The certainty in his tone set her teeth on edge. "You can't afford to brush me off. This is too important."

"I can't think of anything you have to say that I'd consider important."

"Really?" His voice had gone silky, a tip-off, she'd learned, of his rising temper. "Have you talked to Larry Stanton lately? No? You won't, either. Because someone killed him this afternoon. And I'd be willing to bet that you're the reason he's dead."

Ria's own temper was simmering at a dangerous level by the time she entered Hoochees. The hostess she recognized from her previous visit seemed to remember her, or at least had been given her description. At her entrance the brunette sent her a bright smile and led her to a private corner in the dining area, next to the windows overlooking the river. It was hard to gaze at that view and not remember the same sight from Jake's windows in the apartment above.

The memory just fired her temper hotter.

"Mr. Tarrance will be right with you," the hostess promised. Even as she walked away, a waitress, one Ria didn't recognize, hurried over with a bottle of Chivas Regal and two glasses. Setting one down in front of her, she began to pour, before Ria reached out to stop her with a hand to her arm.

"None for me, thanks. I won't be staying long."

The woman continued filling both glasses. "Mr. Tarrance's request, ma'am."

Ria's lips twisted. The man was clearly used to issuing orders and having them obeyed. Problem was, she wasn't used to following them. It had been on the tip of her tongue to tell him to go to hell, but the news about Stanton had taken her off guard. He'd hung up, assuming she'd come as he'd commanded, and it still burned that she'd done exactly that. But a call to Warden Udall had confirmed Jake's news. Like it or not, Tarrance might be able to supply some details that the warden had been lacking.

It hadn't escaped her notice that the rest of the tables in their section were empty. She was certain that, too, had been Jake's directive. They would be alone here, lending an unwanted air of intimacy to the scene. She couldn't fault him for the decision, however. Their conversation needed to be conducted in private.

There was a tingle of awareness at the base of her nape. She guessed the cause intuitively. Involuntarily, she turned to watch him cross the room toward her, all the while damning the slow heat flooding her system.

So she couldn't control her body's response to him. That didn't mean she'd act on it again. She couldn't afford to. She hadn't been out of Fenton County five minutes before she'd realized she'd picked up a tail. It had alarmed her until she recognized the clumsiness of the driver's skill. She'd assumed that if it was the person who wanted her dead, he'd have a little more finesse.

Figuring out that it was Ralston, however, had merely stoked her irritation higher. The man was going to be a nuisance, and she could ill afford any extra scrutiny right now. She'd managed to lose him with minimal effort, which didn't cause him to rise in her estimation.

"Ria." There was genuine pleasure in Jake's voice.

Steeling herself against it, against him, she said, "I talked to Udall. He said the autopsy report wouldn't be finished for a few days, but they believe Stanton's noontime meal was poisoned."

There was a subtle hardening of his expression before he smoothed it and sat down. He chose the chair next to hers rather than opposite, and her pulse leaped. A woman would have to be dead not to respond to his magnetism. And although her existence had, for all intents and purposes, been erased, her femininity appeared alive and well. Under the circumstances, she didn't find that reassuring.

Tonight he wore black trousers and a black collarless dress shirt. There was elegance in the simplicity of the clothing, and she figured they probably cost more than all the garments in her closet put together. For him, crime seemed to be paying quite well.

Because she'd refused to dress up for him, she'd changed

from her uniform into jeans and a simple navy long-sleeved T. But if the look in his eyes was any indication, it wouldn't have mattered what she'd worn. That focus was back, the smoldering intensity that made her feel as if everything around them had ceased to exist.

He reached over with one finger to touch the cheek she'd taken the splinters from. She knew it was still red and angry looking. "You always seem to have a mark on you."

"Hazard of the job." When he didn't move away again, she shifted in her chair, placing a bit of distance between them. "Udall thinks—and I agree—that Alvarez masterminded the poisoning. There will be an investigation—"

"You know as well as I do that nothing will come of it." There was no mistaking the bitterness in Jake's tone. Any hint of tenderness must have been her imagination. Those pale eyes were cool now, guarded.

"Probably not." It was notoriously difficult to get inmates to come forward with information. Prisons were primitive communities, with a basic set of rules for survival. "But someone might hope to trade what he knows for better treatment. A transfer closer to home. Something." She leaned forward, a note of urgency entering her voice. "The fact is, you know as well as I do that Alvarez is the one who wanted him dead. And I resent you trying to lay Stanton's death at my door."

She didn't need anyone else on her conscience. She was haunted enough by Luz's specter as it was.

"I wasn't blaming you. Or maybe I was, but I was angry." He reached out for his glass, brought it to his lips and drank. "I have no doubt that his death was planned to make everyone else come to the same conclusion. There's no way to prove it, one way or another. God knows, Alvarez had the motive, and he's tried it before. But I don't think masterminded this."

"Who else would it be?" she countered. Her glass was in her hand without her even thinking about it. Sipping from it, she continued, "Since you've cleared me, and apparently Alvarez, who does that leave?"

"I'm guessing it was the guy who was in my office this afternoon." His gaze caught hers over the top of the glass. "The man who hired me to kill you."

There was a kick in her chest, strong enough to drive the breath from her lungs. Her hand hesitated an instant in the act of setting the glass back on the table. Then she recovered, looked at him coolly. "Well, what's the going price on a hit these days? Are we talking pocket change or real money?" Her lips twisted. "Call it ego, but I'd like to hear he made it worth your while. No one likes to know their life is worth the price of a couple tickets to Six Flags."

Jake stared at her for a moment. Could she really be that cold? From her reaction, one would think she had ice water running in her veins. But he had reason to know that her blood could, on occasion, run quite hot, indeed.

"He offered me a hundred and fifty thousand."

Amazingly enough, a flash of amusement flickered across her face. "Come to think of it, I'm not certain which of us should be more insulted. Did it occur to you that you might have been lowballed because he's underestimated *you?*"

He sat back in his chair, considered her. "I'm counting on that. And you're taking this amazingly well. Most potential hits could be forgiven for being a bit jumpier."

Her eyes chilled. And he was abruptly reminded that she was as adept at donning masks as he was. "You can try, Tarrance." Her voice was a taunt, a dare. "Do your worst. But the first two men who came for me are dead. And the one who attempted a couple nights ago will be, too, when I catch up with him." She shrugged, picked up her glass again with a steady hand. "You might want to consider that before taking his money."

The first two who had come for her? Ready to follow up on her former statement, he had to take a moment to comprehend the latter one. "What happened a couple nights ago?"

She tossed back the contents of her glass and reached for the bottle. "A sniper was waiting for me when I got home. Under the circumstances, I'm sure you won't be offended if I ask where *you* were at the time."

Ridiculous, given what he'd just told her, to feel an odd pang at the accusation couched in her words. Ridiculous and unacceptable. Jake Tarrance didn't feel anything for anybody. Life was less complicated that way.

"Do you have any leads on the shooter?" At her mocking stare, he sat back. "Okay, I can see where there might be a noticeable lack of trust here. But let's try to connect the dots, shall we? You go to see Larry Stanton—whose death, by the way, seriously inconveniences me—and days later he's dead. And even before his death you're shot at. Professional job?"

"It would have been a perfect head shot from two hundred meters if I hadn't ducked back into the car for something that I forgot."

His stomach knotted. Two hundred meters was nothing for a sniper. Good ones could shoot accurately from five times the distance. And given the events of the last few days, there was no reason to believe this had been anything less than a professional attempt.

"And two days later, I'm contacted by someone who badly wants you dead." His eyes met hers. "Even though we be agree he didn't offer nearly enough for the job. You started something in motion the day you went to see Larry Stanton. Given what I have riding on this thing, I want to know what your business with him was."

"It was exactly that. *My* business."

He shoved his face closer to hers. "It ceased being merely your business about the time my prime informant bit the dust. Right around the time a stranger waltzed into my office, throwing around threats and petty cash. I'd say that as of right now, it's *our* business."

Her expression grew cautious. "He threatened you?"

"Claimed he could arrange an early release for Alvarez. Naturally, I'd find that an inconvenience, too."

She gave a bitter smile. "Such a shame you're being inconvenienced by all this. Why don't you just give me his name and a description, and I'll take it from here."

She was good. A vague sense of admiration filled him. She'd been hit with more in the last few minutes than most people could withstand, and still continued to try and bluff her way through. "Sure. The name he gave me was Colton, but it's doubtful that's genuine. No ID, and his description is remarkably unremarkable." Jake paused, waited for comprehension to flicker across her face. "He's the type of guy that even when you describe him, he doesn't stand out. And I'm fairly certain he can do everything he claimed. When I had him followed he was passed through the airport without clearing security. And that's all I'm telling you without some answers on your part."

"You actually think I'm going to give answers to someone who just told me he's been hired to kill me? You're deluded."

From the mutinous expression on her face, it was clear she was still feeling obstinate. "Larry told me you came to see him about a tattoo he'd done years ago."

Her shrug was casual. "So?"

"So when he described it I remembered seeing it before." He tipped more Scotch into his glass. "On your ankle. If memory serves correctly, it was the only thing you were wearing at the time."

For the first time emotion flashed in her eyes. He felt a fierce sense of satisfaction. Good. Maybe he wasn't the only one who still woke up with the sheets in a tangled heap, his insides tangled over a woman he never should have met. Never should have touched.

And couldn't stop thinking about.

"What else did Larry tell you?"

"He reported your entire conversation," he said bluntly. "He knew better than to keep something like that from me. And damn his soul, when he mentioned someone else who would pay well for the information on you, I should have known that nothing would stop him from making that contact. Even his fear of me was outweighed by his love of money."

She looked as though she would benefit from another glass of Scotch. But when he nudged the bottle toward her, she made no move to pick it up. "Who could have gotten to him so quickly?"

"It wasn't quick at all. Sounded to me like he was approached several years ago and at your visit he figured he was finally going to hit the jackpot. So." Jake sat back in his chair, rested an elbow on its back. "Time for answers, baby. Because this little drama all revolves around you. Start talking."

At her continued silence, frustration rose. "You can skip the part about the foster homes you grew up in." He didn't want to hear her relate her experiences there, at any point. It had been hard enough to contemplate what her life had been like as he pored over the details his information broker had gotten for him. "Your graduation from the Colorado Police Academy was impressive, though. High grades for marksmanship, wasn't it? Very nice."

Her eyes had gone dark and dangerous, like those of a big jungle cat about to pounce.

"And your career in the DPD was similarly impressive, I suppose, for a cop. All you need to tell me is where the tattoo fits into all this and why someone would kill you rather than have you asking questions about it."

"I must be missing something." She cocked her head quizzically. "Tell me again why I would share anything with the man who's been hired to kill me? Or wait. Maybe you're going to try and convince me you didn't accept the job."

"No, I accepted it." He looked around, caught Marta's eye. The waitress hurried toward them with menus. From the looks of things this was going to take awhile, and all of a sudden he was starving.

He glanced back at Ria, enjoying the arrested expression on her face. "I bought us both a week by taking the job. So that's what we've got. Seven days to figure out who wants you dead and why. Then you can go back to…being a cop." His tone reflected his absolute amazement at the choice. "And I can go back my plans." And of course he'd rather the scheme involving Alvarez had several weeks, rather than days, to become finalized.

He accepted the menus, handed one to Ria and flipped his open. It was purely habit. He had the entrées memorized.

She made no move toward hers. "As I said earlier, this is my business. I am sorry you got mixed up in it." He didn't detect a hint of sincerity in her words. "But I have no intention of trusting, or involving, you further."

He lifted a shoulder, as if it didn't matter. "That's up to you, of course. But I assumed you'd want to know the information I've acquired so far about Colton. I know where he lives, and in another twenty-four hours I'll know his real name and place of work, as well."

Chapter 6

Her fingers clenched the menu. Jake couldn't tell if that was a sign of nerves or if Ria was suppressing the urge to throttle him.

"You're bluffing."

"Am I?" He lowered his eyes to his menu again. "Are you a seafood lover? We have the crab and lobster flown in fresh daily. I can recommend either."

"I have some money put away." Her flat tone had his gaze rising, slowly. A dangerous burn ignited inside him. "Not much more than what this Colton offered you, but enough to pay for some simple information, I would think."

"You know, if I were a man to appreciate irony, it might amuse me that I find it so offensive to be offered bribes twice in one day. Considering how often I pay them myself, it's a bit incongruous. But there it is."

"Look at it from my perspective." Her fingers rubbed absently at the condensation on her glass. "I'm naturally reluctant to provide information to a man hired to kill me."

"You said there'd been others." There was a flicker in her eyes before they went blank. Mentally, he damned that ability of hers. His information brokers hadn't dug deep enough, long enough. Nothing in the file they'd put together for him hinted at what was going on in Ria Kingsley's life. Whatever it was, it was deadly.

And as of today, it involved him.

He gestured to Marta, and she crossed to their table, taking her order pad from her apron pocket. "Have you decided what you want?" he asked. "Or shall I order for you?"

Ria glared at him. "I'm not staying."

"Of course you are." To the waitress he said, "I'll have the New York strip, medium rare. Garlic mashed potatoes. No salad. She'll have the Alaskan king crab legs...." He paused, shot her a glance. "Potato?"

"I don't want the crab legs."

"All right. Bring her the same thing I'm having."

"I'm not eating..." She was talking to the waitress's back. Marta had already moved away, and would place the order exactly as he'd told her to. He expected no less. His people did what he asked, or they no longer worked for him.

It was no use wishing that Ria could have just a shred of that same trait. She wasn't a woman to be easily led. And that was one of the reasons he found her so damn enticing. He appreciated women with backbone—women who didn't allow themselves to be victimized, and excuse the behavior in the name of love.

Ria might not need rescuing, but from where he sat, the odds were stacked pretty high against her. She had to realize that, too, but if she did, not a hint of that knowledge showed.

More than was comfortable, he wanted to know where that strength of hers came from.

"Even given the unpopularity of cops in certain segments of society, having three assassins sent after you seems excessive."

She picked up her glass, toasted him with it. "Four," she said pointedly. "Counting you. I don't know why you're surprised. You have enemies of your own."

"Yeah." He gave a slow nod. "But I know who my enemies are. And you don't." With the words, comprehension dawned, and with it, certainty. "You wouldn't need my information on Colton if you already knew who wanted you dead. You wouldn't have needed Stanton, either. You don't know who's out there pulling the strings, do you? If you did, we wouldn't be having this conversation right now."

She picked up her glass, downed the remaining liquor. "I'd give anything to not be having this conversation."

But things were clicking into place. Pieces of information that had never quite added up before were now making sense. "Larry said he thought the group he'd done the tattoos on were army. Funny thing is, the information I got on Rianna Kingsley doesn't show any record of military service. She went right from college to the police academy."

Ria arched a brow. "Since you seem to have all the answers, I'm having a hard time figuring what I'm still doing here."

He stared at her, wondering, more than was comfortable, what lay behind that stoic facade. "Not all the answers," he murmured. "Not by a long shot. Who are you? *What* are you?" He didn't expect an answer, and he didn't get one. But he did get a response.

At his last questions, she flinched as though he'd struck her. And her eyes…for a moment the look in them would have fit perfectly in the collection of photos he had on his apartment wall.

Desolation. Stark and unvarnished. The sight of it stripped his mind of the points he was puzzling over. The expression vanished in the next moment, but he knew he hadn't imagined it. There was a primitive sort of protectiveness welling up inside him in response.

"I'll make you a deal." Ria turned to catch the eye of the waitress, motioned her over. "I'll still pay you for whatever information you gather on this Colton. Give me the week to get answers to some questions I have of him." When Marta arrived at the table, she requested more ice. She waited for the woman to move away before meeting Jake's gaze again. "At the end of that time, if you still want to try to collect from the job he hired you for, as well…" She shrugged. "You're welcome to try."

Jake reached over, picked up her hand, tightening his grip when she would have pulled away. "You're really, really going to have to stop trying to bribe me," he murmured. Her skin was smooth beneath his touch as he skated his thumb across her knuckles. "Call me sensitive, but I'm starting to find it annoying." He watched the irritation flash over her features, and something else. Awareness.

Satisfaction bloomed low in his belly. "You haven't been exactly forthcoming with answers, so I'm having some doubts about the, uh, *veracity* of any information you'd be willing to pass on about your discoveries." He intentionally ignored the sneer on her lips at his words. "Since it would appear that we both have a vested interest in any forthcoming info, as well as a shared lack of trust on both our parts, I suggest that the only real solution is for us to work together to find out what Colton is up to."

"Maybe you're right." Her words came slowly, with just the right amount of hesitation. "It might make sense to join forces. You have to admit, I have the most riding on this, though. You have to give me something, as a mark of good faith." She leaned toward him, the curve of her breast barely grazing his arm. "Tell me anything. Where did Colton go when your men followed him?"

Jake brought her hand to his lips. "They followed him—" he pressed a kiss to her palm "—out of state." When her fingers curled in his, he wisely released her and moved out of range. Given the sparks spitting from her eyes, he'd be wise to be cautious. "Nice try, by the way. I especially liked the almost accidental brush of your breasts on my arm. Distracting *and* devious."

Ria sat back and bared her teeth at him. "Accidental is the only way I'd get that close to you again."

He laughed, picked up his glass. The exchange had put him in a good mood. "I reserve the right to change your mind about that."

"I'm the one with everything to lose here. You realize that, don't you?" She drank as well, as if to douse her temper. "I have to worry about both you and Colton. If there even is such a person. You could have made him up. I'd be a fool to trust you."

"And I you." He waited for her to catch his gaze over the rim of her glass. "For all I know, *you* could have sent Colton to *me.*"

She had the nerve to look offended. "Me? Why would I?"

He shrugged. "I've never pretended to understand how cops think. Entrapment, maybe? Some elaborate scheme you cooked up with Columbus Vice?"

"And I thought I was paranoid," she muttered.

"You are." He delivered the words calmly, surely. "From

what you've said, you have reason to be. And so do I. You're just going to have to decide whom you distrust less. Me or whoever is trying to kill you."

Ria stared at him, refusing to state the obvious. As of a few minutes ago, by his own admission, the two had become one and the same.

Two hours later Ria waited for Jake to get them cleared through the surprisingly complex security at his offices. As they passed by the last guard and headed for the elevator, she said, "Are all the occupants of this building as cautious as you are?"

He punched in a number and the doors began to close. "There are no other occupants. I like having space."

She slanted him a glance. "So you rent the entire building to keep away curious neighbors who might take too much interest in your business, is that it?"

"Sort of. Except I don't rent the building. I own it."

Of course he did, Ria thought dourly. It was becoming obvious that his properties were vast. If he'd been operating for ten years, the length of time Detective Edwards had said Alvarez had been in prison, he'd had ample opportunity to amass a fortune. It was almost inconceivable to her that he'd managed to stay free all that time, despite the Columbus PD's suspicions about his activities. Jake Tarrance was either very very good at what he did, or incredibly lucky.

Either way, he was also incredibly dangerous. This whole thing could be an intricate trap, although try as she might, she couldn't figure out what he could have to gain from involving himself in this mess, other than the reason he'd stated.

But she hadn't stayed alive this long by being careless. And despite his acting as though their partnership was a done deal, she had yet to separate fact from fiction in his tale.

He ushered her through some well-appointed offices and then punched a code into the keypad outside another door. In a few seconds a green light winked and he opened the door, ushered her inside.

When he flipped on the switch, she looked around curiously. Expensive artwork adorned the polished paneled walls. There was an acre wide desk, behind which were floor to ceiling bookcases. A leather couch and several matching chairs sat to the right of the desk. But what caught and held her attention was the lack of windows.

It was a completely interior room. She was certain that was by design. She'd already determined that he was a cautious man. Not for the first time it struck her that in this way, at least, they were similar.

He went to a large mural on one wall and a moment later had the painting sliding aside to reveal a bank of CCTV monitors. He fiddled with some knobs as she stepped to his side. He allowed the tape to reverse some more, then stopped it as it showed a door opening, the same one she'd recently walked through. A man she recognized was showing another inside. It took her a moment, but she finally placed him. It was the man who had been behind the bar the first night she'd gone to Hoochees. The one who'd joined Jake in the parking lot later that night.

"Recognize the man with Cort?"

Ria focused on the second individual on the screen. As Jake had already said, this wouldn't be someone who would stand out in a crowd. But that wasn't the reason she didn't recognize him. Her stomach hollowed out as she searched his features with a knife-edged feeling of desperation. He could be a stranger, or he could be the man who had tried to kill her six years ago. And again a few nights ago.

But there was no way to tell. If she had ever known him, she didn't remember. Disappointment rose, harsh and punishing.

Belatedly, she became aware of Jake's gaze on her. She shook her head. "I don't know him."

But she might have, a sly inner voice whispered. She could have known him at one time, only too well. Could have served with him on some sort of assignments that even now she could only guess at. He might have been the one to explain what those assignments were. Might have been the one to put two bullets in her back.

Her lack of memory had never made her feel so vulnerable. How could she protect herself from an enemy who had no face? One intent on exacting retribution for acts she had no memory of committing? Despite its futility she traced the man's features with her gaze, looking for something, anything familiar. She didn't find it.

Jake reached out, turned on the sound. Ria listened quietly, but there was nothing familiar about the man's voice, either. When he got to the point of asking Jake to kill her, a sheen of ice seemed to settle over her. It provided a sort of numbness that insulated her from emotion, which was just as well. Emotion had a way of clouding judgment, and she needed to think clearly. She watched the tape in its entirety, a part of her marveling at the matter-of-fact way the two men discussed her death.

When it was over, when the screen went dark, Jake reached out to snap it off. Then, still silent, he stared at her, waiting for her to speak.

"Like I said, I don't recognize him. You could have staged the whole thing." She gave a shrug that was far more nonchalant than she was feeling.

"You can't afford to believe that."

No, she couldn't afford to believe it. And it would be incredibly stupid to ignore the coincidence between the shooting incident and this man walking into Jake's offices days later with a contract on her life. After years of watching one lead after another disintegrate upon closer examination, all this had come to a head after she'd interrogated Larry Stanton about the tattoo. There was a common link in all of this, and Stanton just might be it.

"I told you he didn't carry ID. What I didn't say was that he was carrying what looked like a simple gold pen and a calculator."

"You think they were something else?"

"We take…precautions before allowing people in here. Cort found a small camera in the head of the pen. He thinks the calculator was some sort of scrambling device. It would interfere with any attempts to monitor the conversation electronically."

Nodding toward the bank of screens, she said, "Under the circumstances, wise precautions to take."

"We're in the habit of taking precautions ourselves." Motioning her to one of the chairs, Jake seated himself on the couch. "But we've never seen anything like the gadgets he had on him. There's nothing like them on the market." He gave a self-deprecating grin. "And by that I include the black market."

He would know; she was certain of that. "It's still difficult to believe he'd come so prepared, and still make his pitch to you once the devices had been taken from him."

"I think he had to." Jake rolled his shoulders, one hand going to the back of his neck, rubbing. "Stanton was already dead. The deal had been set in motion. This guy was confident that our conversation could never be traced back to him, regardless. We're following up on the name he gave, but as I've said, I'm sure it's phony."

"But you managed to follow him."

Jake gave a modest shrug. "He underestimated who he was dealing with. I alerted Cort to put things in motion after I called the prison. Most wouldn't have had my resources."

She was beginning to wonder about the extent of his resources, herself. "You said you trailed him to the airport." The fact that he'd been waved through security spoke of either immense wealth or high-level clearance.

Jake leaned forward, his hands clasped, arms resting on his knees. "He got into a government-issued helicopter. His flight plan said he was headed to New York, but it was altered midflight."

"And you know that—how?"

He looked impatient. "I have people everywhere paid to furnish me with certain types of information. Try to focus, Ria. That's not important. What *is* important is that Cort and a few of my other men were able to take my jet and follow this Colton to Washington, D.C."

She wrapped her arms around herself, feeling suddenly chilled. The information was coming too fast and hard, seemingly disconnected pieces that somehow had to be linked. And her time for putting it all together was depressingly short.

One week. That was the timeline Colton had given Jake for the hit on her. Glancing at her watch, she mentally amended that to six days and a few hours. Less than a week to solve a mystery that had haunted her for six long years. And to help her she had to set aside a very natural distrust of the man watching her with a mesmerizing ice-blue stare. Had to accept his story as if not truth, at least as possible. Entirely possible.

A familiar core of excitement formed in the pit of her stomach, growing despite her attempt to tamp it down. She'd have to be more cautious than ever. But the prospect of having the answers she'd sought for so long in just a few more days was very nearly dizzying.

Mentally, she reined in her exhilaration. There was a lot to be done before she solved this. The most important thing was staying alive while she gathered the information. Given the events of the last few days, that just might be a far more difficult feat than discovering the answers she sought.

"What do you have on the guy who shot at you the other night?" Jake asked.

"Not much," she admitted. "He set up across the road, waited for me to come home. It would have been a perfect opportunity. He was close enough that he shouldn't have missed." Ducking back into the car for the flashlight had been due to an ingrained sense of caution that was more instinctive than logical. That instinct had saved her life.

"I'm wondering if Colton was the shooter."

She'd wondered the same thing, but there was absolutely no way to be sure. "It could have been one of the drug dealers we arrested." Two of them, at least, had turned out to have extensive hunting experience. That alone, however, didn't narrow them down. Half the males in Alabama had probably hunted at one time or another.

"How did the other two come after you?"

"Knife and garrote. Professional, and above all, quiet."

"A sniper could be a professional, too."

It wasn't like she hadn't thought of that. "I don't know. It doesn't seem to fit with the other two attempts."

"When did they take place?"

That penetrating blue gaze of his made it difficult to dissemble. "Six years ago, thereabouts."

"That would have been—what? A year, half a year before

you started the academy? Why would the attempts stop for all these years and then begin again?"

His words arrowed through her, reminding her that he knew too much about her already. It would be crazy to arm him with even more knowledge. "I don't know."

He looked at her shrewdly. "You're not saying. You need to consider the fact that I'm the one who will have the information about Colton. If you want to get to him, you're going to have to open up to me. I'm not walking into this thing unarmed. I want to know everything."

"Nobody is inviting you into this thing at all," she snapped. She rose, emotion demanding a release. Rounding the chair, she grasped its back, her fingers splayed over the butter-soft leather. "All you have to do is pass on the information your men discover about Colton's identity. I'll do the rest."

The slow negative shake of his head infuriated her. "Why not? Prove to me that you have no intention of following through with the hit. Let me act on the information myself."

"He's going to notice if you're not dead after a week," Jake said dryly, not taking his eyes off her. "Given Stanton's death, I have every reason to believe he can carry through on his threat of getting Alvarez released immediately. I can't allow that to happen. No, we work together. And I'm not going into this blind. I want to know everything you know, or suspect, about this guy. Let's start with the other two attempts. You said they failed. Who were they?"

Ria felt her lungs constrict. It was as though the walls were moving in on her, depriving her of oxygen. It struck her that she'd never had these types of questions leveled at her before. Never found herself talking about what had taken place six years ago. Even Benny knew only what he'd guessed from the type of information he'd gotten for her.

Jake remained silent, watching her, and a chasm of suspicion yawned between them. The thought of telling him anything required an act of trust so huge she couldn't even contemplate it. No, not trust. Never that. If she were to put her faith in anyone, it wouldn't be the man who had accepted a contract to kill her.

But she needed the information he could get for her. Needed to find out for herself if Colton could lead her to the answers she was seeking. Any facts she gave Jake wouldn't be news to Colton, even if Jake passed them on to him. The man wanted her dead. He wouldn't be overly concerned with how much she'd pieced together in the last few years.

In the end, it was less an act of faith than accepting the lesser of two evils. She returned Jake's fathomless gaze, reading nothing in his expression. He might be sincere about helping her, or he might be planning to double-cross her at the worst possible moment. Knowing that, accepting it, was the biggest risk she'd ever taken.

But if it led her to the man who'd left her for dead, who'd had Luz killed, it was a risk well worth taking.

"All right." Despite the hammering in her blood, her voice was steady. "Come to my place tomorrow night, after dark. I'd prefer some discretion. Your presence last time didn't go unnoticed. Bring me the name and any other information your people discover on Colton."

"And you'll give me…?"

"I'll tell you everything I know then." It was, she knew, an uneven exchange. She had bits of information, none with more than a tenuous connection to recent events.

"And we'll decide on a plan of action then." He waited for her gaze to jerk to his before lifting a brow. "I know you, better than you think. You're going to go after Colton as soon as you get your hands on that information. You might as well get used to the fact that you won't be going alone."

"Wait for her to get out of sight of the school." Ria lowered the high-powered Steiner binoculars, speaking into her cell phone. Too many people monitored police chatter with scanners at home. She never used the radio for investigative work.

Deputy Cook's voice sounded dubious. "You sure? Seems easier to pull over as she stops to let the kids out. Neater that way."

"Her children are going to have enough to deal with today. They don't need the memory of their mother being arrested as well." A social worker would be dispatched to the school, and the children would be placed in foster care until their mother's drug trial. Given the information they'd put together on the woman's operation, Ria was certain that Vickie Witherspoon would be serving time. Her kids would be grown up before she got out again.

Ria decided that she could feel sympathy for the child even knowing that they'd be far better off out from under their mother's influence.

"Suspect is leaving the school and traveling east down Dawson." Cook spoke again. "How far you want us to go?"

"Catch her at the next turn." Dawson Avenue would end in another half mile at a T intersection. By the time Ria caught up with Cook and Ralston, they already had the woman out of her car and cuffed. Ralston was reciting the Miranda.

The woman twisted around at Ria's approached and said, "Sheriff! Hey, Sheriff. I wanna talk to you. Private."

"Save it for your lawyer," Ria advised. She nodded for Ralston to complete the recitation, after which Cook opened the back door of the car.

"Wait, you gotta listen to me. This is important."

The insistence in the woman's face had Ria hesitating. After a moment, she motioned for the two men to step away. "All right. What is it?"

Vickie Witherspoon moistened her lips, tried to smile. She had a long narrow face with a smattering of freckles across the bridge of her nose that stood out in sharp relief against her pale skin. "You got a kid? Doesn't matter. I got three. Their daddy ran off years back and we've got no one else. I can't go to jail. What would happen to them?"

"The time to think about that would have been before you started manufacturing meth in your home. The same home your children live in." Ria's voice was as devoid of sympathy as her heart. The explosive nature of the chemicals used in the drug's manufacture was highly dangerous. That the woman subjected her children to that risk day after day didn't speak highly of her motherly concern.

"I had no other choices, don't you get it?" The woman's gaze shifted to the two deputies, who were already moving restlessly. "I had to provide for my kids. I got no skills. What else was there for me to do in this part of the state?"

"Others manage. Have you ever seen a meth lab explode? Do you have any idea what would have happened to your children if that had happened?" Ria shook her head, sick at the thought. She motioned to the two men, who stepped forward and placed the woman in the car.

Witherspoon spat at Ria's feet. "What do you know about trying to find a way to feed your children? You never been faced with the problems of a mother alone."

That was true enough. Whatever else had transpired in her life, Ria had never borne a child. She thought of Luz then, and of how difficult it must have been for her, living on the edge of poverty, not seeing her child for weeks at a time as she tried to carve out a living for them.

Ria reached for the door, shoved her face close to the woman in the back seat. "No, I haven't had that problem. But if I had, I wouldn't have made the choice you did." Straightening, she slammed the door and waved for the deputies to take over.

Ria had never considered herself particularly hard-hearted, but nothing in the woman's tale of woe had touched her on any level. As traumatic as her mother's arrest was going to be on the children, it couldn't come close to inflicting the kind of damage living eight years with the woman would.

Opening her car door, she slid behind the wheel. Maria had been eight when Luz had died. By now she'd be the same age as Luz had told Ria she'd been when she married. In a third world country, choices were even more limited than those Witherspoon had whined about. Not for the first time Ria wondered what kind of options faced Luz's child.

She stopped by D.A. Richmond Davis's office at the courthouse to fill him in on the most recent arrest. "Witherspoon may try to deal," she concluded, her shoulder propped against the wall next to the door. She'd dismissed his offer of a seat, not intending to stay long, and the man didn't seem to know whether to remain standing as well, or seat himself.

"But no plea bargains." He slapped his palm on the desk hard enough to shake his immaculately groomed hair. "This office doesn't go lightly on drug dealers."

Which was, she noted, a far cry from the tune he'd been singing just a few short days ago. "You can listen to what her lawyer has to say. I doubt she's got anything worth dealing. We did pretty intensive surveillance before her arrest. We're rounding up her known customers now. If there's anyone bigger in the picture, we haven't caught word of him. Or her."

Shoving away from the wall, she turned to go.

"Oh, miss, er, Sheriff." Davis's diffident voice stopped her. "That other suit isn't going away as you promised. My office has been buried in paperwork from that man's attorney." At her raised brows, he hastened to add, "Not that we're backing down. This county is tough on crime. We're not going to give an inch."

He'd be more persuasive with even a modicum of conviction in his voice. "Don't worry, Richmond. It will never see trial. But if it does, that little speech you gave a while ago would make a dandy closing argument."

With his mouth opening and closing like a spotted bass, she shot him a grin and headed out the door.

Cook and Ralston had beaten her to the offices with the suspect. There was no sign of Cook or Vickie Witherspoon, but Ralston was in the parking lot talking to a couple of reserve deputies. As Ria walked up to the small group, one of the reservists caught sight of her and elbowed his buddy. The two men looked down and shuffled their feet, but Ralston kept talking, not seeming to notice their restlessness.

"Can you believe that? Thinking you're going to get anywhere appealing to Kingsley as a woman?" He guffawed. "They may have the same equipment, but from what I hear, Kingsley don't play for the same team, know what I mean?"

Ria folded her arms across her chest, cocking her head. "No, Ralston, I don't think I do know what you mean. Would you care to elaborate?"

The man went still, and the two reservists seemed to find the toes of their boots worthy of contemplation.

The tips of Ralston's ears reddened as he slowly spun around. "Sheriff." His voice was insolent. "Haven't you ever heard that eavesdroppers rarely hear good about themselves?"

She pretended to consider, then shook her head. "I don't think I've ever heard that. Today seems chock-full of new learning for me. C'mon." She clapped him on the shoulder, steered him toward the door of the building. "You can teach me all about teams and such."

There was a scrambling of feet behind her. Ria could only assume that the reserve deputies had quickly made themselves scarce. The idea seemed catching. Once inside the building, everyone they came across seemed to have trouble maintaining eye contact. Maybe they could sense danger. If so, their instincts were dead-on. Ria had never been closer to decking a man in her life.

Opening the door to her office, she waited for the deputy to enter before closing it gently behind him. She didn't invite him to sit. "You know, Ralston, I'm getting the feeling you don't like me." She rested her hips against her desk, facing him.

"I don't think this is a job for a woman," he said stiffly, looking somewhere over her shoulder. "Commissioners made their decision, no getting around it. But I'm entitled to my opinion."

"I guess I don't understand. First you say I'm not a real woman, now you're saying I am. Which is it?"

The man's lips flattened, but he said nothing.

Tiring of the game, she straightened. "I can't force you to respect me, but I can demand that you treat me with respect. Until your attitude changes, I'm putting you back on nights." The man's jaw dropped, and he glared at her. Duty rosters typically had the least senior deputies on night duty, supervised by the newest officers. "You'll trade places with Sergeant Morris. Finish out your shift today. You can report for your new hours tomorrow. We'll reevaluate the change in a month." Crossing to the door, she opened it, waited for him to exit.

He did, brushing by her with a defiant air that told her better than words she'd made a bad situation worse.

She swung the door shut behind him. Ralston wasn't going to change his opinion of her, regardless. But she had had to do something about him or risk losing the respect of the other members in the department. She didn't fool herself into thinking the skirmish between the two of them was over. Her action had merely delayed it.

Dismissing the man from her mind, she went to her computer and spent the afternoon combing the databases for a man who went by the name of Colton. She found several matches, but the pictures looked nothing like the individual Jake had caught on his monitors. She hadn't really expected to find anything. Anyone who took the precaution of bringing no ID with him wasn't going to give out his real name.

The air outside when she left held a bite that had her hunching into her leather jacket. Although January in Alabama was a far cry from winters in Denver, it hadn't taken long for Ria to grow accustomed to the milder temperatures. Apparently she had already gotten spoiled.

Dusk turned quickly to night at this time of year. Her headlights speared the falling darkness as she made her way home. As she turned into her lane, she couldn't prevent a quick glance at the stand of trees across the road. The same stand that had given cover to the newest assassin.

How many lives was one person allotted? Had she been a cat, she'd have been a third of the way through hers. The dark humor failed to amuse her. There was a prickle of instinct warning her that sometime soon her luck was bound to run out. Skill and sheer guts would carry her so far, but no one could outrun death forever. She just needed to dodge it a little longer, until she had all the answers she'd been seeking.

With her usual caution, Ria turned off the car and took the flashlight out for the perimeter check. She stepped carefully across the trip wire she'd restrung after the night of the attempted shooting, circling the house, examining the "tells." When she was assured that the security hadn't been breached, she let herself in the back door.

With her mind already on the task ahead, she reengaged the alarm and slipped her coat off, hanging it over the back of one of the kitchen chairs. Then she made her way to the extra bedroom, turned on the computer.

While it whirred and hummed in the act of starting up, she went to the filing cabinet, unlocked it and withdrew the sheaf of papers she'd been painstakingly going through. So far she had a list of one hundred three Army personnel who had been reported dead about the same time she'd been thrown lifeless in the ocean. Twenty-six of those names were women.

Ria didn't want to think of how much work still remained to be done. She'd cross-check the list for similarities in post locations and field of training. But time was running out.

The contract on her life had dictated a week. She had a little over five days left. After spending more than six years on the search, she felt closer than ever before to discovering the truth about her past.

She just had to stay alive a little while longer.

The strand of tiny crystal lights she'd run along the baseboard began to wink. She raised her head, hand going to her gun. The lights were connected to the trip wire around the perimeter of her house. She'd had to pay a pretty sum to a puzzled electrician out of Phenix City to hook it up to her specifications, but anytime something over fifty pounds so much as touched it, the circuit of lights in every room of the house began blinking.

Rising, she flipped off the light switch, throwing the room into total darkness, save the glow from the computer screen. Padding lightly down the stairs, she entered the kitchen, heard the creak of the steps. Someone was on her back porch.

The voice, when it came, wasn't totally unexpected. "C'mon, Ria, open up. It's freezing out here."

Checking the Judas hole, she determined that Jake was alone before unlocking the door, then stepped aside, gun still in her hand. He gave her only a quick glance as he stepped through, using his shoulder to push the door closed after him.

"Reset the alarm," he ordered, going to the kitchen table to drop the sacks he carried. He flipped on the light switch with a familiarity that reminded her he'd been here before.

She reactivated the security system, all the while watching him take small boxes out of the sacks. "I had one of my men drop me off. Crossed the property southwest of here to come in the back. Don't even know if this is still warm, but I figured you weren't going to have anything edible around here."

He rummaged around in her cupboards and drawers, taking out plates and silverware. Quickly setting them on the table, he seemed to notice for the first time that she still had a gun leveled at him. He looked from it to the boxes of Chinese food. "What? You wanted Italian?"

The irony of the scene wasn't lost on her, even as she reholstered her weapon. She was going to sit down and eat dinner with the most notorious criminal in the area. The man who freely admitted he'd accepted a contract to kill her.

The man who, God help her, had just become her partner.

Chapter 7

"Eat up." His tone brooked no arguing. "You're going to need your strength. You've got a lot of explaining to do."

Slowly, she pulled out a chair and sat. Without asking, he pushed a full plate of chicken chow mien toward her.

"Did your men report back on Colton?" she asked. At his curt nod, her frustration grew. "Well? What do we know about him?"

"We—" she didn't miss the inflection he gave the word "—know where he lives. Where he works. By sometime tonight I'll have his real name." Jake shot her a hard look. "Like I said. I want some answers before this goes any further."

She waited for him to begin eating before reaching out to switch their plates. Under the circumstances, she figured her paranoia could be excused. Picking up a fork, she took a bite. "The deal was you were going to get *me* answers, remember?"

His eyes gleamed at her action, but he let it pass. "Tit for tat, baby. I want to know what I'm in for. No more holding out. I need your whole story."

He was managing to annoy her. Especially since she'd spent most of her waking moments today trying to figure a way to avoid giving him just that. "How about a trade? You give me something you learned today, and I'll answer any question you ask."

He looked at her, finished swallowing. "Okay. The man who gave his name as Colton—the same guy who we agree most likely had Stanton killed—works at the Pentagon. So why don't you tell me how the hell you got on the wrong side of someone like that, hmm?"

For a moment she felt as though each one of her organs shut down. Air stopped moving in and out of her lungs. Blood clogged in her veins. Her brain went abruptly blank.

"Ria…" Jake's silky tone held a note of warning.

She blinked, remembered to haul oxygen shakily into her lungs. "I don't know," she said truthfully.

"Bull." Quick as a snake striking, he had her wrist in his hand, and there was nothing loverlike in his grasp. "Don't yank me around. Until you showed up at Donaldson Prison, I had a good thing going with Stanton. Now he's dead and my plans for Alvarez are in jeopardy. And I'm starting to get a real bad feeling that this guy isn't one it pays to double-cross."

Easing her chair back gave her greater mobility in case she needed to draw her weapon again. And from the look on Jake's face, she might have to. With a start, she realized from his grim expression that *he* distrusted *her*. If the situation hadn't been so lethal, it would have been amusing.

She pulled free of him. "Having second thoughts about not following through on that contract? Go ahead," she invited. Every nerve in her body quivered with readiness. "But your plans for Alvarez aren't going to be delivered by a dead man."

Jake brought another forkful of food to his mouth, took his time chewing and swallowing. "I have a feeling that's a possibility either way." He sounded more irritated than frightened. "Whoever this Colton is, he's got powerful contacts. It's getting harder and harder to believe he thinks I'm ever going to get a chance to spend that money he promised me."

She relaxed, inch by infinitesimal inch. "Given that the money is in exchange for killing me, you'll forgive me if I don't get too choked up about that." Finding her appetite returning, she dug into the food on her plate.

"Stanton said he applied those tattoos on a group of six or seven, all men except for one woman." Pointing his fork at her, he continued, "It goes without saying that you're the woman. He thought they were army, but I suppose he could have been wrong about that. But your timeline doesn't add up, regardless. Ria Kingsley was attending the University of Iowa at the time you got that tattoo. She spent seven semesters there, and attended classes every summer so she could graduate early. So that can only mean one thing. You're not Rianna Kingsley."

Ria could feel her blood rushing in her ears, feel the heat of it pounding through her system, sparking fire in its wake. How long had she waited for those words, for that threat of discovery? How long had she dreaded hearing at long last that someone had discovered her secret? At least one of them.

"No. I'm not." There was a disconnected part of herself, one that seemed numb to the emotion crashing and churning inside her system, that saw the irony rife in the moment. In following the first solid lead she'd had in years, she'd blown the cover that had served her so well.

She consoled herself by remembering that if Jake was really involved in an elaborate scheme with Colton, nothing she told him was going to come as any surprise to the other man.

"So who are you really?"

"That's what I'm trying to find out." Ria got up with her plate of food and put it in the microwave to warm. The act gave her something to focus on besides Jake's penetrating stare. "The more you tell me about this Colton, the more I believe he might be the one who can explain everything to me." The microwave dinged, and she removed her plate, strangely loath to turn around and face him again.

But she couldn't put it off forever. Returning to the table, she sat, forced herself to eat. The food tasted like sawdust in her mouth.

"Something tells me that Colton isn't interested in having a conversation with you." He went to the fridge and helped himself to one of the beers he'd left the last time. He set one in front of her, as well, after twisting the top off for her. "Take it," he ordered, as she started to shake her head. "You're going to need it."

He took a long pull from his bottle, returned to his meal. But she didn't fool herself. His mind hadn't stopped working the entire time. "People adopt new identities to disappear or because they can't remember their own. Which was it for you?"

"Both."

The bluntly uttered word, her matter-of-fact voice, was chilling. Jake remained silent, waiting for her to go on. He knew what the information brokers had dug up on her, and what he'd guessed. But he wanted, more than was comfortable, to hear her offer him a piece of the truth. Given the way she'd lived for the last several years, honesty from her would hold far greater value than the rarest of all the black market antiquities he dealt in.

"Six years ago I washed up on a tropical beach with two bullets in my back and no personal memories of my own. I've spent all this time working to discover why someone wanted me dead." Her gaze was direct. "Colton offers me the best chance yet to get those answers."

"Colton offers you a good chance at a body bag," Jake answered grimly. "Did you go to a hospital? See a doctor? Amnesia usually is temporary, isn't it?"

"I don't have amnesia. At least not the kind that's going to be reversed. I think I was injected with something, a designer drug of some sort. Both of the assassins that were sent after me carried a vial of serum and a syringe in a bag. I had…a friend give one of the vials to his friend, who was interning in the University of Iowa Hospital labs several years ago. When he injected a small amount into a lab rat, it no longer remembered where the water bottle was. How to push a tab for feed." Her smile was wry. "I've always felt lucky I can still remember how to make pancakes."

Jake could feel his chest going tight at the calm recitation. He laid his fork down on his plate. He could no longer even feign an appetite. "Maybe there's an antidote. Or maybe hypnosis could—"

She shook her head impatiently. "Don't you get it? There's no antidote because the *drug isn't on the market.* Someone designed it for a specific task. I'm living proof of its effectiveness. I've tried hypnosis. Twice. My memories start six years ago. It's like I didn't even exist before then."

Ria stopped, horrified at just how close she'd come to voicing her greatest fear. Because, of course, if she had no hopes of regaining her memory, and her current identity was a sham, it was easy to wonder, in the darkest hours of the night, whether she really existed at all on any level that mattered.

She'd combed the databases for missing persons dozens of times. No one had missed *her*.

And if Colton succeeded in killing her, she had to question how many would miss Rianna Kingsley, as well.

With the exception of Benny, she'd made acquaintances in the last six years, but no friends. She'd had working colleagues with whom she shared experiences and mutual respect, but none she'd kept in touch with once she'd left Colorado. She'd had lovers, but none had been allowed close to her in any way that mattered.

But Jake Tarrance was proving the exception. He'd not only been her lover, but right now he was the only person in the world she'd given this much information to. There was no trust, but there was necessity. The last two times someone had come for her, she'd run. She had the tools to run again, but this time she wasn't going anywhere without answers.

And the man sitting across from her was going to help her get them.

"What about the bodies?" Jake's question interrupted her thoughts. "Were you able to identify them?"

She shook her head. "The only thing they had in common was the tattoo."

"So three of you are accounted for. Where are the other three or four?"

"If I knew that, I'd know it all."

He leaned back in his chair, studied her. "You must have started working some angle after your interview with Stanton. What are you looking at?"

Her brief hesitation told him she still wasn't sure of him. He wasn't offended. Under the circumstances, she'd be a fool to put her faith in a man like him.

"I'm working the army angle."

He nodded. It's what he would have done himself. "I can get one of my forensic technicians to get personnel files for the time period in question. We could…" He stopped, noting the slight smile on her face. "You've done that." The statement wasn't a question.

"I know a—ah, forensic technician—too."

Admiration bloomed. Despite the seriousness of her plight, this might be the one and only time he admired a woman's mind. If he didn't also have a bad case of raging hormones for her body, he'd really start to worry about himself.

"What have you come up with so far?"

She hesitated, then, as if coming to a decision, rose. "Come upstairs, and I'll show you."

It didn't escape his notice that she deliberately stayed behind him as they made their way down the hallway and up the stairs. And it struck him then that they were two of a kind. He knew she had reason for her wariness. He'd heard her story. He'd touched the scars on her back, scars he'd later attributed to an injury sustained in the line of police duty.

She might not have honed her instincts in the mean alleys of his New York City neighborhood, but she'd endured more than any other person he knew of, and had come out on top. It did no good to wish, for just a moment, that his mother and sister had had even an ounce of Ria's mental toughness.

He'd learned by the time he was eight that wishing never changed a damn thing. Only action could do that. The two of them, it seemed, knew that when life ambushed you, you could accept it or fight back.

He and Ria were both fighters.

"The first door on the right." There were three doors upstairs. One, he figured, would be a bathroom. The space she directed him to had been set up as an office. Even upon first glance he could tell that what money she had spent on the place had been for the equipment in that room.

It wasn't, however, the room he found himself wishing to be invited to. He was tantalized by the thought that her bedroom was just a few strides away.

It might as well be miles. It would easy for her to engage in sex with someone who didn't know her, someone who didn't understand at least a little about her. But true intimacy—that would be impossible. Her defenses would be impenetrable.

They were alike in that regard, as well.

"Looks like you did some serious damage at Best Buy." He paced the room, noting the top-of-the-line computer and peripheral equipment. Like every other part of her house, it lacked any personal stamp. There were no photographs, pictures, or even the useless pretty things women seemed partial to having around. He had a feeling that the most personal part of her life was encased in that computer.

She went to a sheaf of papers she'd left on the desk. "I've got two hundred three army listed as dead within three months of my landing on Santa Cristo. When I widen the search to twelve months the number jumps to five hundred seventy."

His brow creased. "Six years ago. About the time our government was involved with the uprising in Swahana?"

"We had army personnel stationed in eight countries. Five of the locations saw some combat." She sank into the desk chair, swiveled to face him. "My next step is to start looking for similarities between these records. Then I can narrow the search."

Jake nodded, shrugged out of his navy wool jacket. Beneath it he wore a white sweater and well-worn jeans, both of which accentuated his muscled build. Because her eyes wanted to linger, she trained them firmly on the papers in her hand.

Circumstances dictated that they work closely together, at least for a while. Given the situation, she even preferred to have him where she could watch him. But she had to wonder what was wrong with her system that it still responded to him, as strongly as the first time she'd laid eyes on him. There was a connection there she wished she could reject.

Since it couldn't be denied, it would have to be ignored.

"Let's concentrate for now on the smaller list. What would be the easiest? Start a database with different columns for each item to match?"

She nodded, went to the computer and opened up the appropriate application. Quickly she typed in column headings for names, date of service, cause of death and date. Then she got up. "I'll read the material to you and you type it."

When she noted his expression she gave a half smile. "There's not room for any other furniture in here, so I'm saving you from sitting on the floor all night with a magnifying glass. Some of this print is pretty small."

"We'll trade off. Start with the women. It would be easier to see if we can find a couple of men whose date of death matched one of theirs." He went to the computer and she gave him a chance to sit before beginning. "Showalter, Sarah M. Pfc. Date of service…"

Hours later, Ria rolled her aching shoulders and mentally admitted that age could trump physical fitness every time. If she and Jake hadn't taken turns every half hour or so, by now she'd be in a permanently hunched position. She scrubbed her burning eyes with the heels of her palms, dislodged a contact lens, and had to go in gentle pursuit to right it again.

Jake was printing out their completed product, and as she watched the pages spit out of the printer, she felt a familiar flicker of anticipation. How many times had she felt this close? A hundred? A thousand? Each time she'd gotten a lead that had seemed viable at first, tugging on it had eventually led nowhere. But remembering that couldn't dampen her eagerness. Couldn't douse the hope that this time might be different.

She slid a glance at him, unwillingly noting the way his sweater contrasted with his dark coloring. The scar that ran from the corner of one eye down his cheek was nearly as light as the sweater. It looked old, as though it had toughened and weathered with his face for a lot of years.

"When did you get that?" With a shock, she realized she'd voiced the question out loud. She didn't expect him to answer. Certainly she'd never given the truth on the rare occasions she'd been asked about the old wounds on her back.

He touched the scar. "This? When I was fifteen. My stepfather was a handy mechanic when he wasn't drunk. That wasn't often. This time he used a tire iron. It was the last time he ever hit me, though. The last time he ever beat my mom."

His tone was flat, his face expressionless. But Ria could guess at the rest of the story. Compassion bloomed. "He's dead?"

"I killed him." His gaze was steady on hers. "Spent three years in juvie for it, because my mom was pretty pissed at me. It didn't matter to her that he beat her senseless every time he drank, and was threatening to kill her that time. He was her meal ticket, and I took that away." His mouth twisted. "That's when I learned that everyone has their price. She'd traded her kids and her self-respect for groceries and rent."

Jake began to gather up the papers with swift sure movements. And Ria sat there, all too able to imagine the scene as he'd described it. She'd been involved in enough domestic calls to know how easily they could become deadly. And she'd never left one without worrying about the children in the home. The scar on his cheek was likely only the most visible of those he carried.

"You had brothers and sisters?" She was unfamiliar with this compulsion to know more. Given her need for privacy, she'd always scrupulously respected that of others. Maybe it was because Jake already knew more about her than anyone else. Or perhaps it was part of the fascination he held for her. Facts could often be used to defuse mystery.

"I had a sister. She's dead."

His tone said he wasn't going to offer more. But the bleakness in his eyes made Ria sorry she'd pushed. She'd been tortured for the last six years by the loss of any personal memory. He'd been tortured for far longer by memories he couldn't forget. It would be difficult to say which of them was worse off.

"There are highlighters in the middle desk drawer." Her throat was full, so she cleared it. "We can use them on the matches in each column."

He opened the drawer, took out two and tossed one to her. "Where were you when you were found? You said on an island."

The question pulled them out of personal territory. Their task provided a buffer that she seized on gratefully. "Santa Cristo. It shares the island with Puerto de Ponce."

"I believe they mentioned that in sixth grade geography."

Ignoring his wry tone, she went on. "Six years ago Puerto de Ponce was experiencing civil war."

"One of many."

It was true enough. Santo Cristo was still a third world country by anyone's definition, but it had lush jungles and white sand beaches that had become a mecca for tourists. Puerto de Ponce shared little of that natural beauty. Its side of the island was rocky and mountainous, and the poverty rate was among the highest in the world. Time after time in history guerillas had risen up to try and overthrow the government. Whether they succeeded or failed, little had ever changed for the country's people.

"I always considered that I might have been headed for Puerto de Ponce."

Jake looked up from the sheet he was marking. "So you've always figured you might have been military?"

"Not necessarily." She still held out that hope, of course. It would be bitter to discover that she was one of the thousands of mercenaries who hired out to whichever group could afford them. Or worse, part of a group intent on descending on the area to exploit its misery.

"What about Red Cross? You could have been affiliated with it, or any one of a number of international relief organizations."

"I checked that out. I wasn't. And the only medical knowledge I have is basic first aid." She didn't bother to mention that few relief workers had the type of other skills she possessed. Setting the marker down, she rose to stretch her legs. "I haven't exactly been sitting on my hands for the last six years, you know. I've checked the civilian missing persons databases. I've followed leads on possible meanings for the tattoo, as well as the artist. I speak several languages, so I checked out universities with graduates obtaining multilingual degrees. High school academies focusing on languages. Special schools of American children overseas, diplomats and embassy personnel reported kidnapped…."

The frustration of her search sounded in her voice. "Every time I've reached a dead end." And some avenues had never been open to her. If she'd been working covert intelligence, her name would have to be on file somewhere. But she'd never risk Benny's future by asking him to try to hack into Langley's vast database. She didn't doubt he'd relish the task, but the chance of him getting caught far outweighed her need, especially when it was just guesswork on her part.

"I've researched it. There was no openly sanctioned military involvement with Puerto de Ponce at that time. We had no military personnel in the area. Our government took a hands-off diplomatic approach."

"But Stanton thought the group was army." By the understanding in his voice, she knew Jake was realizing just how thin this lead was. It was based on the very shaky word and selective memory of an immoral convict.

A convict who'd been killed shortly after he met with Ria.

Right now, it was the best lead she had.

They worked silently for a time, engaged in the painstaking work. When they'd finished, they exchanged pages and began to discuss the areas where the personnel matched. "More than a third of the males reported dead were trained as Rangers."

"That makes sense, I guess." Ria had noted the same thing. "Special Forces are the first to be sent into any combat situation. They'd be involved in the most dangerous missions."

"But women can't be Rangers, so that can't be the link."

"Military remains a patriarchal system," she said dryly. "Women can receive the same training as men, up to a point. No branch allows females in the special ops programs."

"Given that, I guess we should look for ways any of the males here connect with the females."

"The fact that they went to Stanton as a group suggests they were teamed together for some sort of assignment. I have to figure that the tattoo depicts something about the nature of that mission." She reached for the bottle of now warm beer she'd brought up with her, and drank. "But I keep butting up against the fact that a woman isn't normally going to be tapped for a dangerous assignment."

"So maybe you weren't military at all. You could have been borrowed as an attaché from one of the alphabet agencies."

"Maybe. But their databases are all a little beyond my reach." At least until she had something far more solid linking her to one of them.

She stared at the pages before them. There would be answers of some sort hidden in them. They just had to ask the right questions.

By the time they'd finished, they were able to narrow the list to thirty-seven men, all trained as Army Rangers, who'd died in combat around the time she'd been shot. Only six of the women had died in the same time period. The locations where the individuals had been posted were varied, with some overlap, but none glaringly obvious.

"Maybe we've been at this too long." Ria looked at her watch, saw it was after midnight. "If there's something there, I'm not seeing it. I think we need more information on these individuals." She went to the desk, had to lean across Jake to open a drawer and take out the private cell phone she kept for only one purpose.

"I'm going to contact my—what'd you call it?—forensic technician."

Jake looked at his own watch. "Isn't it a little late?"

"He'll be up." She was certain of that. Benny had always been a night owl, cruising cyberspace and chatting with others of like interests. She remembered he'd once told her they preferred to be called "crackers," rather than hackers. She didn't care what he called himself. She only knew that he was a genius with computers.

She dialed the number from memory. "Hi." Aware of Jake's intent stare, she turned her back, strode across the room to rest her hip against the door. "You almost sound asleep.

Don't tell me you started keeping normal hours like everyone else?"

"Ria? Damn!" She could picture Benny in her mind, searching for his glasses, which he often removed when he was at the computer. "I can't believe it's you. Do you know how long it's been since you called last?"

Seven months. Thirteen days. "Not exactly," she lied. "You know why, though. It's too risky."

He was silent for a moment. "Still? Ria, it's been…geez. About six years. How long can you live like this?"

"As long as it takes. But hopefully it won't be much longer. I need your help again. So what's new, right?"

"Just a minute. Let me get a piece of paper."

Her brows rose. "Paper? You really aren't at the computer? Are you sick?" She was only half joking.

"No. I was in bed." Then she heard another voice, a female, asking a question. Heard Benny shushing her. Comprehension slammed into Ria, and with it, astonishment. "You're not alone. Talk about bad timing." She'd never given a thought to Benny's social life. If she had, she would have questioned whether he had one at all. He'd just always been there, dependable, slightly wacky, but undeniably brilliant.

"No, it's okay. It's…that was my fiancée. Greta. We're getting married this summer."

"Married?" Ria repeated weakly, her thoughts in a whirl. "That's…great. Really great." Voice stronger, she added, "Don't tell me that you found someone who's as crazy about computer game design as you are?"

There was a slight hesitation. "Actually, that's my hobby now. I started working for a software security company a couple months ago. Not as much fun, but the paycheck is steady and it has great benefits."

Steady paycheck. Great benefits. Ria was beginning to wonder just who she was talking to. It sounded like Benny's voice, but the content was totally foreign.

But then he said eagerly, "So what have you got for me? I've been working on a great little firewall infiltrator. You wouldn't believe some of the places I've been with it!"

There, she thought with a feeling of relief, was the Benny she was more familiar with. "You can get some use out of it then. I want you to get me more detailed information for some former army personnel."

"OMPF/PERMS?" Disappointment was rife in his voice. "A ten-year-old could handle that."

"I'd prefer you didn't contract it out," she said dryly. The Electronic Records Management System for the Official Military Personnel Files might seem like child's play to him, but Ria was hoping it would contain the information she lacked. "Are you ready?" She pushed away from the wall, crossed back to Jake, who scooped up the pages they'd highlighted and handed them to her. "I've got quite a list."

She read off all the names, waiting for him to write them down. "I've got dates of service and death dates, training and post locations from the last time. But I need you to get me 2-1's for units and posts timelines, 201 files with their evaluations, DD214's for the last unit they were assigned to…anything you can get your hands on for each of those individuals."

"How long do they keep those kinds of records?"

"Guess you'll find out, won't you?"

"Are you kidding? If it's in a computer system, I'll find it. How soon do you need it?"

Again, Ria heard a female voice. She imagined the woman was complaining. Ria couldn't really blame her. "Whenever you can get to it. It sounds like you're otherwise occupied tonight."

Benny's voice was sheepish. "Yeah. But I'll get at it first thing tomorrow morning. I don't have to be at work till nine. Same e-mail address?"

"That's right. I really appreciate this. And...congratulations. I mean that." She hoped the words didn't sound as awkward as they felt. "You deserve this."

"Thanks. I know I'm lucky." The joint laughter on the other end made her feel as distant as if she were on another planet. "I wish more than anything you would think about coming to the wedding. It'd mean a lot to me."

It was a bit disorienting to even think that far ahead. To plan on attending a nice normal occasion for normal people leading normal lives. Lives free of assassins and full of the kinds of memories that made a person complete. She couldn't fathom it. But neither could she deny him this one thing. Not after all he'd done for her.

"If it's at all possible, I'll be there," she heard herself promise. She was aware that Jake's attention had sharpened. It wasn't overt. He wasn't even looking at her. But he was like a large jungle animal scenting prey. Muscles ready. Instincts alert.

Forcing her attention back to the phone, she spoke for another few seconds, then ended the conversation. Deliberately avoiding Jake's gaze, she crossed to the desk, replaced the phone and shut the desk drawer. "We should get it by tomorrow."

"I hope so. We're kind of under the gun here."

She was still a little unsettled from Benny's news. Not that she begrudged him his obvious happiness. But she had a sudden image of herself on the outside looking in at others living regular lives. Falling in love. Getting married. Having children. All while she existed in a vacuum of sorts. Afraid to get too close to anyone for fear of bringing death to their doorstep. Afraid to trust.

But this waiting was almost over. She had to believe that. For better or worse, within the week she'd either have the answers she'd long sought, or she'd be dead. She could almost face that prospect if only she got the facts she needed first.

Jake watched her, growing grimmer by the moment. No matter what face she put on it, the phone call had disturbed her in some way. Instead of her usual guarded expression, she looked almost…forlorn. An odd word to come to him, but apt in this case. What had the man on the other end of the phone meant to her?

Because it had been a man, he was certain of that. And Ria probably wasn't even aware that her voice had warmed when she spoke to him, that her face had held an animation he'd never see there. And if it were possible to be jealous of a faceless, nameless voice on a telephone, then this burning knot in the pit of his gut must surely be jealousy.

Except that he'd never been jealous of a woman in his life. So he was ready to blame the sensation on bad Chinese food eaten too late in the evening.

Brooding, he watched her bend to pick up the papers, putting them into some sort of order. "You seem to enjoy a closer relationship with your forensic technician than I do with mine."

Her smile held a hint of sadness. "He's great. Probably as close to a friend as I have, if you can apply the term to someone you never see and rarely talk to."

"Friend?" Jake had meant the word to sound lighter than it did. "Or something more?"

Her gaze flew to meet his. "Don't tell me that you're one of those people who don't believe men and women can be platonic friends."

His shrug was far more casual than he was feeling. "Never

really thought about it. But no, I think most men would want more."

She went to the filing cabinet and replaced the papers in a folder there, then shut the drawer. "Well, maybe he did once. At first. But when he saw I wasn't interested, he didn't push. And he's never failed to do anything I ask of him. So I guess that's pretty one-sided, as far as friendships go."

She'd never seen Jake move so fast. One moment he was standing by the desk, the next he was by her side, looming over her. "Maybe it's enough for him. It wouldn't be for me. I don't want to be your 'friend,' Ria."

Instantly wary, she moved backward, until she could feel the cool smooth face of the cabinet behind her. "I'm still not quite sure what you want."

He gave her a grim smile. "That makes two of us. But whatever it is, it's more—a helluva lot more—than I've ever wanted from any other woman."

It would have been easy to resist a more polished line. Simple to evade a well-rehearsed move meant to disarm. But the genuine bafflement in his voice struck a chord deep within her. Because she felt the same attraction, even while her inner alarm shrilled a warning.

The heat suffusing her owed nothing to the approaching danger, and everything to the man standing before her. And she, who had taken only the most calculated risks in her life, took a step away from her customary caution and into his arms.

The instant his lips covered hers she felt the effect spiral through her, desire hurling flaming fireballs through her veins. His mouth ate at hers without finesse, all raw hunger and savage power. And in just a moment it reignited the smoldering embers of the last time they'd been this close. Closer.

She'd almost convinced herself that the memory of last

time couldn't have been real. No man could elicit that fierce a reaction from her, that quickly. No man, it seemed, but Jake.

Her hands slipped inside his sweater, in search of smooth warm skin stretched over taut muscle. He was just as impatient. He made quick work of the buttons on her uniform shirt, and shoved it apart, releasing the front clasp of her bra in the same motion.

And then his warm palms were cupping her breasts, his mouth lowering to take one turgid tip between his teeth. His jaw rasped her skin as his mouth worked at her, and her fingers flexed, the nails biting into his skin.

Her life, what she could remember of it, had been a study in patience. Following lead after lead, waiting years to discover the one piece of information that would answer everything. Strange then that impatience should burn through her now, etching a blazing path that demanded gratification.

She deliberately gentled her touch, brushing the back of her hand against his hard belly, then lower. She dipped her fingers inside the waistband of his jeans, her knees nearly buckling as his teeth scraped her nipple.

Passion like this, instantaneous and bright, could burn out, couldn't it? She tried to seize the thought, felt logic slip away, as evasive as wisps of fog. She'd known desire before but had never experienced this need, so hot and vibrant that it was a whipping of her pulse and a hammering in her blood. Had never felt it fueled by a man's response, primitively carnal, stripped of even the semblance of finesse. For a woman who'd lived her life demanding control, its imminent loss shouldn't feel so exhilarating.

He nudged her thighs apart with one of his, and the position brought their hips into excruciatingly intimate contact. At the feel of his hard masculine length against her, a thousand points of flame burst beneath her skin. She knew there was only one way to douse them.

A phone shrilled, and the sound had them both going tense, bodies still, breathing choppy. By the third ring Jake was easing away, a long breath sawing out of him. "It's mine." His words were laced with frustration, reflecting her own. It took far longer than it should have for the riot in her pulse to calm.

With quick, jerky movements she righted her clothing, turning away from him to do so. She made the mistake of looking at Jake once, and forgot to breathe. The smoldering expression in his eyes could turn the recipient to flame.

"Yeah."

Because she was watching him, she noted the instant his mind shifted away from what had almost happened and focused on the person who'd phoned. "How sure are you? Good. No, that's good." His gaze had returned to her, and there was no trace of the man who had nearly scorched her alive with his hunger.

Then she noted the tightness of his jaw, the flare of his nostrils, and revised her estimation. Jake was keeping rigid check on his passion. But the traces were still there.

"Excellent. You have? Are you prepared for that? Great. I'll talk to you tomorrow." He disconnected the call, flipped the phone shut. "We got a name. Should give us enough to move on."

If he could make the switch back to normal, so could she. "Okay. What is it?"

"Does the name Chad Hendricks mean anything to you?"

She lifted a shoulder. "That's Colton?"

"That's it. So we've got his name, we've got where he lives and where he works."

Excitement began to hum, originating from a far different source than a few moments ago. "What's the address?"

Too late she saw the half smile on his face, the too knowing look in his eyes, and knew she should have gone for subtlety.

"I think that's one piece of information I'm gonna hang on to. Because I know exactly what you're thinking, baby." With one hand he reached out, cupped her chin in his hand. "But there's no way you're going anywhere without me."

Chapter 8

"You need to reconsider. There's absolutely no need for you to take any risk at all in this." Ria felt as if she were talking to a slab of granite. Certainly her arguments for the last half hour had had no effect on him.

Jake had his arms folded across his chest, his shoulder leaning against the wall. And although his listening air gave the impression of reasonableness, he wasn't giving an inch. "You're not going alone."

She sprang from her chair, strode across the room in frustration. "You're not hearing a damn thing I'm saying."

"I'm hearing it. I'm just saying no."

She bared her teeth. His previous answers hadn't escaped her. "This doesn't really involve you at all. I can get the information I need on my own. And then if this goes wrong, you wouldn't be anywhere around."

"And you actually think that's going to convince me?"

Something about his low voice had her nape prickling. There was danger here, even if she couldn't guess where it stemmed from. "I'm just saying if I get caught, it would be smarter for you to be in Georgia. Then Colton—Hendricks—can't hold you accountable."

"You act as though this doesn't concern me at all. He's threatening to spring Alvarez immediately. I can't let that happen. At least not until I'm ready for it. My plans have been years in the making. He's got a lot to pay for, but I need more time to get everything in place."

She looked at Jake oddly. "Some might say that spending ten years in prison was payment enough."

"Not nearly." The lethal tone sent a shiver sprinting over her skin. "He's still alive, isn't he?"

Their gazes locked. And in that moment, seeing his mask of utter ruthlessness, Ria didn't doubt that Jake Tarrance could be deadly. "Your plans for revenge can't be carried out if you're six feet under, either."

His smile was chilling. "Can't they? My plans…are extensive. And I think I've taken every contingency into consideration. But that doesn't matter. Even you can't pull this off without my help."

His words were a slap at her ego. "I've been doing fine on my own for six years."

"Exactly. Six years. You've got a little over four days now. Less if he gets impatient. I have over a dozen of my men on this thing in D.C. at this very moment. Within another twelve hours, give or take, I'll have the keypad code to his house alarm. We can have you inside fifteen hours after that. But you need my manpower, my data and my resources. Face it, Ria. You *need* me."

Everything inside her rejected his assertion. She didn't

need anyone. Never had. And she certainly didn't want to be forced to trust Jake any more than she already had. It hadn't escaped her that by breaking into Hendricks's home to look for the missing pieces to this puzzle, she might be delivered neatly into the man's hands. All it would take was one act of betrayal.

"My men are wiring a device to his keypad as we speak. We have to come up with a plausible reason for getting you inside, because it'll have to be during the day. No use tipping him off before we have to."

"Cleaning service," she said automatically. "Get a van with a phony logo on the side to park out front. Visible, but forgettable."

He paused, looked thoughtful. "Possible." Seeming to remember his argument then, he returned to it with a vengeance. "And I've got the money and employees in place to take care of all those details. When the time comes we can make a trip on my private jet, getting there and back in a matter of hours. Tell me how you'd manage all that on your own, given the time frame."

With every sentence he was boxing her more neatly into a corner. The situation was made even more untenable because she could see the logic in his argument.

She had that money saved. Arranging all the details he'd mentioned would put a serious dent in it, yet it could be done. But the timeline was like a ticking bomb in this case. He was right. Even if she could get it arranged in a little over four days that gave her no time to connect all the dots.

It gave her no time to defend herself against the next assassination attempt.

"Maybe it would be better for me to go in at night. Be there when he got home," she mused. She could put the thing to rest once and for all. Demand the answers she needed, and get the threat he posed out of the way, one way or another.

Jake was at her side in three quick steps. "Not a chance in hell. We'll decide what to do about him once we know how he figures in all this. But you aren't going to confront him. I'm not letting you take that kind of risk."

He was standing much too close. She wasn't going to back down from him, so she angled her chin. "I'm not sure just when you began thinking you had a say in what I do."

"Neither am I." His tone sounded rueful, halfway irritated. "But you better get used to it, baby. You're not alone in this. Not anymore." Seconds ticked by, and his gaze never left hers. A slumberous warmth crept back into it. "What are the chances you're going to invite me to spend the night and finish what we started a little while ago?"

From any other man the words would have seemed unbelievably arrogant. And they were. But accompanied by the reigniting heat in his eyes, they were also tempting. It was far harder than it should have been to say, "Nonexistent."

There was a moment when she thought he would try and convince her. But a second later he was backing away, reaching for his phone. "I'll call for my car. My driver will pick me up where he dropped me off."

There didn't seem to be anything else to say, so she just nodded. She nearly flinched when he reached out, ran a gentle finger along her jaw. "Get some sleep."

Then, as if embarrassed at the gesture, he turned and picked up his coat, shrugged into it. "I'll call you tomorrow."

She nodded. It seemed impossible to speak. She just stood staring at the door long after he'd passed through it. Long after the sound of his steps down the stairway had faded away.

It was as if she were poised on a precipice of discovery.

The long sought information was there, just out of reach. But never when she'd envisioned this moment had she imagined herself anything other than alone.

For better or worse, Jake was intricately involved in this. And she still wasn't sure how she felt about that.

For the first time in her law enforcement career, Ria found it difficult to concentrate at work the next day. She'd become adept at compartmentalizing the personal aspect of her life from the professional. It was the only way she could stay sane all those years.

But today the duty rosters couldn't hold her interest. Nor could the employee yearly evaluation forms that would be coming due next month. Since she'd been on the job such a short time they would take a great deal of research. At the moment she didn't have the concentration required.

Instead, she kept wondering about the information she'd requested from Benny. She didn't doubt that it would be in her e-mail in-box when she got home. He'd never failed her yet. Would the more detailed military records yield answers or spawn more questions?

When the intercom buzzed in the middle of the afternoon, she was still staring blankly at the half-completed duty roster for March. "Unidentified caller for you on line two," Marlyss announced.

"I've got it." With a thrum of anticipation in her veins, she picked up the receiver.

"Ria." Just the sound of Jake's voice had anticipation firing through his veins. "Everything's set. We leave at 7:00 a.m. tomorrow."

"Where should I meet you?" She marveled that her tone was so steady when every nerve of her body quivered in readiness.

"Columbus Metropolitan. I'll meet you in the terminal. Gate F. You'll need to arrive a couple hours early to deal with the parking and security."

"So all the arrangements are made?"

"They will be." He sounded distant, as if his mind were somewhere else. "I'll fill you in when we're on the jet. And you can brief me on what you discover from the new information you get from your friend today."

"What about Hendricks? Have your men discovered anything else about him?"

"Amazingly little," he said grimly. "Other than the deed to his home, a pricey one at that, there's not a lot available in the databases. Which means we go deeper, but that takes time. There's usually a reason for that level of security. I think at least we figured out what that reason is."

"What?" Her fingers were clenched so tightly around her pen that her knuckles were white.

"His job at the Pentagon. He's special aide to the Secretary of Defense. From what we learned, he's Kent Samson's right-hand man."

Any hope of concentrating for the rest of the day had been shattered by Jake's news. Well after she'd left the sheriff's office and gone home she could hear his words continue to echo over and over in her head.

He's special aide to the Secretary of Defense.

She sat at her desk, printouts of the attachments Benny had sent spread out in front of her. As jobs went, they didn't get much more powerful than Secretary of Defense. Samson was entering his third decade in public service. He'd spent the last eleven years in the position he held now, under three consecutive administrations—a rare feat for any politically appointed official. Although he'd been coy about his plans, it was generally believed that he was positioning himself for a run at the presidency. The primaries were a mere eighteen months away. With his name recognition, he wouldn't have to do a lot of early campaigning.

But what could that have to do with Hendricks? And, by association, with her?

Her gaze dropped to the copies of officer evaluations. As expected, there was far more detail included in them than in what they'd already accessed. These were the records that would have been used to make decisions about promotions and special assignments. Commanding officers wrote detailed reports about each officer or enlisted person's strengths and weaknesses.

The first thing Ria did was read through the six females' reports, scanning each of the narrative evaluations. Distantly, she noted that her hands were trembling slightly. She hadn't admitted, even to herself, how much she was banking on finding something in them that could reasonably describe her, six years earlier.

After the first time through, she started over, reading more slowly and carefully. But by the end of the task she had to admit that nothing sounded in the least familiar.

Disappointment bloomed, too strong to be ignored. There were those that had some of the training she'd obviously picked up along the way. A couple of the women were expert marksmen, but their ages didn't seem right. One would be older than she guessed her own age, by at least a decade. Another was the mother of two. One of the few things Ria could at least be scientifically certain of was that she'd never borne a child. Three of the women were bilingual, but no reports described a woman who could speak six languages.

Try as she might, she couldn't make any of the women's

reports fit her situation. Whoever she'd been back then, it wasn't anyone detailed in these pages.

She was missing something. Shoving away from the desk, she rose to pace the small area. Either her identity was hidden on one of these sheets, and she just wasn't interpreting things correctly, or she'd made an error in her original thinking.

That thought had merit, so she pursued it. She'd originally decided to have Benny search for deceased military personnel because she'd figured she was connected in some way to the two men who'd been sent after her. Since she'd killed them, she'd figured their deaths would have to show up on the massive military record management system.

It went without saying that she wasn't dead. Yet. The dark thought intruded, a shadowy reminder of the three days and some hours remaining in the week Jake had been given. So if she'd been army, how had her disappearance been explained? She'd imagined since it hadn't been made public that they would have wanted to hide it in some way. What better way than to list her as dead?

Ria grappled with the question for a long moment. She wouldn't have been left on the enlisted rolls. There would be pay records, assignment rosters…too many possible pitfalls to try to hide a military person missing from duty.

Unless they'd reported her that way…

Once the thought occurred to her, she couldn't believe it hadn't before. She could have been reported as AWOL or Missing in Action. That would have galvanized military resources in the search. Would have been a red flag to any law enforcement agency or hospital she might have gone to for help.

And it would have ensured that she would be handed over to the army had she ever requested assistance.

Galvanized by the possibility, she went to her cell phone,

put another call through to Benny. But although she waited impatiently through a half-dozen rings, she ended up getting an answering machine.

Caution was too ingrained for her to risk leaving a message. Instead she replaced the phone and sat down at the computer, sending Benny an urgent e-mail request. She hit the send button, fairly certain that she'd have a reply within twenty-four hours. But with the time ticking resolutely by, they were twenty-four hours she couldn't spare.

Deliberately, she set the records of the females aside and started in on the males'. At one point, eyes aching, she got up and retrieved a magnifying glass to aid her. Much of the print was poor quality.

Several of the men had the background and training in skills similar to those she possessed. She recognized the military jargon. Skilled in formal and informal weaponry. Superior surveillance techniques. Successfully engaged and subdued enemy forces. She focused on finding similarities in post locations, deployment orders or other timelines.

It was fairly easy to start placing pages in sequence according to post locations. Soon she had several piles, symbolizing different spots internationally. She picked up each stack, rereading the reports, discarding records that seemed dissimilar to the others. This task went more easily and she was able to move through the piles quickly.

Perhaps too quickly. She almost missed it. She had to backtrack to see what it was that had alerted her subconscious. She scanned halfway down one page before a single name jumped out at her.

C. Albert Hendricks.

She stared at the name, blood pounding in her temples. With her index finger she traced the scrawled signature on the

officer's report. Looked at the typed name above it. There was
no mistake. Every officer had to fill out reports evaluating the
performance of each of the personnel they supervised. There,
under commanding officer, was the name C. Albert Hendricks.

C as in Chad?

Furiously, Ria flipped through the other pages, ran her finger down each until she identified the commanding officer.
When she was done, four of the deceased men whose records
lay before her had at least one evaluation signed by Hendricks.

Same post. Same commanding officer. She'd been looking for something that connected these men and she'd found
it. The commanding officer might well be the same man who
had gone to Jake Tarrance and hired him to kill her.

Ria had never flown first class, much less in a private jet.
She looked around at the lavish appointments speculatively.
From what Jake had said, he'd grown up teetering on the
brink of poverty. His childhood was a far cry from the luxury
he now seemed to take for granted.

He walked down the aisle, returning from the captain's
cabin, having just conversed with his pilot. "We're not expecting any turbulence. Should set down in Dulles in an hour and
a half."

"You still have your men in D.C.?"

He nodded. "They attached a tiny recorder to the keypad
alarm system of Hendricks's house at night. He returned home
from work yesterday evening about six-thirty, punched in his
code. The recorder was retrieved and hooked to a computer,
which identified the numbers and sequence by their pitches.
And simple as that—you have the code to get in."

Ria looked at Jake, outrage battling admiration. "You seem
to have access to all sorts of odd skills." She'd worked sev-

eral B and Es in Denver, but none of the burglars had risen to this level of proficiency.

Jake gave a self-deprecating shrug. "What can I say? Where inventiveness fails, a little research often does the trick. It doesn't hurt that I have employees with, uh, varied interests."

She snorted. "Interests that will land them in a federal pen one of these days, no doubt." But in this case, she had little reason to feel superior. She had no qualms about using the knowledge to engage in an illegal act herself. She'd be the one going inside. If caught, she'd be the one prosecuted.

Ria didn't give the possibility much consideration. If Hendricks was who she thought he was, if caught she'd never live to be tried.

Rather than choosing one of the plush chairs across the aisle, Jake settled on the couch beside her. "Did you call in sick today?"

"Of course not." It hadn't even occurred to her. "After you phoned yesterday I filed to take a vacation day."

His teeth flashed. He seemed in abnormally high spirits, given the circumstances. "Some vacation. Did your friend come through with the information you requested?"

"Yes. And I realized I'd been spinning my wheels searching for a female listed as dead around the same time I was shot." Quickly she filled him in on her lack of success with the records of the females and the conclusions she'd drawn about how her absence might have been explained.

"That's possible," he said. "Actually, it seems pretty likely, since you've exhausted the reported-deceased angle. The military has to be like any other government bureaucracy. Paperwork in triplicate, all of it leaving trails. AWOL or MIA, either would have you turned over to them once you were found."

"That's what I thought, too." Not even to herself did Ria like to admit there was comfort in having someone else to discuss the possibilities with. It wouldn't do to get used to the sensation. But since the opportunity was there, she might as well take advantage of it.

"I've brought along some things you might need when you go into Hendricks's place," Jake told her.

Thinking of the weapons she'd packed in her small carry-on, she smiled grimly. "So did I." In any undercover operation, there were a number of things that could go wrong. She wanted to be prepared for all of them.

"You know how to run a digital camera?"

"Of course. I brought my own."

"As long as it's got a USB cord, it should work. What's the card hold?"

She thought. "About four dozen images, I think."

"We'll use mine then. It takes closer to a hundred pictures." Seeming not to notice the look she sent him, he went on. "I've also brought you a mini scanner in case there are documents you want to copy, and of course you'll wear a wire."

"A wire?" Trepidation began to mingle with anticipation. "Just how sure are your men that Hendricks will be gone?"

"I've got a half-dozen on him. We'll know if he doesn't leave for work, or starts home early for some reason. The house should be empty. He seems to live alone. At least he hasn't had any visitors since surveillance began. But to bar against any unforeseen complications, you'll wear the wire. And that's not negotiable."

The suggestion made sense, but she found his tone objectionable. "And who will be monitoring the electronic surveillance?"

"I'll be in the van with a couple of my men. If anything looks wrong, anything at all, you'll get the hell out of there."

He took her chin in his hand, turned her face to him until she met his gaze. "I mean it, Ria." His expression was grim. "At the first hint of trouble, you're out of there. Don't take any chances."

"I'm not going to take unnecessary risks," she snapped, moving away from his touch.

"Bull. If you find anything in there, you'll stay as long as it takes to finish the job."

Annoyance flared. "You think you know me so well?"

"It's what I would do." She stilled at the certainty in his voice. "We're alike that way. But you may as well come to terms with this right now. If the situation calls for it, you'll abort and get out to safety."

"I can handle myself."

He searched her gaze for some minutes before finally nodding. "The wire will ensure that we'll know if you need help. If anything looks odd, you can let us know, and we'll find a way to get you out."

Nerves were bunched in her stomach, adrenaline already starting its heady march through her veins. She was barely two hours away from discovering if Chad Hendricks and C. Albert Hendricks were one and the same. If they were, the pieces would begin clicking into place more and more rapidly.

A thought occurred to her. "What was the name on the deed to Hendricks's house?"

Jake slipped out of the heavyweight leather jacket he'd been wearing. January could be a bit more unforgiving in D.C. than in Alabama. "I already told you. That's how we discovered his name. Chad Hendricks."

"No middle initial?" she persisted. She told him about the signature she'd found on a few of the personnel evaluations last night, of the commanding officer a few of the men had shared.

"C. Albert?" He shook his head, but already was reaching to dig the cell phone from his coat pocket. "I know the deed reads Chad, but..." He broke off to dial a number. "Cort? Read the name off that deed for me again, would you? The full name."

Ria read the answer to her question in the stillness that crept over his face. After a few more moments, he disconnected, looked at her. "The deed is recorded in the name Chad A. Hendricks."

A rush of exhilaration went barreling through her with the speed and intensity of a locomotive. "They're the same person. They have to be."

"Hopefully. But there's still the difference in the way he signs his name."

"It could be an effort to distance his new persona from that of his military one." Excitement grew, and with it, certainty. "Maybe it momentarily stalls any search on him, if people do start digging. Could be he hoped it would throw off anyone looking at military records from making a connection to the aide to the Secretary of Defense."

"It's possible." The caution in Jake's tone was meant to douse her enthusiasm. But she didn't heed it. Things were starting to solidify. She was surer than ever that she was on the right track. And despite Jake's warnings, if there was anything in Hendricks's home that connected him to this whole thing, she was going to find it, regardless of the cost.

"It's 1244. The redbrick colonial home."

Ria looked out the window of the midsize white van as they slowly rolled through the Old Town Alexandria neighborhood. The cobblestone street and two-century-old architecture gave the feel of a bygone era. Hendricks's home was one of a few nestled among pubs and museums, restaurants and specialty shops. Although the weather was cold, there were a number of people on the streets, perhaps visitors touring the historic area.

"What's real estate go for around here?" she asked.

Jake looked at the man driving. "Cort?"

"The place is presently valued at just under three million." Ria started in surprise as the man went on. "Said on the deed that the place is listed on the National Register of Historic Places. He bought it four years ago."

So where, she wondered as they moved slowly past the home toward the corner, did an ex-military man come up with that kind of cash? Family money? Government jobs, including aides to those in high-level positions, wouldn't pay the kind of salary that would allow a person to afford this.

It was one more area to check into. But she was well aware that her time was running out.

"Ready to do this?"

Ria looked at Jake, nodded. They were in the back of the van, both sides of which were equipped with large windows customized with one-way glass. Each door bore a large magnetic sign with a Tidy Brooms Cleaning Service logo.

"Turn on Ramsay and go around the block. There's a parking spot fairly close to the front of the house," Jake stated.

"I saw it, too." Cort turned as instructed.

Ria could feel her heart hammering. Anticipation had been growing steadily until it was almost an unbearable weight in her chest. But her thinking was clear. This was her best chance at finding answers that had eluded her for six long years. She was going to make the most of the opportunity.

"Here's the house's layout." Jake unfolded a large piece of paper, handed it to her. "Three bedrooms and a bath upstairs.

Downstairs has a living room, dining room, half bath and another room described on the deed as family room-slash-office." With his index finger, he indicated the different areas. "How are you at picking locks?"

"Competent."

His mouth quirked. "Well, there's a zippered instrument holder in the false bottom of the cleaning bucket, in case you need it. Are you armed?"

"Yes." The dowdy maid's uniform he'd given her to change into was sufficiently roomy to hide the stiletto fastened to a sheathe around her thigh. Her gun was tucked at the small of her back, concealed by her coat. But neither would be immediately available as she entered the house. The most dangerous time for her would likely be the first minute, as she disengaged the alarm and walked inside.

"The house is empty. Hendricks entered the Pentagon an hour ago and hasn't been seen since. I've got men watching every exit. There's no way he could show up here unexpectedly."

Jake's words were meant to reassure her, she realized. And though that wasn't necessary, she was touched.

"I'll be fine. Should be in and out in no more than twenty minutes, half an hour."

"Hopefully sooner," he muttered. His mouth was a thin flat line. "I'd feel better if I were in there with you."

Ria cocked a brow, something inside her lightening. "Although I'd give quite a bit to see you in a matching uniform, it isn't necessary. You've taken every precaution. I'll do the rest." Each of them wore a tiny transmitter and crystal-controlled wireless in-ear receiver that was more advanced than any of the equipment the sheriff's department had. It would allow them to communicate while she was inside.

The van pulled to a halt along the curb. Ria pulled on the

white frilled cap that matched her uniform, and tucked her hair up inside it.

"You remember how to open the false bottom of the cleaning bucket?"

Because she could detect the worry in his voice, she answered patiently. "I remember. And before you ask, I recall the security code, too." She looked out at the street. Although people were scattered up and down both sides of it, none were close. There would be no better time to go in. "I'm ready."

She reached for the bucket, and the compact carrier that held a mop, broom and hand sweeper. Setting them near the door, she grasped the handle.

"Ria."

With a frown, she turned her head, patience near an end. But instead of issuing yet another warning, Jake dragged her close, covering her lips with his in a bruising kiss. It was over in an instant, but thorough enough to have heat spiraling crazily through her system.

He released her, sitting back. "Be careful."

It took a moment for her to recover. Because she wasn't sure she could manage a reply, she just nodded, opened the door. She got out and he handed her the bucket and tool caddy.

The sound of the van door closing behind her sent a keen-edged eagerness snapping through her veins. The rest was up to her now.

From her experience in law enforcement she knew that the approach of a dangerous operation elicited certain physical effects. The adrenaline rush was accompanied by clarity of mind. Time seemed to slow, each second ticking by with exquisite precision. And action, when it followed, would change all that to a mind-numbing blur of perceptions, reactions and responses made more by instinct than training.

Ria was professional enough to make sure none of this showed. If anyone noticed her on the street they'd see a cleaning woman on her way to work, wearing a cheap overcoat flapping open to reveal a maid's uniform. Her air was slightly harried, as if she had a schedule to keep to, but her step was purposeful.

Climbing the three stone stairs, she set her load down and looked at the touch pad security device mounted next to the door. Jake had warned her that it allowed only two attempts before activating a silent alarm to the security company. She didn't expect to need more than one.

She tapped the code in. Waited a couple of seconds. A green light winked and she drew a breath, every nerve in her body ready. Reaching out, she turned the knob, pushed the door open.

The house was still, save for the ticking of a clock in one of the nearby rooms. Ria stepped inside, setting the bucket and tool caddy on the floor and pushing the door closed with one foot. In the next moment, the gun was in her hand.

Toeing her heavy black shoes off, she moved silently through the house, checking to be sure it was as empty as it seemed. Once she'd satisfied herself that no one was hiding on either floor, she relaxed a fraction. "All clear," she murmured.

"Good." Jake's voice came through with amazing clarity. "Let's get this over with."

Although there was a pressure in her chest demanding she begin her search, caution was too ingrained to be discarded easily. Not until she'd checked for escape avenues from the back of the house and the second floor, did she allow herself to give in to the demand. Slipping the gun into the pocket of her coat, she left her leather gloves on for the search, checked her watch. The entire process had taken less than five minutes.

Leaving the tool caddy inside the door, she swiftly removed the cleaning supplies and set them on the floor. Then she picked up the bucket and entered the living room, which was equipped with comfortable overstuffed furniture and obviously expensive stereo equipment. Thick rugs were scattered over the gleaming oak floors. An ornately carved oak fireplace with copper inlay dominated one wall, a large screen TV another.

The room looked lived in but not messy. A copy of today's *Washington Post* lay folded on the arm of the couch. There was a half-empty cup of coffee on the table next to it, as if Hendricks had relaxed in here before going to work.

Staying clear of the windows, Ria went to the fireplace mantel, looked at the collection of pictures displayed on it. Unlike her own home, his had the personal stamp of someone with a history. With family and loved ones.

She slid open the false bottom of the bucket and withdrew the compact digital camera, taking several shots of the collection of framed photos. She recognized the person appearing in most of them as the man who'd passed himself off in Jake's office as Colton, aka Hendricks himself. Studying his image, she realized Jake had described him accurately. Average height, average build…his features were pleasant enough but hardly memorable. But that wouldn't be why *she* didn't remember him from her past.

"Where are you?"

Jake's voice gave her a start. For a moment she'd forgotten he was waiting on the other end of the transmitter. "Taking pictures of his photos in the living room."

There were several shots of him with an older man who bore his likeness, a couple of him, much younger, with a woman Ria assumed was his mother. There was none of him with a woman his age, so she was guessing Hendricks was single. His had been the only name on the deed.

After a glance around, she headed to the next room. What Jake had predicted would be an office was instead, a collector's room. It was crammed with glass display cases filled with antique military items.

Each piece had a computer-generated label beside it. She walked up and down the rows of cases, taking pictures of each. A Samurai helmet. A pair of Walther P-38s. An 1898 "potato digger" machine gun. An 1852 Patt sword. World War II German bayonets. A Remington split-breech carbine. Including the collection of knives, swords and handguns hanging on the walls, Ria estimated that there were close to two hundred pieces displayed in the room.

"What do antique weapons run, ballpark?" she asked Jake.

His voice sounded in her ear, half-irritated. "What the heck are you doing now?"

"The other room on the main floor is filled with old military weapons. From the looks of the security system on the cases, this stuff is valuable."

He was silent for a moment. "How old?"

"World War I and more recent."

"Antique weapons and other collector items can run pretty steep, depending on their rarity and condition. Most range from a couple hundred to several thousand, although some pieces go for well over that."

In other words, it was an expensive little hobby. She'd dearly love to know where Hendricks's money came from.

She knew from her preliminary check of the house that the formal dining room, kitchen and half bath seemed normal. She headed upstairs, to a spare bedroom that was equipped as an office.

One wall was covered with pictures. She ignored it for the time being and crossed to the desk. The drawers were all locked, so she took out the case Jake had mentioned and unzipped it. Withdrawing a pick, she inserted it into the lock of the top drawer and with a few swift movements had it open. The thought occurred to her that she shared more than a few of Jake's criminal skills.

There was so little contained in the drawers that she figured the small black, leather-bound notebook inside must be valuable. Flipping it open, she saw it was less than a third full, and held names, addresses and phone numbers. Using the scanner, she recorded each page, then set the book back inside and turned to the filing cabinets nearby.

Neither of them was locked, which made Ria doubt there would be anything of interest inside. But she went quickly through them anyway. Most files, she soon discovered, held receipts and written histories on the weapons housed downstairs. With eyebrows climbing, she noted that Jake's estimation on the value had been close.

Other folders showed routine bills and payment stubs, all for the previous year. She scanned the stubs and mentally calculated Hendricks's annual salary. As she'd guessed, it fell enormously short of enabling him to afford a house like this.

She went to the wall of pictures, and saw that most detailed Hendricks's own military history. There was a younger, unsmiling picture of him, newly enlisted, standing in front of a U.S. Army barracks. In another he was grinning, pointing to the gleaming captain's bars on his uniform. Still others showed him shaking hands with various army officials.

One large framed case held what she assumed were his army insignias, medals and patches. Brows rising, she saw he'd reached the level of colonel before leaving the military.

From the most recent of the pictures, she guessed him to be about forty-five today. He'd been out of the military at least four years, according to Jake. A fairly rapid rise, but certainly not unprecedented.

She took pictures of the wall, then replaced the camera in the bucket. A thought struck her then, and she went back to the desk, searching above and below each drawer for anything taped to the interior. She discovered nothing. Undeterred, she probed at each of the drawer linings, looking for a false bottom. Her search was rewarded in the bottom drawer.

It was deep enough to hold hanging files, though it contained only computer, printer and software manuals. But once she'd taken out the contents and looked more closely, she was able to release a spring-loaded panel and push the false bottom aside.

There in the space lay a bankbook.

Ria's heart began hammering. Hendricks kept his pay stubs and bank records in the filing cabinet, so she knew she'd discovered something else. Flipping it open, she saw it was the bank record for an offshore account. Monthly deposits had been made each of the last five years.

She might not have discovered the source of his money, but she could be fairly certain it wasn't legitimate.

Retrieving the scanner, she copied each page before putting the book back in the drawer and replacing the false bottom. Then she piled the manuals back inside and locked the drawers again, a fierce feeling of satisfaction coursing through her.

"I've got you, you black-hearted bastard," she muttered.

"I'm going to assume you're not talking to me." Jake's sardonic voice sounded in her ear. "You found something?"

"Looks to me like Chad Hendricks is blackmailing someone. I wondered where all this money was coming from." She gazed at the computer. "I wish I had the know-how to break into his electronic files."

"Not this trip. Finish up and get back out here. It's been twenty-five minutes already."

She didn't need the reminder. But before she left the room she stopped in front of the pictures one more time. Scanned rapidly, they were a collage that spanned the younger Hendricks's steady rise in the military. His achievements, his friendships. One photo showed him with his arm thrown around the shoulders of a younger man wearing a uniform with a Ranger's tab. Noting the insignia, Ria gazed more closely at the man's face.

Her breath stalled in her lungs as recognition slammed into her. The man in the picture was none other than the one who'd come to kill her on Santa Cristo. The same man who'd murdered Luz.

Chapter 9

Other than a few snarled comments, the trip back to the airport was accomplished in silence. There was no mistaking Jake's mood, however. It was lethally menacing.

Ria ignored him as much as she was able. With her thoughts in tumult, she welcomed the quiet, even when it was as charged as a stick of dynamite. Once on the plane she changed back into her own clothes, putting the transmitter and receiver on top of the folded maid's uniform. Entering the cabin again, she dropped heavily to the couch, welcoming the moment of solitude while Jake talked to his pilot.

Leaning her head back against the cushion, she let her eyelids slide closed. At least two of the men on the team she'd been a part of were dead, by her hand. It shouldn't be too difficult to match the man in the picture to one of the deceased soldiers on her list at home.

Things were starting to come together, at warp speed. The

dizzying avalanche of information and conclusions needed to be sorted out, and new options explored.

She felt Jake sit down next to her, and her eyes popped open. Given his mood earlier, she figured she needed all her wits about her. "Feeling civil yet?"

The look he sent her was smoldering. "You were in there for an hour. That's more than twice what we'd planned. I almost came in after you twice."

Her lips curved. "So you said." Other statements, much less polite, had been muttered, as well. A more timid person would have considered them threats.

"After finding the bankbook in the false bottom of a desk drawer, I decided to look more thoroughly, in case he had documents hidden elsewhere in his house." She'd done a careful search of everything she could think of, including the appliances, walls and floorboards, to no avail.

"What in the hell made you do that?" His tone was biting. "This was supposed to be an in-and-out venture. You've got the bankbook. You know he was the commanding officer at the posts of at least two of the men."

"I recognized someone in a picture with Hendricks," she said baldly. That had been the catalyst that sent her hunting for even more tangible evidence. "It was the first assassin sent after me, in Santa Cristo. He killed the woman who saved my life, then came for me."

There was no change in Jake's expression, but she felt the charged air between them defuse slightly. "You're sure?"

"I remember that face." Her gaze was turned inward. She could still picture both men who had been sent after her. The scenes replayed endlessly in her nightmares, in vivid Technicolor. "He spoke, the other assassin never did. Said I was a traitor. That more would be sent after me. He was right."

Until she'd dived so deeply undercover that no one could find her. Before now.

A thought struck her then, and she straightened abruptly. "He said something else. Something about Sammy sending his regards." The idea that occurred then arrowed through her with caution-laced accuracy. "You don't think...he couldn't be referring to Secretary of Defense Samson, could he?"

The words chilled Jake straight to the core. God Almighty, when it came to enemies, they didn't come much more powerful than that. "I hope not," he muttered feelingly. But the possibility couldn't be ignored. Hendricks was the man's closest aide. Hendricks had been C.O. at the base where at least two of the deceased soldiers had been stationed at one time. Both soldiers, Ria said, had been Army Rangers.

"The man in the picture," he asked suddenly, turning to look at her. "The guy with Hendricks. Was he a Ranger?" At her nod, his gut tightened into knots. He'd hoped this excursion would clear up some of their questions, but damned if he liked the answers.

Coming to a sudden decision, he said, "We have to get you somewhere safe. The contract on you expires the day after tomorrow. If we don't convince Hendricks you're dead, he'll go after you again himself, or hire someone else."

"He'll come back to you first," she predicted. If Jake wasn't imagining things, he saw worry in her eyes. Even while he called himself every kind of a fool, that flicker of anxiety warmed him.

"I'm counting on that. But we can get you out of the country first."

"And what's to stop him from going after you? Or following through on his threat to spring Alvarez early, knowing *he'll* go after you?"

It was probably what Hendricks had planned all along. Stanton would have told him at least some of the history between the two of them. Jake knew Alvarez had been plotting his death for ten years. Even without help, his chances of succeeding were better than Jake liked to admit.

"I already have safety precautions in place." Nothing was fail-proof; he knew that as well as anyone. But he had resources at his disposal far beyond anything Ria could have. Of the two of them he liked his chances better.

He wasn't willing to chance *her.*

"I can have my jet take you anywhere in the world. I know a guy who's a master at creating false identification documents. We keep you hidden for a day, two at the most, and he can have yours ready. If Hendricks believes you're dead, we buy ourselves some time. With any luck, we both stay alive."

She swallowed hard and looked away. "I was determined that if I had to run again, I'd be prepared. So I have money put aside, and two different sets of ID."

The news should have put him at ease. Instead, he was filled with a sense of foreboding. Her next words made it worse. "But since then I changed my mind. I've been running all my life. At least," she corrected, "for as long as I can remember. I was determined to get answers and now I'm getting them. I'm not running anymore. Since Hendricks seems involved in this up to his neck, he's the man who's going to give them to me."

"You won't get those answers if you're dead." Jake knew the words were blunt, but there was no use sugarcoating it. "Let me put you somewhere safe. You're too close to the truth now to risk dying. You want someone to pay for everything that's happened? For that woman's death? Then you have to stay alive to be sure he does."

She was silent long enough for him to start considering alternatives in case she refused. Kidnapping her was starting to look like a damn fine option before she finally responded.

"The first time someone came after me, an innocent got hurt. I won't let that happen again." By removing herself as a target, Ria thought bleakly, she could protect those around her. It wasn't much, but it was something. She hated to admit it, but Jake's plan sounded the most feasible.

If Hendricks were convinced that Jake had killed her, he would have no reason to harm him. Hendricks had no idea his real identity had been discovered. And she wouldn't go far, definitely not out of the country. When she left, it would be on her own terms. To a place of her choosing, a location she wouldn't share with anyone else. Not even Jake.

Especially not Jake.

She could continue her search from anywhere. And she would. She was close enough now to almost taste success.

"I'll go tomorrow night." When he seemed ready to argue, she went on, resolve stiffening her spine. "I want to leave things in reasonable order at the sheriff's office." The thought of leaving Fenton County in the lurch filled her with remorse. The other times she'd run she'd had no responsibilities, no ties. She had people depending on her now. But better to walk away from them than to put any of them at risk.

"All right," he said grudgingly. "I'll call you tomorrow to make the arrangements."

She was already making plans. For her disappearance to look reasonable, she'd have to leave everything in her home. It wouldn't be too difficult. She deliberately led a pretty Spartan existence. But she'd first download everything on the computer to CDs and then wipe the hard drive clean. The CDs and all records pertaining to the search would go with her.

Wherever she ended up, she wanted to be able to continue the investigation without losing any time. Too much had passed already.

But the pang in her heart was new. She was used to recognizing what had to be done and then doing it. This regret was different, and difficult to shake.

She slid a glance to the man beside her. He was the cause of more than a little of it. She almost…not *trusted* him; she wasn't sure she was capable of that. But he stirred a welter of feelings that were foreign to her. Feelings that left her more than a little sorrowful that they'd be separated before she'd had the opportunity to explore them.

He looked at her then and the expression on his face drove the breath from her lungs. His pale blue eyes were softer, deeper than she'd ever seen them. And she knew she wasn't imagining the regret shimmering in their depths.

Frozen in time, she waited for him to speak, half hoping he would say something to shatter the spell weaving inexorably between them. But instead he remained silent, even as he reached over and scooped her into his lap.

Ria stiffened at the unfamiliar position. She wasn't a lap sitter. But any hint of awkwardness was dissipated in the next moment, when he buried his face in her neck.

There was an air of weariness to the act that tugged on something deep within her. And the fingers she threaded through his hair were gentle. She'd rarely given in to self-pity or railed against the circumstances that had stripped her of memory, of possible family and friends. She'd regarded each new experience as a step toward regaining what she'd lost. But never before had she been so achingly aware of the sweetness of each moment. Perhaps she'd been given another chance to relish these feelings. Or perhaps, more frighteningly, she'd never felt this storm of emotion before.

Whichever was the truth, she'd savor this one. Each bittersweet instant of it.

When his mouth came in search of hers, the touch was whisper light, a mere brush of movement before he halted, lips suspended a fraction of an inch away. Their breaths mingled, the moment spinning into liquid gold. And she understood, even without words, that this would be the only real goodbye between them.

Linking her arms around his neck, she pulled him closer, moving her lips sweetly, achingly on his. A thousand might-have-beens hovered between them. For the next little while she was going to turn aside from regret and fear and defenses.

She was going to begin saving for an uncertain future by making memories right now. Memories to warm her in the cool shadows that fell across her bed when she lay awake at night, her mind too full to sleep. When the pressure of being alone was too suffocating.

His tongue moved against hers, his flavor racing through her system. But he didn't rush, didn't take the kiss deeper. He cupped her face in both his hands, and this tenderness from him was devastating to the senses.

Jake felt Ria go boneless, and her tiny sigh of surrender sparked the need that was never quite extinguished. Still he toyed delicately with her lips, drawing out the pleasure for both of them.

His mouth cruised along her jawline, rediscovering smooth skin and soft flesh. He knew now that sex could be easy when it was mindless and urgent. When logic was blinded by passion and doubts stilled by need. There was a distant sort of alarm at the realization, but it couldn't compete with the enjoyment in this instant.

He swept his hand beneath the simple black sweater she wore, felt the individual vertebrae, their delicacy belying the strength of her will. The skin there was warm and sleek, heating his palm. He traced the ridges of her scars with his thumb. She arched beneath his touch and her reaction caused little drumbeats of demand to sound in his blood. Even the most leisurely buildup could torch control.

Drawing the sweater over her head, he tossed it aside, following in the next moment with her bra. Tormenting them both, he cupped her breasts, brushing his thumbs along their sides, stopping short of her nipples before retreating again. A tiny gasp escaped her, and she pressed into his touch, urging him to take more.

There was a dark and reckless side of him that wanted to do just that. A part that wanted to take and take until he could satiate himself in her. Until he could be certain that he wouldn't be tormented later by memories that held a sharp edge.

He wouldn't miss her once she'd gone, he'd told himself, rolling her satiny nipples between thumbs and forefingers. Regrets were a foolish waste of time. He wouldn't close his eyes and recall her face, or be left trying to banish the scent of her from his system. He had the thought and tried to believe it.

Ria pressed closer, little demons of need firing through her veins, making her sizzle. His hands were incinerating any attempt at control, one moment caressing and the next just a few degrees shy of rough. She yearned to feel them racing down her body, his touch possessive.

She turned to straddle him, even as she took his mouth with hers. Her tongue darted between his lips, sneaky tempting forays designed to make him think twice about restraint. When his mouth twisted under hers and his body tensed, she knew she'd succeeded.

Her fingers went to his shirt, and her movements deliberately slowed. Where before she'd urged a faster, deeper response, now she reined back, baring each inch of his skin with excruciating care.

When she finally spread his shirt open he released her to press her closer. She was still for a moment, the exquisite sensation of bare flesh against bare flesh a keen-edged pleasure she wanted to savor. But too soon a greedy need for more rose up, and she twisted against him, his chest hair rasping against her sensitized nipples.

Jake felt arousal surge through him, shattering all intentions to move slowly. Rising, he set her on her feet and finished stripping her, then turned into a quivering heap when she returned the favor.

When they were both nude she stepped close enough for her breasts to slightly graze his chest. He took a moment to enjoy the sight of her—slender torso, rounded hips, long slender thighs. His hands went in pursuit of pleasure, roaming her body to explore every curve, every secret pulse, every sleek muscle quivering beneath her skin. And he recognized, in some distant part of his mind, that vows were useless and resolve ineffective. Ria would linger in his system despite his best efforts to banish her. He wondered if he'd even have the will to try.

She bent to retrieve the condom he'd taken from his pocket, and, gaze fixed on his, rolled the latex over the straining length of him. Then he dropped to the couch, pulling her with him, wrapping his hands in her hair as desire burst low in his belly and scorched a path of fire through him.

Ria settled in his lap facing him. Jake bent his head, took

one of her nipples in his mouth and suckled deeply. Control abruptly receded. Her back arched and she rocked against him, the motion bringing her into intimate contact with his hardness.

Sensations careened through her. There was the scrape of his teeth on her breast, the slight roughness of his touch as he gripped her hips. And there was pleasure in the knowledge that the memory of this moment would etch his mind as deeply as it did hers, and be as impossible to erase.

She could feel her heart hammering in rhythm with his. The blood thundered in her veins. His muscles were tight beneath her touch, quivering with barely leashed control. The air between them thrummed with a dark and desperate passion.

She rose to her knees, reached for him, nearly going limp at the leap of hunger she felt in his pulsing strength. With trembling fingers she positioned herself to take him in, one slow inch at a time.

Jake's back pressed into the cushion, sweat beading on his forehead. The languid, velvet slide of sweet flesh clenching around him had his raw nerves screaming. But there was more than the savage need clawing through him. There was the sight of her—spine arched, expression absorbed, as if she were focusing on each individual sensation.

And he knew in that instant that this would be the picture branded on his mind. This would be the image of her he'd be doomed to remember. There'd be no keeping the thought of her from sneaking in at odd times, shattering his guard, melting his defenses.

He clenched her hips, more than a little desperate. But she wouldn't be rushed. By the time she took him completely, his control was ragged and his vision hazed.

Her forehead rested against his, and his muscles ached with the need to surge blindly upward. Finally, when his senses were all but screaming, she straightened, began to move.

He tried to let her set the pace, even as his mind reeled and greed welled inside him. But at her first broken cry, something inside him snapped.

His hands gripping her hips, he drove upward, filling her with a completeness that tore a low groan from him. He'd never known such violent desire, which burned even as it pleasured. Ruled by a primal need to get closer, he swallowed her low throaty moans, then buried his face against her neck as he drove them both to madness.

Damp flesh slapped against damp flesh. The air sawed out of his lungs. And when at last he felt her tense muscles quivering, he took savage delight in watching her climax around him.

But the sound of his name on her lips had his own release springing forth, with a possessiveness he didn't even recognize. After one last savage thrust, he followed her into a free-fall of mind-shattering pleasure.

They lay on the couch for a long time after, naked limbs tangled, waiting for their blood to stop raging. Her fingers were tangled in the hair on his chest, while he stroked a palm over the curve of her hip.

He thought he could guess the direction of her thoughts, but when she spoke her words surprised him. "What happens when Alvarez is freed?"

His hand stilled. "I've told you. He has a lot to account for."

"Detectives Edwards and Renard know about the rivalry between you. You're the first person the police will look at if something happens to him."

Jake wasn't convinced. It was just as likely they'd hope the two of them did each other in, and call it community improvement. "I'm going to be careful."

Ria propped herself on one elbow, looked at him steadily. "Who are you kidding? He's been planning his revenge on you as long as you have his. If there's one thing I've learned over the years it's that no security is foolproof. If someone wants you dead badly enough, if they're good enough, you're dead."

"I know." He'd accepted the prospect a long time ago. "I'm going to gamble that I'm better than he is, though."

His tone was light, but her expression didn't change. "What can be worth that kind of risk? Surely not money. You're practically swimming in it as it is."

He traced the crease of her thigh with his finger. "Spoken like someone who doesn't respect wealth."

"It's not worth it, Jake." Her tone was certain, her gaze direct. "Whatever he did to you, revenge isn't worth having to look over your shoulder for the rest of your life."

If anyone would know about life on the run, it was Ria. But she didn't know everything. Not even close. "It's not about revenge." He disentangled himself from her, sat up and reached for his clothes.

"What do you call it, then?"

"I call it justice." An all too familiar block of icy anger was back, settling in his chest. For more years than he could count it had lodged there, cold and unrelenting. "He got away with murder. And one way or another, he's going to pay for that." Jake pulled on his jeans, shrugged into his shirt.

Ria was slower to follow suit. She had her clothes clutched in her hands, her gaze still on him. "Whose murder?"

"Jilly's. My sister." Grief and guilt could still swamp him, he discovered, the years doing nothing to dilute their tide. He buttoned his shirt and shoved the tails into his jeans. "She was older than me, but...maybe too much like my mom." Especially when it came to her poor choice in men. "I always had to kind of look after her. When I got out of juvie she'd already moved away, gone south."

But he hadn't worried about her. Remorse flickered, and he let it burn. He'd believed her stories of the great job she had in Columbus, hostess in some fancy restaurant. When she'd talked about her wealthy boyfriend, Jake's instincts should have alerted him. But he'd been glad to accept her stories as truth. Had wanted to think that she, at least, had escaped the poverty and violence they'd grown up with.

"The first few years she came back at Christmas, but then she started making excuses. After the second year she didn't come home I went down to see her."

With crystal clarity he remembered his shock at the difference in her. Jilly had always been vibrant, proud of her dark good looks, but the woman he'd encountered in the run-down apartment she shared with two other women seemed to have aged ten years in the time since he'd last seen her. He'd recognized immediately what her brittle air, and the tracks on her arms, had meant.

But it had taken a couple days before he understood just how far her job was from "hostessing."

"The man she introduced as her boyfriend was nothing more than a drug pushing pimp." The look Jake shot Ria was full of the bitterness that had long ridden him. "Alvarez reeled her in with a promise of money and attention. He got her hooked on drugs and then he put her on the street. She died of an overdose when she was twenty-six, two weeks after I got to town. And maybe Alvarez didn't put the needle in her arm that time, but you'll never convince me he isn't responsible for her death."

There was compassion in Ria's eyes, and something else

he recognized. Regret. "Yes, he's responsible. Directly, indirectly, it doesn't matter. She's just as dead either way. But *your* death isn't going to right hers. You can't convince me she would have wanted you to take that kind of risk."

His mouth twisted. "No, Jilly was never much for risks." Like their mother, she'd put her faith in the wrong man because she'd needed so badly to be taken care of. Had allowed the mistreatment because she lacked the strength to walk away, even if she'd been allowed to.

He'd known her well enough not to accept her story at face value. If he'd done something sooner, gotten her away, she might still be alive. And that fact would haunt him to the grave.

The law wouldn't hold Alvarez responsible for Jilly's death, so it was up to Jake. And from his experience with his stepfather, he knew just how careful he'd have to be. So he accepted a low-level position in Alvarez's organization, and used the opportunity to learn as much as he could about the man's illegal sidelines. Then he'd tipped off Vice, and they'd done the rest.

He'd arranged for a great deal of the cocaine Alvarez had intended for the street pushers to be found in the trunk of his car. It was, he thought, a sort of poetic justice. And the moment the man had had the cuffs slapped on him, Jake had moved in and reshaped Alvarez's empire into his own.

Alvarez had had ten years to suffer, but even that wasn't enough to pay for his part in Jilly's death. When he was released from prison, he'd be a dead man. It was only a matter of time.

He glanced at Ria, found her almost dressed. "You better than anyone should know that sometimes the only choice we have is to play the cards we're dealt." And even if he wished for a different hand now, nothing would change. This had been set in motion too long ago. Win or lose, he had to see it through.

Ria stopped at the sheriff's office to catch up with as much paperwork as she could. She was mindful of the fact that every minute that ticked by counted down her remaining time here. So she stayed later than she'd planned, getting her files in order so the transition to a new sheriff would be as seamless as possible.

With grim humor she reflected that Ralston just might get his wish. With her sudden disappearance, the county commissioners might look upon his job bid a bit more favorably.

As she pulled into the lane leading up to her home, though, thoughts of the Fenton County Sheriff's Department were far behind her. Although it seemed like a lifetime ago, it had only been last night when she'd requested the new information from Benny. She had no doubt it was in her in-box right this moment.

Even the surge of anticipation tightening her stomach, however, wasn't enough to have her skirting her usual security check. Given all that she and Jake had discovered the last few days, caution remained imperative.

When she got inside she bypassed the kitchen, even though her stomach was growling violently. Food, if she could find any, would have to wait. Quickly she strode upstairs and booted up the computer. While she waited, she got a briefcase out of the closet and began to empty the filing cabinet of the papers she'd been working on.

Once she'd finished the task, she sat down and typed in the password needed for her e-mail account. A quick flare of satisfaction filled her when she saw the expected message with attachments from Benny. Impatiently, she tapped in a command, waited for the documents to download.

And despite her best efforts, her mind returned, over and over, to Jake.

It seemed bitterly ironic that while she was planning to protect him, he was openly embracing the danger that Alvarez's release would mean. She pressed the keys for the documents to print.

She planned to slip away without taking him up on his offer of a jet and protected location. As long as Hendricks was free, she was at risk, and so was anyone around her. But her efforts would probably be in vain. The deadly game Jake was engaged in with Alvarez was every bit as lethal as the links she was discovering to Hendricks.

Snatching up the papers as the printer spat them out on the tray, she scanned the first two quickly. They listed the only MIA reports involving female soldiers in the time period of her own disappearance. Although women weren't sent into combat, that didn't mean they weren't sometimes caught up in danger during the course of their assignments.

But it didn't take long to ascertain that neither of these women could be her. One was too old and the other had the wrong eye color. Setting the reports aside, she went to the next printouts.

There were more female soldiers listed as AWOL than she would have expected. Twelve in all, with all but two eventually caught and dishonorably discharged. It was the records for the remaining two that captured her attention.

It wasn't the names of the women she looked at first; her gaze zeroed in on the C.O. at their last post location. Recognition punched through her, like a sneaky left jab.

The commanding officer on one of the records read Colonel C. Albert Hendricks.

Her system seemed to freeze, a paralysis that shut down organs. Clogged breathing. She stumbled backward, dropped into the chair, eyes sweeping down the pages.

Starkey, Karen L., Sgt. FC.

Performed leadership duties in a decisive and positive manner with exceptional results.

Her mental toughness and integrity are beyond reproach.

Ria's gaze riveted on another paragraph, a dull roar sounding in her ears.

Fluent in multiple languages. This, along with her ASVAB score, makes her an ideal candidate for military intelligence.

Ria flipped through the pages numbly. Her mind seemed frozen; she couldn't take it all in. But she didn't need to read any further to know that she held the key to her real identity in her hands.

Smoke rolled from the old barn, billowing black clouds of it filling the air and blocking vision. Flames shot triumphant spikes skyward, evading the streams of water pumping through the fire hoses. There was a steady crackling as the conflagration greedily consumed more of the structure, hissing blankets of steam rising from the area Tripolo firefighters were targeting.

Hearing another siren in the distance, Ria spoke into her radio. "Parker, roll that emergency fencing back. Sounds like Bakersfield's trucks are on the way." Noting the crowd had swelled appreciably, she radioed the deputy she had stationed at the mouth of the driveway. "Clark? Have you checked the road to make sure it's clear for the emergency vehicles?"

There was a burst of static before Clark's response came through. "…use another officer out here for traffic management. Don't know where all these people are coming from."

"I'll get one out there." Ria looked up and scanned the crowd. "Cook. Clark could use a hand keeping the traffic moving."

The man nodded, started off. Ria made her way to where a pair of her deputies stood with the owner of the property, Darrell Hempsted. The old man was gazing at the blaze with a scowl on his face. Of course, she couldn't be certain the present situation was the cause for his mood. She'd met him a couple of other times, when he'd come into the office to lodge a complaint. He was, according to Marlyss's shared confidence, a faultin' sort of person.

When he saw her coming toward them, Hempsted's expression grew truculent. "If you'd done what I told you the last time I was in, Sheriff, this wouldn'ta happened. I hold you personally responsible."

To her deputies she said, "Simpson looks like he could use a hand with crowd control." Then she shifted her attention to the older man. "You'll have to refresh my memory, Mr. Hempsted. What was it you requested?"

The man sent a stream of chewing tobacco to the ground. "It's them damn Yarrow boys, I done told you that. Hangin' out here all the time, smoking cigarettes and drinking what beer they can steal. Wouldn't be a bit surprised if they played hooky again and spent the day holed up in there, and look what they done now." He nodded toward the blaze, a losing battle being fought by the firefighters.

Memory came to her aid, supplying her with details. She had sent a deputy to talk to the brothers, and they'd admitted to being in the barn "once or twice." Since the old man had more suspicions than real evidence, there had been little the sheriff's department could do other than issue the boys a warning.

"We'll talk to them tomorrow." At least, she mentally corrected, someone would. She wouldn't be there. It wasn't the first time she'd had to issue herself that reminder today.

"If'n you'd done something before, this wouldn'ta happened." He stomped off.

The Bakersfield truck joined Tripolo's emergency vehicles, but Ria could tell the fire was a lost cause. Now the biggest concern would be to keep it from spreading. Fortunately, the building was several hundred yards away from the Hempsted home. The family wasn't in any danger, unless it was from Darrell's ire.

Several hours later the barn was little more than smoldering cinders and most of the crowd had dispersed. Ria thanked the fire chief and his men and headed down the driveway, cognizant of the time. She had less than an hour before Jake was to send a car for her. They'd discussed the plan for several minutes when he'd called that afternoon, interrupting her as she was finishing the employee evaluations.

He'd sounded distant, although his interest had sharpened when she'd briefed him on what she'd discovered the night before. They'd decided that she'd meet the car he sent for her on the road along the adjacent property. She didn't want any neighbor to spot a strange car at her place. Her disappearance needed to be absolute. It would be better that way for everyone.

And though Jake's resources would help spirit her away, at the first opportunity she'd settle on a different location from which to conduct the rest of her investigation. She refused to put him at risk by allowing him knowledge of her whereabouts.

That morning, she'd downloaded all her information onto a CD. The hard drive had been wiped, then a few innocuous files placed back on it. On her way to work that morning she'd stopped at the post office and mailed the CD to the anonymous mail drop she used. Once she returned home, there was little left to do but wait for the time she was to meet Jake.

Since there was nothing more to be done here, she began radioing each officer to give them their orders as she headed to her car.

At the end of the driveway, Scott Carter hailed her. "Sheriff. How long you want for us to stick around?"

She halted. "I'm sending everyone home but Simpson and Cook. They'll stay as long as the fire crew does."

The man gave a nod. "I'm not going to argue. Missed supper by several hours tonight. Can I drop you anywhere?"

"I drove, but thanks anyway." She'd been using a spare cruiser ever since her department issue car had been shot up.

He fell into step with her as they walked to their respective cars. "You bought the Haskell place a couple miles down the road, didn't you? My grandparents used to live in that house. It's been sold a couple times since, but I have lots of good memories of running around that old place when I was a kid."

She halted, her hand on the car door. "Why did your grandparents sell it?"

He propped an elbow on the hood. "Oh, they got older, moved to town. Didn't want to be so isolated anymore, I guess." He gave her a wave and climbed into his vehicle.

She thought of his words as she got in the car. She hadn't been seeking isolation when she'd looked at the place as much as she had privacy. It was the first property she'd bought in the last six years, but there were few memories she'd take away from there. Perhaps of finding Jake ensconced in her easy chair, gun hidden beneath the newspaper. His unexplained presence that night had seemed to linger, despite her efforts to expel it. Of the two of them poring over the military files upstairs.

Or of the moment in her office last night when she'd first become certain she'd discovered her real name.

She pulled the car to a stop next to the house, reached for the flashlight. The perimeter check would be another last in a day that had been full of them. She switched the light on, circled the house, playing the beam over the ground. Seeing nothing out of the ordinary, she climbed the back steps, carefully checking the position of the mat, the paint chip she'd repositioned on the doorknob. Satisfied, she descended the steps again and rounded the house to examine the front door before heading inside.

The dog seemed to come out of nowhere, snarling and barking. Ria jumped back, raised the flashlight threateningly. The animal was huge, some cross lab mix, and judging from the collar it wore, probably belonged to one of the neighbors.

More annoyed than frightened, she held her ground until the animal backed away, still barking. Keeping a cautious eye on it, she continued toward the front of the house. The animal was large enough to have triggered the silent alarm system she had rigged up. It wouldn't be the first time that had happened.

She passed by the window of the living room, half expecting to see the lights blinking their warning. But the interior of the house was dark. She frowned, switching her flashlight off, and looked again. The house remained in shadows.

Backtracking, she headed around the house to look in the kitchen window. No lights flickered near the baseboards there, either.

A cold blade of fear scraped down her spine. She'd deliberately bypassed electricity as a power supply for all her security precautions, so she couldn't blame this failure on a power outage.

She stepped away from the window and flattened herself against the house, dread pooling in her stomach. There could be a short in the wiring. A flaw in the system itself.

Or it could have been deliberately deactivated. Which could only be done by someone in her house.

Chapter 10

Ria collected her thoughts for a moment, tried to still the nasty little fingers of dread gripping her. Surely this leap to paranoia was a product of the recent events. But she'd survived this long by listening to her instincts.

And they were screaming at her now.

She could slip across the property adjacent to hers and wait for Jake. In less than an hour she'd be well away from here. Far away from the danger that might await her inside.

But the records were in there, bundled in a small briefcase she'd intended to bring with her, along with the vials and syringes she'd taken off the two assassins. Ria hesitated, torn. She could get the records sent to her again, after she'd taken the precaution of establishing a different e-mail account. Benny had managed it once. There was no reason to think that he...

Realization arrowed into her with dizzying accuracy. Benny. Her disposable cell phone, the one she kept only to contact him, was in the briefcase, as well. It was supposed to be untraceable, but could it be used to track a person Ria had called? Fear circled in her chest as she considered the possibility. And thoughts of creeping away withered and vanished. For someone with enough money and power, there was no telling the kind of technology that could be used to retrieve Benny's number. From there he was only a heartbeat away from suffering the same fate Luz had.

Ria had sworn no innocent would ever die because of her again.

Having made the decision, she turned her mind to how to get inside and take the intruder by surprise. He had to know she was out here; he would have seen the headlights. He must have tripped the wire on his approach to the house, and disengaged the lights she'd rigged up, in case they tipped her off.

She'd taken other precautions. There was an escape route from the house, although she'd always considered using it to get away, not as an alternate means to get inside. But if she was going to ambush the intruder by surprise, it was her only hope.

She set the flashlight on the ground, and swiftly removed one boot, then the other. Creeping toward the front of the house, she hoisted herself up on the porch railing and to the roof.

By standing on the porch roof she could just reach the overhang above. With a leap Ria grabbed the edge and pulled herself up, far enough to swing one leg over the side.

Moments later she lay flat against the slanted roof, her lungs heaving from her efforts. But there was no time to linger. He'd be in there waiting. Had probably already figured out she'd been tipped off to his presence. Would he come outside for her? She thought he would. She was hoping that he'd never dream she'd come in after him.

She rose to a crouched position, began making her way up

to the peak. In the center, directly above the attic, the roofline flattened. There was a trapdoor in that flat section, probably put there to allow the owner to get to the chimney for cleaning. It would provide her with the access she needed now.

She lifted the small door, set it aside. Climbing down the old wire-rung ladder on the side of the chimney, Ria stepped onto the attic floor, praying her entry had gone undetected. If the intruder stayed downstairs, if he was watching doors and windows rather than the upper level…

Finally able to draw her gun, she released the safety and tiptoed down the attic steps. At the door, she took a deep breath, turned the knob and pushed it open slowly. She went through it low, both hands on her weapon as she secured the area. Finding herself alone there, she shut the door quietly behind her and went hunting.

First she determined that the rest of the upstairs was unoccupied. Her quick scan of the office showed her that not only was it empty, but her briefcase was gone. Her mouth abruptly dried out. The last thread of hope that her security system had somehow malfunctioned withered and died.

From her bedroom she took a long body pillow off the bed, and then crept to the stairs. There was no way to avoid the squeak of floorboards as she descended. She didn't even try. Gun steady, she crept down the steps, watching both sides at its base for signs of movement. There was nothing.

She drew closer. Her heart was jackhammering in her chest, deafening her to any slight sounds the intruder might make. Still she watched, knowing a killer lay in wait at the bottom. She just needed one hint of the direction the attack would come from.

She was four steps up now. Pausing, she scanned the darkness. There. A shadow had moved just a bit, as if readying to pounce. One more step. A breath caught and held.

She leaped, throwing the pillow ahead of her. A dark figure jumped out, hands outstretched. It was only an instant before he realized his mistake, but it was time Ria used to her advantage. She hit the floor of the hallway, spun, catching him in the kidneys with a kick that had the force of her weight behind it.

He stumbled but didn't go down. He raised his arm and there was a slight thud as something lodged in the plaster beside her head. His gun had a silencer. She squeezed off two shots in quick succession, dived to the floor, rolling for cover in the next room.

Emboldened, he ducked out from the corner he'd taken refuge in and fired again. A lamp above her head shattered.

Raising the gun in her left hand, she shot two more times, hearing his grunt of pain when a bullet caught him in the arm, spinning him back against the wall. She heard something hit the floor. Pain exploded in her hand, and her nerveless fingers had opened, almost dropping the weapon before she scooped it up with her other hand.

She sprang at the intruder, swiping viciously at his head with the butt of her gun. He dodged that blow, but wasn't quick enough to evade the next one, which slammed into the bridge of his nose. Her knee drew up with savage intent, but missed its mark when the man lunged at her, grabbing her throat and swiveling a hip to bring them both crashing to the floor. They rolled, each battling for control of her gun. The man's mask came off in the struggle, and they were locked close enough for Ria to recognize the man who had hired Jake to kill her.

She landed on top of him, using her knee to ram him in the crotch. But despite her position she could feel herself losing ground. Her right hand was useless, and although he, too, was wounded, he had far more strength in his good arm than she did. Little by little, the gun was being wrested away from her.

A voice split the darkness, interrupting the deadly battle. "Colton, I'm disappointed. If I didn't know better, I'd say you were trying to screw me out of the job you hired me for." A figure stepped into the room, too shadowy to make out at this distance.

But his voice was instantly familiar. Jake stepped over to the combatants on the floor and pointed his Glock at her temple. "Drop the gun, Ria," he advised. "Very carefully."

Fragments of ice splintered through her, along with a shattering sense of disbelief. How had Jake gotten in here?

But on the heels of that thought came a feeling of betrayal so intense it clutched at her heart. Self-condemnation scorched a path through her as she searched his eyes, saw no mercy in their depths. It should come as no surprise that a man who'd sneaked beneath her defenses was shrewd enough to use that to his advantage.

But he couldn't betray a trust that hadn't been given. The thought carved a cruel furrow through her chest. In the end, then, it wasn't Jake who was to blame here, but Ria herself for giving him the weapon to use against her.

His finger squeezed the trigger slightly. "Don't make me say it again."

"Tarrance, what the hell are you doing here?" Hendricks seemed to finally find his voice.

"The job I was hired for, remember? I had a week, Colton." His tone was silky. "And I don't appreciate you changing the rules without telling me."

"Then what the hell are you waiting for? Shoot her!"

"Now?"

As Jake seemed about to comply, Hendricks said hurriedly, "Wait, you idiot. Let me get up."

Jake reached down to grab the gun that was still clutched

between them, jamming it in his waistband. Ria climbed slowly to her feet, backing away, her gaze going from one of them to the other. It would be the height of bitterness to die here like this, on the verge of discovering every answer she'd sought for six long years.

But even more bitter would be dying at the hand of the one man who had filled a bit of the emptiness inside her and made her feel, at least for a little while, almost whole.

"What are you waiting for?" Hendricks used the sleeve of his black turtleneck to swipe at the blood still coursing down his face. He sent a murderous look at Ria. "Kill her now."

"I'd prefer to be paid first." Jake's smile was lethal. "Finding you here, you can understand why I wouldn't be too trusting."

The man hesitated. "I can have the money wired to your account right away. You're mere hours away from your deadline. You can't blame me for figuring you'd changed your mind."

"You figured a lot of things wrong." With a sense of confusion, Ria saw him swing the gun in Hendricks's direction. "Ria, come and get the other gun."

"You son of a bitch!" Hendricks lunged forward, stopped abruptly by Jake's Glock.

Jake smiled grimly. "Let's leave my mother's morals out of it. Why don't you give me a reason to shoot? After what you've done to Ria, I wouldn't be hard to convince."

Pain was fogging comprehension, but she stepped forward, took the extra gun he'd stuck in his waistband. Hendricks's lip curled at her action. "You don't know who you're dealing with. If you kill me there isn't a corner of the earth far enough away to hide you."

"Actually, I do know," Ria corrected him, still keeping a wary distance from Jake. A dizzying welter of relief mingled with a baffling sense of joy. Hendricks hadn't been the only one convinced by Jake's act a moment ago. "Colonel C. Albert Hendricks. But as a civilian you go by Chad Hendricks, don't you? Special aide to Secretary of Defense Samson."

She stared into the face of the man who had cost her so much, and wondered at the lack of passion she felt. "If he's the one you've been blackmailing for the last four years, something tells me he won't be sorry to hear of your death."

Deputy Ralston pulled alongside the SUV at the side of the road, craned his neck to look inside. There was no one in the front seat, but that didn't necessarily mean it was empty. He cruised on by, a tuneless whistle escaping his lips. He'd radioed in the plate number on his last pass along the road, and couldn't say he was too surprised to find the Georgia license was listed to one Jake Tarrance.

It wasn't the first time he'd discovered one of Tarrance's vehicles parked nearby. And he knew exactly how far it was from here to the Kingsley property. The bitch could come up with any excuse she wanted. No way was there a legitimate reason for her to keep meeting with the Columbus crime boss.

And after tonight, no one would believe it even if she did have one.

With a little chuckle, Ralston patted the digital camera on the seat next to him. A picture was worth a thousand words. And the shots he was going to get tonight would tell a helluva story.

Hendricks's eyes flickered, but he kept his attention focused on Ria. "You don't know what you're talking about."

"Don't I?" The emotion she'd thought lacking a moment ago returned with jet force, churning and bubbling inside her. "You put together your own little team, didn't you? Was it at

Samson's request, or was it your own idea? Each of us had to have been handpicked by you, because you're the one linking us all together. What was our mission? Who did we answer to?"

"You still don't know? That drug was almost as good as a bullet, then, wasn't it?"

One moment Jake was standing beside her, silent, and the next he'd holstered his gun and grabbed Hendricks by the shirt, slamming a fist into his face. The man fell to the floor, then sprang to his feet, only to be knocked down again. "Reminding us of what you did to her isn't a good way to stay alive," Jake advised, his tone deadly, as he stood over the man. With expert movements he patted him down, took a set of car keys from one pocket, and a slim dark plastic case from the other. A green light winked from the corner of it.

"What's this?"

When the man remained silent, Jake went to the wall, flipped on a light switch. When Ria saw what he held in his hand, her blood turned glacial.

"It's a detonator."

"So you do remember some things from your past." Hendricks smiled unpleasantly. One hand was clapped over his upper arm to staunch the flow of blood from the bullet wound there. "Perhaps you'll also remember what the green light means. If the two of you want to stay alive, we'll need to leave in the next ten minutes or so."

"He's bluffing." Jake's eyes were narrowed. "He wouldn't set up an explosive that he could get caught in, too."

"Maybe he'll be more willing to supply some answers as the minutes count down." Ria looked at the man. "How about it, Colonel? There's nothing stopping Jake and me from walking out to safety and leaving you here."

"If you want answers, we're all leaving." The tone of command still came easily to the man's voice. "I've documents that will explain everything, all put away someplace safe. Come on." His tone dropped persuasively, his gaze on Ria. "Don't you want to know what your real name is? Don't you want to finally discover if you have family waiting somewhere?"

He was not only a traitorous son of a bitch, he was a masterful psychological manipulator.

"I already know my name." She was aware of Jake's head swiveling toward her in surprise. But she didn't look at him. She didn't take her eyes off Hendricks. "Karen Starkey. You're the one who recommended me for military intelligence." She saw the shock on his face. "I wouldn't be surprised to learn you had a hand in my assignment to the Defense Intelligence Agency, as well."

Hendricks took a step toward her, his face twisted in a mask of hate. "Yes, I recommended you. Dammit, everything you became you owed to me. And what did you do? You betrayed your country and your team."

Adrenaline mixed with dread in her stomach. Here, then, would be the truth behind what she was. If this man could be believed. "Tell me what happened."

Headlights flickered up the lane, approaching her house. Hendrick's attention was diverted as Jake walked to the window, pushed aside the curtain. "Someone from your department."

But her patience was at an end. "Tell me now, Hendricks."

"He's getting out of the car," Jake reported from the window.

It was as if Jake's words were the only catalyst needed to spur Hendricks into action. "The men were SOCOM, Special Operations Command. They were a specialized unit put together by Samson, upon my recommendation, answering only to him. The team was designed to carry out missions that were too politically risky to advocate for publicity. Unfortunately for all of us, the second mission required a woman." His glare speared through her. "I thought of you."

"You've got a deputy coming up to the house," Jake advised.

Panic showed on Hendrick's face. "Come with me and I'll show you every bit of evidence you could want!" He got up off the floor despite the gun she still held on him. "You want money? I've got millions. Just leave now so we have a chance to spend it."

The sound of a boot on the front walk had the man leaping toward the doorway. Jake punched him, sent him sprawling.

Comprehension slammed into Ria as she heard the first porch step creak. "He's got the secondary device wired to the front door." She ran toward Jake, shoved at him to get him moving. "The dining room window. Go!"

They raced to the next room, where Jake grabbed a chair and shattered the glass. He all but threw Ria through the opening before diving after her. The fall knocked the air from her lungs, but he was dragging her up, pulling her after him.

"Get away from the door," she yelled at the deputy on the porch as they raced to put distance between them and the house. "Get away from the door. Don't touch it—"

The explosion ripped through the night, the force of the blast lifting her off her feet and sending her sailing through the air. There was an instant of terror before everything went black.

Chapter 11

Three months later

The foamy waves eddied and swirled around Ria's ankles as she walked barefoot down the sparsely populated stretch of white sand beach. Most of the tourists who'd chosen Costa Verde over Rio de Janeiro for its beauty and solitude would be dining now, or enjoying the resort's nightly entertainment. On her rare time off, this was always her favorite part of the day, when the sun was bleeding into the pink and gold sky, preparing for its rapid descent beyond the horizon.

With the cluster of hotels at her back, and her gaze turned toward the seam where ocean met sky, it was easy to forget that she'd be back on the job, handling hotel security, in a few short hours. Instead, her mind was filled with the latest news from the States.

The American media was still filled with reports about former Secretary of Defense Samson. The beleaguered ex-secretary hadn't stood a chance of withstanding the firestorm of speculation and criticism that had arisen in recent weeks. The death of his aide had drawn little national attention, but Hendricks's passing hadn't come without a steep cost to his boss.

Ria had imagined the man had acquired a pretty thick cover-your-ass file in order to blackmail Samson about the Pegasus missions. So it hadn't come as a real surprise to find that he'd left the proof with his lawyer, with orders to make it public upon his death. The first news report had aired just days after the explosion that had destroyed her home.

For the first few weeks she'd haunted the newscasts, buying a TV and VCR so she could tape the twenty-four hour news channels. Most of the answers she'd still been missing had been gleaned from that coverage. But she'd never been able to shed the feeling that she was listening and reading about someone else.

With her toe she traced a line in the sand, watched the water wash in and erase it in the next moment. Karen Starkey, she realized, had been like that line for much too long—all but eradicated by events beyond her control. The moment she'd refused to carry out that last assignment as ordered, she'd signed her own death warrant.

The details had all been contained in Hendricks's files. How for their sixth mission, Samson had sent them to Puerto de Ponce to assassinate the embattled prime minister, helping the guerillas affect a change in government that would then owe allegiance to the United States. But when they'd approached the island, she'd challenged the need for blowing up the prime minister's home and killing his whole family. According to the documents, Starkey—*she*—had wanted to take Prime Minister LeLaue the next day, when he would be alone.

There had been no place for dissension in the Pegasus ranks.

One of her former teammates had injected her with the drug designed specifically for their unit, intending to spare her life, if to commit her to one without a past. But the team leader had insisted on following the protocol demanded by Samson: dissension meant death.

And so Karen Starkey had died that day, the moment the needle had pricked her skin, the instant she'd dived into the waters of the deep Atlantic to escape her fate. The act had merely selected another fate, as unavoidable as the first.

A few remaining gulls wheeled slowly against the eye-shattering sky, their raucous cries quieted for the day. But there was no quieting the questions that still lingered, despite the research she'd done into her life, and the conclusions she'd drawn.

She thought Hendricks had most likely been the sniper who'd nearly killed her at her house. He would have had to have done some surveillance on her to realize she never entered the place through the front door. When he'd failed in his attempt, he'd searched for someone else to do the job.

Because thoughts of Jake were too painful, she focused instead on what she'd discovered about her past.

The orphan Karen Starkey had been as alone as had the real Rianna Kingsley. Her father had been an army general who had raised her by himself once her mother had died. Her childhood had been a checkerboard of military bases across Europe and Southeast Asia. General Arnold Starkey had died of a stroke a year after Karen had joined the army. Two years before she'd been tapped by Colonel Hendricks for military intelligence.

She imagined she'd been proud to be requested to be part of Samson's elite team. A team charged with carrying out top-secret assignments designed to make the world safer, while dodging international politics. Missions ordered by Samson himself, and even now being decried by the current president.

In a strange way, the more she learned about the Pegasus team and its task of delivering Samson's perception of justice and honor, the more grateful she became for her blank memory. She could still recall every feature of the men who'd come to kill her. How much more haunted would she be if she also remembered being trained by them; going into danger with them; trusting them at her back; being trusted to cover theirs?

She'd once naively thought that the simple act of *knowing* would put to rest the gnawing questions that had driven her life for the last six years. Would begin to fill the void she'd carried within her for as long. And there was closure, of sorts, to discovering many of the answers. According to the files Hendricks kept, Samson had ordered the deaths of the rest of the team after two of them had come after her and failed. Even then he'd attempted to shield himself from any consequences. Now Hendricks himself was dead, along with Ralston, in the explosion. Samson was left to watch his career crumble, along with his presidential ambitions.

But the inescapable fact remained that Luz was still dead. And despite the mystery still puzzling Fenton County residents, so were Rianna Kingsley and Karen Starkey. Somehow, when she'd imagined the conclusion of this chapter of her life, it hadn't ended with her donning yet another identity, this time as Andrea Clauson. Running once more.

The waves were stronger now, tugging at the edge of her simple white lace shift. Absently, she gathered up material in both hands to rescue the garment from the water. It had been at Jake's insistence that she'd run again, and, dazed and reeling, she'd allowed him to bully her into the car he'd had waiting. Had sat unresisting while he bit out orders about her retrieving her sets of ID and taking his jet to an estate he had on Jamaica. Neither of them had been able to foresee the repercussions once Hendricks was out of the picture.

The memory of Jake seared a path across her heart. She hadn't been willing to sacrifice him when the fallout from the Pegasus team came to light. So she'd used her skill, ID and money to walk away from his estate one night and make her way to South America. If it meant she never saw him again, at least she could make certain that Samson would never be able to hurt him to get at her.

And she could almost convince herself that she could live without the prospect of seeing him again if she could just be certain he was safe.

But news of Jake Tarrance had been much more difficult to come by than reports of Secretary of Defense Samson. There had been nothing in the media regarding him, although she'd combed the Internet and Columbus newspapers daily. A few weeks ago she'd found reference to the release of Enrico Alvarez from Donaldson Prison, however.

While it would be soothing to believe that no news meant Jake was probably still alive, she knew better than most how easily some people could disappear without it raising any questions.

Had he gone underground to play a deadly cat and mouse game with Alvarez? Or had he engaged the man in one last lethal battle and lost? This was the hardest question of all to face, because she was only too aware it might never be answered.

Shading her eyes with her hand, she turned to look back

up the beach. Seeing how far she'd roamed, she started back again. The answers she'd been seeking about her past for so long were just that, answers. They relieved her mind, not her pain. They changed nothing, much as she'd predicted to Jake. And discovering them had emptied her life of direction.

Without the search that had driven her for so long, she often felt as though she was just floating along, waiting for life to happen. And it was time for that to stop. She'd felt like a spectator of other people's lives for far too long. It was time for her to carve out one of her own, even if she couldn't yet decide what it would entail.

Even though she was certain it wouldn't include the only man she could imagine sharing it with.

Ria paused to watch the brilliant ball of crimson sink into the sea. But she wasn't so lost in the sight that her instincts failed to warn her she was no longer alone. She looked over her shoulder to see a man in the distance walking toward her. It was impossible to see his features from here, but his stance was familiar. She frowned. It wouldn't be unusual for Carlos to seek her out and try to coax her into taking his shift tomorrow if he'd found a tourist that caught his eye.

But in the glow of the fading sunset, she could almost convince herself that it wasn't Carlos. That this man was taller, broader, and walked with a sense of purpose that was absent in the flirtatious security guard. It was as if, on cue, her mind had conjured up a mirage of Jake Tarrance, to reflect the focus of her thoughts. She knew the illusion would vanish in the blink of an eye, so she stared, watching the man's face take on detail as he came closer. It was harmless enough, even as she recalled that Jake was most likely... Her mind skirted the word *dead*. But if alive, he had no way of knowing where she was. And less reason for following her.

The man drew closer. He was barefoot, his black pants rolled to midcalf, the sleeves of his white shirt pushed up. Sunglasses obscured his face. She closed her eyes, opened them again. She really couldn't fault her mind for playing tricks on her, because this man did resemble Jake, down to the swept-back dark hair and well-formed mouth.

Ria's breath caught in her throat. As he closed the distance between them she could see the thin white scar darting across his cheekbone, beneath the glasses. She grappled with disbelief. Because it *was* Jake Tarrance, appearing against a spectacular backdrop of color that contrasted sharply with the shadows he'd disappeared into when they'd parted. Her gaze raced over him hungrily. With the exception of a slight limp, he didn't appear any different.

Joy sprinted through her, so pure and strong it nearly dizzied her. Amazement wasn't far behind. But neither emotion was reflected in the first mundane words to escape her. "How did you find me?"

The corner of his mouth quirked, and his pace quickened. "Damned if I didn't guess that'd be the first thing you'd say to me." He reached up to remove the sunglasses, and his pale blue gaze did a slow, thorough scan of her form that had her nerve endings prickling. Upon reaching her his arms snaked out, pulling her into an embrace that was strong and tight. "Hello, Ria." She had a moment to recognize the glint in his eyes before his mouth crushed hers.

The earth rocked beneath her feet as sensations burst through her. His lips were demanding, her response more so. It had been simple to tell herself that memory had exaggerated her reaction to him. But the reality made a mockery of the rationalization. Tongues tangled. Teeth clashed. Her hands were fisted in his hair to pull him closer, and her stomach was doing cartwheels as his lethal, heated flavor seeped through her.

It was long luscious moments before he tore away to gulp a breath. But he didn't release her. He kept her body snugged close to his. "Well, I gotta say, that was a far better welcome than I'd hoped for. Maybe now would be a good time to admit that I had you followed."

Her brain fogged, she blinked. "What? Where?"

As if he recognized the exact moment comprehension filtered in, he stepped back a bit, released her waist to glide his hands up her arms. "Here. From my place. I figured you'd run and you did. I've had a couple people watching you since you left Jamaica."

The leap of emotion she'd experienced upon seeing him abruptly cooled. "Did you now."

The menace in her tone didn't seem to faze him. He gave a slow nod, still watching her. "That's right. I didn't want to lose you for good, and given your greeting, you'll have a hard time convincing me you aren't glad I was able to find you. I'd say the ends justified the means this time, wouldn't you?"

He was looking entirely too pleased with himself. And she was feeling a bit put out to think how easily he'd managed the feat. "You tend to think the ends justify the means every time, don't you?" Her eyes searched his. "I knew Alvarez had been released, but there wasn't a word in the media about either of you. I didn't know—"

"There was nothing to report." She thought that was regret in his expression, but it was there and gone so quickly she couldn't be sure. "He was released early. Hendricks had arranged it before he broke into your house. Probably thought we'd take care of each other and he'd never have to worry about me talking."

Remembering the slight limp she'd noticed in his approach, she felt worry take precedence over irritation. "What happened between the two of you?"

Jake hesitated, choosing his words carefully. The bullet wound he sported on his leg was a legacy of the first clash with Alvarez in ten years. But the other man hadn't escaped unscathed. Jake had it on good authority that the knife injury the man had sustained would require several more surgeries to repair the muscle damage. "Our meeting was cut short. Vice has been all over me since he was sprung. Edwards and Renard are convinced there's some kind of gang war in the making. Their scrutiny made it logical to pull back and reassess."

With the kind of attention he was getting from the Columbus PD, he knew it was going to require quite a bit more patience before he could arrange an appropriate end for Alvarez. After waiting ten years, the prospect shouldn't have had him so restless.

But watching the news about Samson, knowing what every detail was doing to Ria, had him increasingly impatient. It might take years before he could make a move on Alvarez without having it come back to him. He didn't have years.

What he had was a nearly uncontainable desire to go to Ria. The thought of revenge had sustained him for a decade, but it proved ineffective at erasing memories of her. With the lingering danger still swirling around her, he couldn't think of going to her if there was a chance someone would come after him about Alvarez. The choice in the end had been simple.

"So…he's still alive."

"He's been given a stay of execution," Jake corrected. But the statement failed to summon the familiar burn of resentment. The man had been stripped of everything. Vice was watching every move he made. There was no way Alvarez was going to be able to assemble an operation in what had been, for the last ten years, Jake's town. It wasn't enough. But it might be close.

"I've made some changes in my operation," he said abruptly. He cupped her elbows, thumbs caressing the delicate skin along the inside crease. "It'll take awhile, but I have some legitimate sources of income forming." And the less legal components would, eventually, be turned over to Cort. The pang that accompanied the thought was far slighter than it would have been six months ago. "I won't be completely legit for a couple years, but it will happen. I figured that would be important to you."

From the expression on her face, she'd missed the import of his news. "Well, if it keeps you alive and out of prison, I'm for that, I guess."

"The question is, will it be enough to keep me in your life?" Even as he heard the words, Jake gave a slight wince. Finesse had never been so difficult to summon until it became all-important.

Already the sunset was fading into night. He had the fleeting thought that his chances were fading with it. "Nothing in Hendricks's documents indicate otherwise, so we have to figure Samson knows you're still alive. You'll have to remain hidden for several more months. Possibly years, if there is a criminal proceeding, which is looking more and more likely. Are you planning to go public? God knows, the government owes you for the last six years. You could testify against Samson."

She gave a half smile. Nothing in her life, it seemed, was ever that simple. "Could I? What would I have to say? Hendricks's files have far more information than I can give. I can't recall anything about the missions, and I have no way of linking Samson to any of it. I may be a target either way, but I like my chances better if I just stay lost."

He stared at her for a moment, then gave a slow nod. "Then I'll stay lost with you."

Ria tried to speak, had to clear her throat. A crazy little pin-wheel of emotion was whirling inside her chest. "You...want to stay here?"

Jake lifted a shoulder, his gaze intent on her face. "Here. Somewhere else. It doesn't matter. With you. That's the impor-tant thing." Women needed words, he knew. Ria was different from any other woman he knew, but he doubted she was *that* different. And he wasn't certain he had the words to give her.

"All I know about love is what I felt for my sister. But there was something about you that spoke to me the first moment I saw you in my restaurant." Something more than lust, he re-membered. Like an instant recognition that went deeper than attraction and took root. "I want to keep you safe. I want to be there by your side as you sort through all this craziness. And when you decide what it is you want to do with the rest of your life, I want your decision to include me."

It wasn't a poetic expression of love. He wouldn't have the experience with those sentiments, Ria knew. Neither would she. But his statement went a ways toward filling that yawn-ing void inside her. And it was suddenly far easier to contem-plate the future that stretched before her.

With little urging she walked back into his arms, rested her head on his chest. "What a pair we are. How can we hope to find our way when neither of us has the slightest idea where we're going?"

Hope eddied through him, a quick spiral banishing the desolation that he'd lived with for far too long. "We'll figure it out together. At least, if that's what you want, too."

She tilted her head back to look at him. Trust had never come easily for her, and trusting him had seemed suicidal. But for once her emotions had ventured where her mind wouldn't. If there hadn't already been the seeds of trust planted back in Alabama, surely she wouldn't have felt that staggering shock, that heart-wrenching sense of betrayal when she'd first thought he'd sided with Hendricks at her house. She still didn't understand the bond that had been forged between them despite her well-constructed defenses. But she knew she wanted him at her side as they explored whatever the future held.

"I don't know much about this love thing."

There was a slight smile on his face as he cupped her jaw in his palm. "Me, either. But I have a feeling you and I are going to learn all about it together."

And as his mouth covered hers, his last word resounded in Ria's ears like a bright and shiny promise.

Together.

Epilogue

The fourteen-year-old girl closed her book guiltily when she heard her grandmother at the door. The small home hadn't been swept yet, and dinner wasn't ready. Once again she'd been lost in the wonders of biology and anatomy while reality had receded.

She dashed to the crude kitchen, began to cut up the fresh vegetables she'd bought at the market on the way home from school that day. The older woman entered the room and sent a quick look around, before seeing the books on the table and heaving a sigh. The girl was as headstrong as her mother had been, although it wasn't a boy who had turned Maria's head, but something even less attainable.

"*Nieta,* you waste your time with those books. College will not be for one such as you." She went to the girl and shooed her away from the counter. Her hands moved quickly and surely as she diced the vegetables. "Did you get meat?"

"It was too expensive today. I thought a vegetable stew."

The older woman nodded sagely. Meat was a luxury that could be afforded perhaps twice a week if her husband earned many tips driving his taxi. They had potatoes tonight, and they would be filling.

"There is mail for you, on the table. You haven't been applying to universities again, have you?"

The girl's hesitation was a shade too long. "No, *Abuela.*" She picked up the lone envelope. Although it was long and narrow, there was no school address on it. In fact—she frowned, turned it over curiously—there was no return address at all.

With quick motions she opened it, took out the single sheet of paper inside. Curiosity was swiftly drowned by a tide of anger, followed by an all-too-familiar sorrow.

Dear Maria,
You can't imagine how often I've thought of you over the years. How often I wished that my life had been taken instead of your mother's. Luz had a big heart and because of her assistance to a stranger, she died. I've never forgiven myself for bringing danger to your tiny part of the island.
For many years I've sought to discover answers to what happened that day, and I've finally found them. They don't change anything. You were still robbed of a parent who devoted her life to you. Nothing can change that.

Maria's eyes misted, and she wiped at them impatiently. The loss of her mother had devastated her young life and it was a wound that continued to throb. Nothing would ever change that.

The debt I owe your mother cannot be repaid. That fact continues to haunt me. But I remember well how proud

she was of you. What she sacrificed for you. And I know
she would have done everything in her power to provide
you with every opportunity.

I've kept track of you over the years, and I've learned
you wish to be a nurse. I think your mother would be
very proud. The account number listed below has been
set up in your name at the noted bank. There is enough
money in it to pay for a college education, either on the
island or off it.

Under her grandmother's questioning eye, Maria pulled out
a chair, sank into it. The letter was clutched tightly in her hand.
A tiny kernel of hope was beginning to bloom where once
there had been a grudgingly bleak acceptance.

I know what it's like to live with a hollow inside you that
you doubt can ever be filled. Each of us has to find our
own way to come to peace with the past. I've only recently
accepted that myself. I hope by following your dream,
Luz's dream for you, you'll discover that yourself.

                                                    Angel

A tear dripped onto the paper, smearing the ink. Then another. Alarmed, her grandmother exclaimed, "*Nieta,* what is
it? Bad news?" She bustled around the small table, slipped an
arm around Maria's shoulders.

The girl shook her head, held the paper up for her grandmother to read. "No, *Abuela,* not bad news. I think…I think
it might be a miracle."

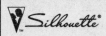

INTIMATE MOMENTS™

Bounty hunter Ike Walker needed his ex-wife,
Lindsay Hollis, to help prove her brother was
the victim of a cold-blooded murder.

But would working together to resolve the
heart-wrenching crime take them down
passionate—and deadly—paths they
wanted to avoid at all costs?

Deadly Reunion
by
LAUREN NICHOLS

Intimate Moments #1374, June 2005

If you enjoyed what you just read,
then we've got an offer you can't resist!

Take 2 bestselling love stories FREE!

Plus get a FREE surprise gift!

Clip this page and mail it to Silhouette Reader Service™

IN U.S.A.	IN CANADA
3010 Walden Ave.	P.O. Box 609
P.O. Box 1867	Fort Erie, Ontario
Buffalo, N.Y. 14240-1867	L2A 5X3

YES! Please send me 2 free Silhouette Intimate Moments® novels and my free surprise gift. After receiving them, if I don't wish to receive anymore, I can return the shipping statement marked cancel. If I don't cancel, I will receive 6 brand-new novels every month, before they're available in stores! In the U.S.A., bill me at the bargain price of $4.24 plus 25¢ shipping and handling per book and applicable sales tax, if any*. In Canada, bill me at the bargain price of $4.99 plus 25¢ shipping and handling per book and applicable taxes**. That's the complete price and a savings of at least 10% off the cover prices—what a great deal! I understand that accepting the 2 free books and gift places me under no obligation ever to buy any books. I can always return a shipment and cancel at any time. Even if I never buy another book from Silhouette, the 2 free books and gift are mine to keep forever.

245 SDN DZ9A
345 SDN DZ9C

Name	(PLEASE PRINT)	
Address	Apt.#	
City	State/Prov.	Zip/Postal Code

Not valid to current Silhouette Intimate Moments® subscribers.

Want to try two free books from another series?
Call 1-800-873-8635 or visit www.morefreebooks.com.

* Terms and prices subject to change without notice. Sales tax applicable in N.Y.
** Canadian residents will be charged applicable provincial taxes and GST.
   All orders subject to approval. Offer limited to one per household].
   ® are registered trademarks owned and used by the trademark owner or its licensee.

INMOM04R   ©2004 Harlequin Enterprises Limited